The Demon King's Destiny
Fate of Imperium
Book 3

By C.A. Worley

ACKNOWLEDGEMENTS

A huge thank you to my readers! This has been my most successful series to date, and I'm feeling indebted to those who took a chance with me.

I'd also like to thank the Indie Author community for all the encouragement, kind words, and advice. I've yet to meet a self-published author who wasn't supportive.

Lastly, a big shout out to my Beta Buddy and Critique Partner, Kay Uno, for her feedback and encouragement. You've been a blessing.

Map of Imperium

Northland
Kingdom of Burghard

Westland
Kingdom of Gwydion

Sanctus Femina

Eastland
Kingdom of Prajna

Southland
Kingdom of Sundari

"Three days and this house shall fall.
One menace to kill them all.
Northland, Eastland, and Southland quest.
Heed the threat from the West."

~Prophecy from Elora, Evelyn's mother

Prologue

"Come closer, little one," the hoarse voice reverberated through the woods.

The hairs on Evelyn's neck and arms stood at full attention as the demon's ensorcelled vocals echoed off her skin. Thankfully, his voice was the only thing he'd managed to get through her protective barrier.

She ignored the male, lowering her head and concentrating on her doll. Her long auburn hair fell over her shoulder, like a dark silky curtain hiding her face from the insidious creature.

More and more he had been visiting her dreams. With each visit, he grew bolder. Tonight, he'd ventured all the way to the edge of the clearing, watching her from the tree line. It was the furthest he'd ever dared.

In this dream, she was sitting on a blanket, playing with a handful of toys. Her two sisters were nearby, chasing each other through the tall goldenrod of the small field beside their home. Evelyn didn't bother calling to them. They weren't capable of seeing the demon when he visited.

He wasn't like her sisters in this dreamworld. Eden and Nora weren't actually here. They were pieces of Evelyn's subconscious, intangible and incapable of being anything other than what her imagination deemed them to be.

The demon was real. Corporeal. He'd meant to be here. He had somehow broken through and now lurked in her forest.

She'd yet to get a good look at him, but she could sense his magic. Dark and dangerous, matching the exaggerated bass of his speech. Demons were known for their low tenor, but this one's was aberrant, almost otherworldly.

The first time he'd broken through, she reached out with her senses to get a feel for his power. It felt cold and crude when he pushed back, like a cold wet tongue testing her flavor.

It had made her feel sick. Something about it was ... wrong.

"Let me into the meadow, girl. I only want to talk."

It was obvious he was lying. Her magics whispered to her and warned her to keep him away.

Evelyn wanted him to go away forever. She'd never been able to make him, no matter how many times she wished him gone.

Being unable to control her dreams was maddening. All she could do was put up a barrier and wait him out.

The demon had shown every night for a week now. Evelyn was worried he would eventually figure out how to reach her in the clearing.

Tonight, before she closed her eyes, she prayed to the Goddess of Sanctus Femina to either keep her safe or to make her strong enough to keep him at bay. She had an ominous feeling she was getting ready to find out if either of her wishes would be granted.

The male growled in frustration and Evelyn's grip on her doll tightened. Still, she refused to look up.

Silence stretched as she sat on her gold and black blanket. She knew he was still there, probably pretending to be gone. Evelyn was not to be tricked. She could still feel his ugly magic.

Demons could use their powers to creep into the minds of others. They could control those they held under compulsion. Evelyn believed such powers were unnatural.

Her father, King Edward, had assured her she could shield against an attack, that her will was strong and she would not be vulnerable. Evelyn wasn't keen on testing his theory.

Her strategy was to figure out how to simply make the demon go away, or to learn how to wake herself from her dreams. Despite her strong will, she hadn't been able to do either. It didn't mean she wouldn't continue trying, or that she wouldn't stand her ground when push came to shove.

Evelyn waited patiently for him to leave. Staring at the worn and ragged figure in her hands, her fingers itched. Her powers were swirling, waiting, anticipating a confrontation.

Though she was young, only six years of age, she was not weak. If he broke through the barrier, she would be ready.

Something hummed through the atmosphere in the distance. Steadily, it grew louder, reminding her of a fast-approaching storm. The air thickened with electrical currents and Evelyn raised her face to the heavens.

A blinding light shot across the sky. She tracked it with her eyes until it disappeared, landing among the treetops, somewhere behind the trespasser.

The bad male growled again and ran towards the place where the traveling light vanished among the greenery. It was just beyond her line of sight.

Tempted as she was to investigate, Evelyn remained on her blanket. The sounds of her sisters' play vanished, replaced by the echoes of snarls and grunts coming through the trees.

The noises disrupted the quiet of the forest. It sounded like two ferocious beasts locked in battle. A loud crash echoed, then silence fell.

Evelyn stood, concerned. Through the break in the trees, she could now see the shadow of a form rising to its feet.

"You've gone too far, Uncle!" the voice roared.

"No, I haven't gone far enough! You'll never be King, Marrok. Over my dead body will you take this throne from me."

"I didn't want the bloody throne, Brennen. Now you've left me no choice."

The two males moved far too fast for her to track. Suddenly, a body landed against the magical barrier separating the clearing from the forest, the one she'd built to protect herself.

The invisible shield pulsed with purple and white sparks. An enormous male jumped to his feet, black eyes glaring at her through shiny black strands of disheveled hair.

Marrok. The bad male had called him Marrok.

For a heartbeat, he remained locked on her and she couldn't draw a breath. His eyes widened slightly before quickly slanting down in displeasure.

Movement behind him caught Evelyn's attention. "Look out!" she yelled.

Brennen's eerie tentacles of magic flew out of the woods. Marrok dove to the side and the ethereal appendages battered against Evelyn's shield, trying to punch through it.

"You'll never get to her," Marrok seethed, searching the shadows for signs of his uncle's location.

"Then neither shall you."

A huge vortex of murky grey magics came out of nowhere, whirling like a nest of vipers around Brennen as he stepped out of the underbrush. His eyes were wide, crazed. His mouth contorted as if he was lifting a great load.

Shite! Marrok cursed to himself. Brennen was completely out of control. He looked one last time at the youngling, praying he could hold off the menace.

"Run!" he hissed at her.

Dropping the doll, Evelyn ran for her life.

* * *

Marrok jackknifed off his thin bedding on the cave floor, clutching at his chest. His pulse raced as he felt for his heart.

Still there.

He could feel the pounding of his blood against his palm. A sheen of sweat covered his skin, cooling him in the damp air. The pain from the dream remained.

His pectoral was sensitive to his touch, burning with irritation. Marrok's trembling hand lifted and came away bloody. Deep gashes from his uncle's claws had shredded his shirt, easily slicing through the skin and muscle below.

He'd dreamwalked—or had he been summoned? His uncle had been surprised to see him, so it wasn't Brennen who sought him.

The girl. It had to have been the youngling with the strange eyes.

Some demons could enter the minds of others, especially when they were sleeping and relaxed. Sleep made more than just the physical form vulnerable.

He could only imagine the terrible things Brennen must have done to obtain knowledge of who the girl was. The male had purposefully broken into the child's dreamworld.

To do what? Marrok didn't know. Whatever Brennen had planned, his uncle deserved the consequences he'd brought upon his own head.

Marrok lowered himself to his back, grinning at the thought of the Sundari royal guards finding Brennen's open chest. Missing a heart.

"All is well, Sire?"

Marrok's head jerked towards the sound of Favin's voice. He could barely see the dark-haired male lying across the alcove. The night's fire was almost completely out.

"All is well, Favin. Tomorrow we shall return home."

"Truly?" his Second whispered.

"Truly. We'll tell the men in the morning."

"But, how ...?"

"In the morning, Favin."

"Very well, Sire."

Marrok closed his eyes, dreaming of the child who'd just handed him the kingdom.

Chapter 1

Evelyn, Age 16

"You don't seem at all disappointed, if you don't mind my saying," Evelyn noted to her older sister as they walked arm-in-arm along the walking path.

Eden's mouth curved downward at Evelyn's observation. She must have hit a nerve. It was her forte, even though she hadn't meant to nettle Eden about the King of Burghard.

"How can one argue with Fate?" Eden replied.

"Ooh, kudos for evasiveness. You're good at this game."

"It's not a game," Eden sighed.

Evelyn twisted her lips. "I know it's not."

They meandered through the trees surrounding their home. Several wide walking paths had been created long ago so the children would not get lost in the woods.

The people of Gwydion loved being in nature. They were elementals and had an affinity to the natural state of the things in the world.

It was calming to be among the greenery. It was why Eden and Evelyn had ventured outdoors after what had been a rather taxing day for their family.

"I—I am loathe to admit I am relieved," Eden finally acknowledged.

"Why? You are certainly entitled to your feelings."

"It hardly seems fair to Nora."

Evelyn mulled over Eden's words. Today, Kellan, King of Burghard, had come to visit Eden. They'd been betrothed to one another Eden's entire life. Now that she was eighteen, their father wanted the engaged pair to get to know one another.

The Wolf King arrived this afternoon, along with his Second, Foley. They'd barely made it through introductions when Fate decided to intervene.

Everyone was beyond shocked when Kellan scented his fated mate in their home—and it wasn't Eden. The male was a wolf. Once his beast picked up the scent of their younger sister, Nora, and knew her to be his, all bets were off and the betrothal to Eden was dissolved.

The issue was Nora was only fourteen years old and far too young to marry. She was also a sickly little thing. But these were obstacles that could be overcome.

Probably, Evelyn thought to herself.

Eventually, Nora would grow up. With any luck, she'd also find a way to be healthy. Evelyn chose to be hopeful. It was, after all, preordained that Nora belonged to the wolf.

She patted Eden's hand. "You're only saying that because Nora is young and looks so fragile."

"She *is* fragile."

"Physically. Not emotionally. I think we all forget sometimes."

"Perhaps. Yet it is still the physical that bothers me. She's going to live among the wolves in the Northland, Evelyn. What if she's challenged? She can hardly defend herself against a wolf."

"You're right."

Eden did a double take. "I'm right?"

Evelyn laughed. Those were not words anyone heard out of her mouth very often.

"It's obvious. Nora is tiny, especially compared to a wolf. She could easily be harmed."

Evelyn didn't bring up the damage to Nora's soul inflicted upon her the day she was born. It wasn't a time for the reminder of how they'd lost their mother or the fact Nora could not wield magic like every other elemental in the Kingdom of Gwydion could.

"Then why are you so accepting of this, Evie?"

"Simple. It's Fate."

Eden huffed.

"I'm serious. Fate. Destiny. The Goddess above. Whatever forces of the world that create such things as mates, such wonders as the ability to shift into an animal, the magic to control the elements, to hypnotize others, or to ... wait, what exactly do the demons do? Compulsion? It sounds exactly like hypnotizing. Don't you think?"

Eden rolled her eyes. Only Evelyn would boil complex powers of the mind down to such simplicity.

Evelyn ignored her sister.

"It doesn't matter," she continued. "There are forces at play we will never understand. I can hardly believe two beings fated for one another would not be well-suited for one another. Or, in fact, perfect for one another. Why else would they be fated?"

Eden looked at Evelyn with newfound respect. She'd always assumed her sister was a hopeless romantic. Maybe there was some degree of practicality in Evelyn, after all.

"I can't believe I'm going to say this, Evie, but you actually make sense."

"Of course, I make sense. You just refuse to listen to me."

They both giggled, continuing their long walk as they did many an evening after dinner. Nora rarely, if ever, joined them, preferring not to venture into the forest and accidently pull energies into herself. It was how she repaired her soul and it took a toll on everything around her.

After a time, Evelyn yawned and Eden steered them back toward the manor. Keeping their arms locked, they stepped off the path and into the golden field surrounding their home.

Feeling some part of the universe had been set right today, Evelyn looked forward to what else the future might bring.

* * *

Evelyn's bare toes wiggled atop the soft grass at the edge of the forest. The summer moon's light created unnatural beams of purple and blue spearing through the trees.

Bright and shimmering, these were the colors of her dreams. Ever since her mother died, the forest and moonlight had been the backdrop of every sleeping fantasy she could remember.

She always came back to this spot, at the edge of the clearing near her home. It was a familiar place, a location she visited often with Eden and Nora during her waking hours. In the meadow, they played as sisters did. Echoes of their laughter often broke through to her dreamworld.

Evelyn did not know what was so special about the area or why she was anchored to it when she slept. She'd tried over the years to drift along the edge or back to her house. Each attempt landed her back in this exact spot.

She wiggled her fingers, testing the elements. As always, she could feel the magic floating in the air. She had been taught from a young age to trust the elements and listen when they spoke.

When she had finally learned to control her powers, somewhere around the age of five, she'd opened herself up in her dreams, allowing her magics into her dreamworld.

Even in sleep the elements spoke. Only whispers of what they were when she was awake, but they were with her in her dreams. Always.

By now, she'd figured out her nocturnal activities weren't normal. Something, other than her own power, pulled her here, again and again. Some force hauled her here every time she drifted off.

A few times, she'd not been alone. Evelyn didn't like thinking about those particular nights from her childhood. She could still feel the phantom cold of the malevolent demon's power.

A noise off to the left caught her attention. A wolf stood not twenty yards away, staring at her. She wasn't surprised. She'd met a wolf today, so her mind was creating images of the familiar.

Evelyn's mouth stretched, thinking of when their younger sister, Nora, came barreling into the room and stole the show, or, in this case, the wolf.

There was something terribly romantic about finding the one being the Universe created just for you, especially when you were of a species who did not have fated mates.

The tiniest pang of jealousy had crept into Evelyn's heart and she quickly froze it out. Their poor father had been beside himself and it would only make things worse for him if he thought Evelyn was unhappy.

A twig cracked to her right and she swung her head around. She was met with a vampire's hypnotic gaze. He was as tall as the trees and carried a flame in his open palm.

It was further proof she was in her dreamworld. No vampire was this size in real life, nor could they wield fire. Her sister, Eden, could. It was her greatest power.

The elements vibrated across the meadow, moving and shifting of their own accord.

Evelyn quickly realized this dream was not going to be like the others. She forced herself to pay attention, to commit it all to memory. Magic was speaking and she would not discount it's story.

Up ahead, Evelyn could make out the outline of an elderly male. Long, scraggly, hair framed the face of what had to be Theron, the temple priest of Sanctus Femina. He'd visited her dreams before. Slowly, he raised his finger to his lips in a silencing gesture.

A shadow stepped out from behind the priest. It grew bigger as it strode confidently towards her, showing the distinct outline of a warrior's figure.

Through the glimmering light, she saw the reflecting shine off dark hair. So dark, it gave off an almost bluish tint. Tanned skin stretched over toned muscles. The shirt he wore did nothing to hide his physique.

He was exactly as she'd remembered. *Well, maybe a little less enraged.*

Moonbeams danced upon his face, revealing obsidian eyes. She didn't like it when his eyes fully dilated, covering what she knew were golden irises. Evelyn had only seen eyes bleed black like that once. Once had been more than enough.

"Hello, poppet," his abnormally deep voice rubbed like velvet against her skin, taking her by surprise.

"My name is not poppet. It's Evelyn."

"Bold as ever, I see."

"You—you remember me?" she stammered, surprised he recognized her. Much had changed on her body since she was six.

It had been nearly a decade since she'd seen him in her dreamworld. Even then, it had only been the briefest of encounters.

"How could I forget?"

His voice was laced with some emotion she couldn't name, causing her to blush. "I suppose you would recognize your surroundings. They're always the same here. Nothing ever changes."

Marrok ignored her misinterpretation of his wording. His eyes wandered while he spoke, noting both a wolf and a vampire were close.

"It's your dream, little one. I imagine you can make anything happen here."

"One would think," she scoffed.

Marrok's steady regard swung back to the female, studying her intently. The girl was an elemental. She was a teenager now, but there was no question she was the same female who had summoned him that night a decade ago.

The same long auburn hair now hung in loose braids. Her mismatched eyes were ones Fate would never allow him to forget.

One eye was green, the shade of the spring fields in the Westland. It was the coloring of the elementals who lived in Gwydion.

The other eye was of a color he'd only seen on a demon. Amber with flecks of gold and russet, identical to his own. Even her skin was darker than other elementals. Bronzed—like a demon's. Like his.

If not for her one green eye and the color of her silky tresses, he might think the female a she-demon. The hair of both Sundari females and males only came in two colors. Black or white. Never any other variation.

Her long locks of auburn were striking. Her peculiar eyes fascinating. Yet it was the attraction of his soul to hers currently tying him in knots.

23

His saatus was a vision, one he'd studiously avoided, refusing to seek her out. He'd been tempted to check on her many a night, but he'd kept his shields up, trusting his iron will to hold.

How easily he'd forgotten her show of strength. As a youngling, she'd managed to keep a rogue demon out of this clearing. Her shields and magics had been impressive, even in sleep.

It was no coincidence he'd not been able to prevent her from pulling him into her dream again. Feeling the presence of the old man at his back, he wondered if she'd had help.

"What am I doing here?" he asked, stopping inches from the transparent forcefield separating the forest from the small meadow.

"You tell me."

"I'm not the one summoning people in the middle of the night."

"I did no such thing."

"Are you sure about that?"

Eden's chest rose and fell. Prickles of sweat seeped from her pores. His voice was magic itself, pushing against her, cocooning her in its warmth.

"Stop doing that," she commanded.

His eyes narrowed. "I'm not doing anything to you."

"You are. Your voice ... it's ..." she couldn't finish. The things his timber were doing to her were too embarrassing to articulate.

Marrok couldn't see the flush under her olive skin, but he was sure it was there. It was the early signs of the saatus bond. The moment he had first seen her, even though she'd been a small child, he'd known what she was to him.

He should try to keep his magics out of his intonations. Demons naturally released power when they spoke. Being an elemental, and his mate to boot, it probably had a greater impact on Evelyn than was fair.

Fate was in no way subtle with its signs of matehood, especially with the demons. No, when a demon saw his saatus—his true mate—he knew. She might not realize it, but she would feel something when his magics touched her.

Now that she was closing in on adulthood, he could feel the mild pull. Luckily, the little witch was still too young for it to push either of them into the mating frenzy.

It was dangerous for her to be dragging him into her dreams. He wasn't sure how powerful the draw would be while their bodies weren't touching, or if it would matter while he dreamwalked. If this was any indication, it would become a problem if she was but a little older.

If circumstances were different, in a few years, he would bring an army to her father's doorstep and demand her hand. Nothing, not even the Goddess herself, would keep him away from her.

Alas, he did not have that luxury. It was starting to look like he never would. His past being what it was ... coupled with the troubles of the present? He couldn't afford to look hopefully into the future.

The Sundari Kingdom was in the middle of a crisis, one he was barely containing. His worst fear was this calamity would spill over the Southland's borders and spread throughout Imperium.

His drastic measures had barely made a dent. At least the madness hadn't gone further than the Corak Peninsula. Minus the random rogues showing up here and there, or the ones making it past the wall.

He'd resorted to setting up a penal colony on the southernmost tip of Sundari. He'd built a blockade, cutting off the isthmus from the rest of the kingdom.

The cliffs around Corak held ancient magics originally created to protect the area from invasion. No one could cross through the invisible partition to reach the land. This also meant no one could leave the land to reach the water.

With so many demons falling into madness, he didn't have anyplace else to put them. He was discovering more rogues with each passing day and his life had become one of constant battles in his determination to maintain peace. His days were spent hunting rogues, killing them, or transporting them to Corak.

Life was too dangerous in the Southland for an elemental. It was better for the girl to forget she'd ever met him, even if only in a dream. His demon soul protested and, with effort, Marrok silenced it.

"What's wrong?" she questioned, taking a step towards him. She noted his thick lashes and how starkly they demarcated the shape of his eyes. Females would be jealous.

"Nothing. Why do you ask?" He hadn't so much as blinked while wrestling with his inner demon.

"Your pupils constricted. Usually, they're so big I can't see the amber of your eyes ... or, they were the last time I saw you. I think it's because you're easily agitated."

"Then what, pray tell, am I if not agitated for being dragged here? Unwillingly, I might add."

"Sad? At the very least, you're unhappy. Whatever it is, you're lamenting. It's not your best look."

His lips quirked. She was precocious, especially for a female of her age. Females rarely spoke so informally in his presence, if they spoke at all.

All demons, especially she-demons, could intuitively sense the emotional state of others. Their powers were rooted in the energies of the mind. Though those around him could sense his mood, they knew better than to call him out on it. Marrok was King.

Little Evelyn—a virtual stranger—had been able to do it with a single look, and she'd had no difficulty saying it aloud.

27

"Observant little thing, aren't you?"

"Yes."

Marrok chuckled, tempted to continue the conversation. She was captivating. He could tell her mind was sharp. A beguiling intellect was a very dangerous thing. Demons valued mental prowess above all else, even physical beauty. That she possessed both was a temptation he might not be capable of fighting.

Standing this close, mere feet apart, his nostrils flared. Even through the barrier he could pick up her scent. She smelled like midnight dew on a desert rose.

He shouldn't be here. Marrok needed to make sure she didn't call to him in her sleep again. If, by some miracle, he found a way to quell the insurrection occurring in Sundari, he would consider seeking her out once she was of age.

If not, well, he didn't want to think about what would happen if he and his people turned rogue. He needed to be very clear with Evelyn to stay away from him.

Fate was playing a perilous game bringing them together. Marrok would never do anything to endanger his mate, even if it cost him his own sanity. She didn't deserve to be caught up in his struggles.

"Listen to me carefully, Evelyn. Do not call for me again. This game, it's not one you can win."

"What game?" Her eyebrows drew tight, irritated by his incessant presumption she was somehow responsible for his arrival.

"The one you don't even know you're playing," he clipped.

Marrok turned and marched into the forest. Evelyn wanted to call out to him, but Theron drifted back into sight, his kaleidoscope eyes swirled with shades of violet and silver.

He pointed towards the wolf, who was now standing next to Nora. Then to the vampire. Eden stood at his side. All four were focused on the demon's retreating back.

Theron's eyes sparkled with magic as he once again made a silencing gesture. *Saatus* he whispered in her mind.

The pieces clicked into place and Evelyn smiled.

Chapter 2

Evelyn, Age 18

"Again," King Edward commanded.

Evelyn exhaled harshly. Her father was taking his daughters' training far too seriously. What, exactly, did he think was going to happen where they would need to use their powers in such a way? It was always better safe than sorry, but still.

"There are only two left, Father," she pointed towards the straw targets across the courtyard, eight of which were either riddled with precisely-made burn holes, missing their heads, or blown to smithereens.

"I'll have more made."

Evelyn squeezed her eyes shut to stop herself from rolling them. They'd spent the entire morning fighting hand-to-hand with Nora. Her training was their father's primary focus these days.

The youngest sister's hands or a physical weapon were her only defenses because of her lack of magic. Admittedly, Nora had become quite proficient and the payoff was evident.

Edward had recently decided all three of his children should sharpen their skills. So, this morning, Eden and Evelyn were forced to join Nora. He'd sent them out behind the barn where many of his men trained.

After getting tossed on her backside one too many times, Evelyn chose to cheat and sent a current of air to distract her opponent. Unfortunately, her opponent happened to be Eden, the one least likely to appreciate Evelyn's humor.

The oldest didn't think having her own hair attack her face was as funny as Evelyn thought it was. Eden retaliated by singeing off one of Evelyn's eyebrows. Eden grew even more frustrated when Evelyn only laughed in response.

Their father's men had watched in amusement. Edward simply made them start over, muttering under his breath about the Goddess giving him such ill-behaved daughters. His eyes were alit with merriment, betraying his true feelings on the matter.

Hours later, however, he was no longer amused. Evelyn thought he might be a little disturbed by his offspring's show of aggression.

"Eden, this time aim for the heart," Edward ordered.

"As you wish, Father."

31

As the oldest, Eden was the most serious of the three. Yet even she had grown tired of today's training and started burning holes in the targets where no male would want to be burned.

The guards stopped laughing. Evelyn, however, could hardly stop snickering over the glorious attack. She was liking Eden more and more with each round.

Evelyn watched Eden blast the straw man from fifty yards away with a smooth and meticulously created beam of fire. She cut out a heart-shaped hole, nearly perfect in symmetry. *Impressive*, Evelyn thought.

Before Edward could give the next order, an arrow shot through the shape Eden had made. Evelyn clapped at Nora's perfect shot.

"Well done, Nora!" she praised.

Nora took a dramatic bow then turned to her father and asked, "If I remove the last one's head, may we end this for today? I'm exhausted."

"Nora, why do you continuously insist on decapitating the targets?" Edward sighed.

"I—"

"It was rhetorical," he said without feeling. "Let's end here for today. Don't think any of you are off the hook."

"I'm not leaving Gwydion for another four years, Father. I think we have time."

Edward patted Nora on the shoulder. "We always believe there is time, daughter. Sometimes things come at you that you never saw coming, and you wish you had been better prepared. Trust me in this."

Nora's face dropped and she nodded. Evelyn felt a pang, knowing her father was referring to their mother's murder. Nora was the only one who didn't know it wasn't childbirth that had killed Queen Elora.

An ancient brotherhood, Sephtis Kenelm, had banded together to ensure a balance of power was maintained across Imperium. No single kingdom could be more powerful than the others. Elora was the most powerful elemental to ever live—and she paid for her natural talents with her life.

Their father, along with King Kellan, whose own father had lost his life to the group's misguided mission, had long ago hunted them down and avenged his queen's death.

Evelyn didn't agree with his keeping the truth from Nora. She hoped someday, he would see Nora's inner strength and tell her the truth.

"Come on, Nora," Eden cajoled, pulling Evelyn's attention back to her youngest sister.

"I'm famished," Eden put her arm around Nora. "I'm sure breaking for sustenance will do us good. Evelyn, are you coming?"

"I'll join you later. I have something to see to first."

As the group scattered, Evelyn headed to one of the larger paths at the south end of the tree line. She followed it until it turned near the small creek.

Several boulders sat in the bend of the stream, worn with time. She climbed to the top of the tallest one and sat, staring at the lazy current below.

She closed her eyes and listened to the melody of the bubbling brook. Gradually, her muscles relaxed and her spirit settled.

Evelyn's strongest power was her affinity with water. For the past few days, the creek had been calling to her. All Gwydions had some connection to a specific element. Evelyn had control over many, but water was her greatest bond.

She'd had a restless mind lately. More and more she had been unable to focus, feeling uneasy. There was no explanation for the knot of anxiety she felt.

Even her dreams had been affected. Mainly, she wasn't dreaming. For the first time in many years, she wasn't being pulled into the clearing nightly.

As she drifted off each night, she was met with darkness. It swirled and danced around her in murky shades of grey and black. She could see nothing beyond the force holding her in its clutches.

Concerned by what it meant, she'd remained close to her sisters instead of coming to the stream to meditate. Yet the water called for her.

Trusting her connection to her element, she returned today. As always, it calmed and centered her. She found herself drifting off to sleep, lulled by nature's symphony.

"You probably shouldn't fall asleep up there," a male voice suggested.

Evelyn's eyes popped open and she swung her head to the right. She recoiled when she realized she was only inches from the sometimes annoying, yet unfairly attractive, face of Jasper Rollands.

She bolted upright, his presence too close for her comfort. Jasper was a young man from town, training to be a soldier in her father's army—training hard from the looks of him. His body bore the fruits of his labors. Tall and muscular, he was the center of much attention, particularly from the young females.

Evelyn, much to her dismay, wasn't immune to his charms. She kept her distance because of it. She had plans for herself, and they didn't involve a roll in the hayloft with the gorgeous male beside her.

"I'm perfectly safe," she retorted once she had her wits about her.

"Even from rolling off? I'd hate for you to hit your pretty little head, hard as it may be."

Evelyn snorted and he chuckled. Jasper was usually good natured, at least, he had been before his teen years. When they were small they'd been playmates. Once he hit puberty, he stopped coming around as much, but she still considered him a friend of sorts.

"Move over," he grunted, hopping up onto the boulder beside her.

Evelyn scooted as far as she could without falling over the edge.

He frowned, brushing his sandy blonde hair off his brow. "I'm not contagious."

She laughed and shook her head. "I know. But your large body barely fits up here."

"Right." His focus drifted above her discolored eye. "What happened there?"

"Eden happened."

"Your sister attacked you?"

"Yes. It was hilarious."

"Looks like it."

They grinned at one another. Jasper turned away first, throwing some pebbles he was holding into the stream.

"What are you doing out here?" he asked.

"I was meditating."

"With your mouth wide open and drool coming out? Doubtful."

She playfully swatted his arm. "It wasn't that bad."

"It was."

Parts of Evelyn's body warmed in reaction to the timbre of his voice. All the wrong parts. She should not be feeling anything for this male, or any male for that matter.

Except for one.

"What were you doing, aside from interrupting my rest?" she scolded.

"I had the afternoon off and was on my way to help out the Greycen family with the summer harvest."

"Ah, out being a pillar of the community."

"I try."

"And it wouldn't have anything at all to do with watching Maggie Greycen work the field? I hear it's quite a sight."

Jasper smirked. "The ladies talk of her ample ... assets, do they?"

Evelyn barked out a laugh and swatted him again. "You are terrible."

"I can be. But to answer your question, no, I'm not going to help because of Maggie. I owe her father a debt and this is how I'll repay it."

"How admirable."

"Not really. Besides," he said, staring intently at her mouth, "she's not half as lovely as the female who always seems to run in the opposite direction when she sees me approaching."

Evelyn's eyes grew big as he leaned closer. She reflexively leaned away from him, but he kept coming. Before she could demand to know what, exactly, he thought he was doing, she tipped backwards and fell off the rock.

Too late, she tried to twist and get her arms under her to break her fall. All Evelyn managed was to slam her cheek into one of the smaller boulders just before her body continued its descent to the ground.

She landed awkwardly, with her rear on the dirt and her front plastered to the side of the rock. She did a quick check of her person. Nothing hurt too much other than her cheek.

"Damn, that smarts," Evelyn cursed, reaching up to inspect the damage.

Already swelling. A little bloody. Likely starting to bruise. It would be just like her to go through hours of rigorous training unscathed—aside from one missing eyebrow—only to be injured by her reaction to some moron's idea of a sexual advance.

Two large boots landed with a soft thud beside her. *Speaking of said moron.*

"Ah, Goddess. I'm sorry, Evelyn," Jasper apologized, kneeling and placing a hand on her shoulder. "Here, let me see," he cajoled.

His fingers gently lifted her chin. Evelyn turned her face so he could get a better look at the damage and he flinched. The big bad warrior-in-training flinched. Hard. Her shoulders shook as she tried to hold in her amusement.

The corner of his mouth lifted. "You're a cruel one, Miss Evelyn, laughing at me."

"I'm not the one knocking ladies off of boulders."

"Yes, well, I'm not used to such gross aversion to my advances."

"I imagine not. But really, what were you thinking? You can't just go around kissing every girl who crosses your path. I mean, sure, convenience is important, but did you think thirty seconds of my time warranted our faces making contact?"

His guffaw was loud enough to knock over a tree. "You are not like other females," he chuckled once he had enough air to speak.

Evelyn twisted her lips, uncomfortable with his comment. He was right. She wasn't like the other females she knew. She was good at playing her role well in her father's court, but outside of those formalities, Evelyn had always been a little rough around the edges. Blunt. A jokester.

She wasn't sure she liked Jasper calling attention to it. If a handsome male such as he thought her odd, what would *he* think of her, the one who never strayed far from her mind?

Jasper was a stark contrast to her dream male. Where Marrok was dark and broody, both in looks and personality, Jasper was light and fun. Light and fun might be more akin to her personality than dark and broody. Evelyn didn't like the thought she wasn't capable of attracting a male like Marrok.

"I should probably head home and clean myself up," she said quietly.

"Let me escort you," he insisted, offering his hand and pulling her up to her feet.

Jasper looked down the path, the one leading to the Greycen's farm. It was in the opposite direction of Evelyn's home. He would be late, but he didn't like the idea of sending her off alone after that fall.

Evelyn shook her head. "I'm fine, Jasper. You've got a further trek than I, anyway. I'd hate for you to be late."

He opened his mouth to protest and she pushed him backwards with air currents. "Go, before I dump you in the stream."

"Alright, alright. No need for violence," he jested. "Are you sure you're okay?"

"I'm fine. Now leave."

"As you wish, my lady." Jasper bowed gracefully. When he straightened, his expression was serious. "I really am very sorry, Evie."

He hadn't called her Evie since they were young. She liked it, in a brotherly sort of way. A tiny part of her thought life would be easier if she simply gave in to a male like Jasper, explored the potential for something more with another elemental.

It would never work. She didn't want any of the males she knew. Even if she'd allowed the kiss, she knew Jasper well enough to know he wasn't seeking something permanent.

Besides, she'd been waiting two years for the demon to return to her dreamworld or, preferably, knock on her father's door. How long was she expected to wait? Having faith in Fate was no simple task.

With a shrug she waved him off. "It's fine. If it will make you feel better, you can owe me a favor."

"Anything."

"Oh, you really shouldn't make such promises. I might just take you up on it."

"Are you flirting with me?"

"What? No!"

He chuckled and saluted her as he walked backwards. "Until we meet again, fair Evelyn." Then turned and jogged away.

Once he was out of sight, Evelyn sagged against the boulder, covering her eyes with her hands. Her face was throbbing and she now had a terrible headache. Even her bottom was becoming sore. Her adrenaline must have started to wear off.

She traced her lips with her fingers, wondering what it would have felt like to have Jasper's mouth touch hers. She argued it was out of curiosity. Any female her age would want to know what it was like to be kissed.

A prick of guilt struck her and she destroyed the thought. She was positive—mostly—Fate had marked her for another. She should not entertain such fantasies.

So much for relaxing meditation. At least the ordeal would make for an entertaining story with her sisters.

She stood upright and blew out a sighing breath, taking one last look at the water. A flash of something caught her attention. Evelyn walked closer to the bank, searching below the surface for whatever had caught the sun's rays.

A glint of silver glimmered and she bent, peering closer. She lowered herself to her hands and knees. Opening her mind, she called to the elements to bring her the item.

With a plop, the reflective piece sailed out of the water and landed in her hand. It was a circular medallion attached to a thick, silver chain.

Evelyn wiped away the silt with her thumbs. She dipped it in the water to rinse away the last of the sand and mud. Putting it in her palm, she brought it close to her face.

In the center of the medallion was an intricate design of a tree. The trunk was wide and the roots visible. Woven into the pattern of bark was the letter M.

Marrok, the name skirted across her mind. The elements buzzed around her in agreement.

Her hands shook. Marrok was a demon. Yes, he'd visited her dreams twice, but he hadn't really been out here in the forest.

She turned the medallion over. There were words engraved across the surface.

ISTINA NIKAD NE UMIRE

The truth never dies.

It was a saying in the old language, one she hadn't heard since childhood. Sitting back on her heels, she waited for the elements to tell her something. Anything.

They remained silent.

Unsure what to do with the seemingly valuable trinket, Evelyn decided to keep it. It was a puzzle she could work on at a later time.

She dried it off using the bottom of her shirt. Her trousers lacked pockets, so she lifted the chain around her neck. As she rose to her feet, she tucked the cool metal into her shirt, hiding it from anyone who might happen upon her.

During her walk home, she debated the merits of showing the necklace to her family. The elements whirred in dissent and she sighed.

Evelyn trusted her magic. It didn't mean she always liked it.

Chapter 3

"Are you sure you're alright?" Nora asked from where she was perched next to Eden at the foot of Evelyn's bed.

"I'm fine. Really. I only wish I'd given Jasper some injury to match."

"Oh, I think you injured him plenty by rebuffing his … encroachment into your personal space."

"Ha! Encroachment? That's perfect, Eden. Yes, I do believe he was launching an invasion, encroaching on my face like that."

"Well, he's lucky Father hasn't paid him a visit. Or that I haven't."

Nora, wanting to be helpful in her own way, had offered to try some of her new combat moves on the male, but was quickly shot down. Evelyn thought it was a grand idea. Their father had not. No, he wanted to deal with the situation himself.

Edward was, to say the least, furious with young Jasper. Evelyn's insistence the male hadn't technically knocked her off the rock had only calmed him enough to where he'd promised not to have Jasper flogged.

Eden nodded. "Oh, I think he'll confront him eventually. He's giving Jasper time enough to let the guilt build. Father is good at messing with people's minds."

Evelyn's hand instinctively reached for the chain around her neck. It was under her nightgown, but she could feel it through the thin material.

"Well it serves him right," Nora agreed. "At least you didn't break any teeth. Or your eye socket. You just look like you've been in a fight."

"One I lost."

Nora patted Evelyn's feet, which were snuggled under the covers in front of her. "There, there. Not many can fight the mighty boulder and walk away intact."

Evelyn pointed to the massive puff of purple flesh on her face. "Do I really look like I'm intact?"

Nora shook her head solemnly. "No. You look positively dreadful, which is good. You should hope for some permanent damage so the fool won't try to kiss you again."

Eden slapped Nora's arm and Evelyn grinned, wincing when her cheek protested the action. It was typically Evelyn's job to lighten the mood. She was thankful Nora's wit had improved with her age.

"Okay, mother hens. You can see I'm in no danger of anything more than the possibility of a scar. The elixir Father gave me is kicking in and I'd like to close my eyes. Off you go."

Eden scooted off the bed and started adjusting the blankets snugly around Evelyn's body. She ran a hand over her sister's head in the mothering way she always did. "Good night, Evie."

"G'night."

"Come on, Nora. Let's let Evie get some rest."

Begrudgingly, Nora slid off the bed. She approached Evelyn for a goodnight hug, unable to hide her grimace at the sight of the damage from the fall. Faces weren't meant to take impact. She averted her stare.

A hint of silver caught the light near Evelyn's collarbone. Nora leaned forward, drawn to it. "Evie ..."

The world blanked and rapid-fire images flashed in front of Nora's face. Her body remained suspended in motion until the onslaught of mental pictures ended.

"Nora!" Eden whisper-yelled, not wanting to draw attention from any of the guards in the house. She grabbed Nora's biceps, trying to pull her out of her trance.

"Stop shaking me," the youngest droned.

"Sorry."

Evelyn's eyes lifted to Eden's. Nora occasionally saw things—visions—as had their mother, Elora. Unlike their mother, when Nora's came, they were quick and she zoned out until they passed.

"Can I let go of you?"

"Yes. I'm steady."

Nora took several deep breaths, concentrating on what she'd seen. She rarely was able to make sense of anything she saw in her visions. It was like she was being teased with power she couldn't use, which was appalling to a Gwydion who could not wield magic.

Nora licked her lips. "Demon. With you, Evie. I think you were dancing with a demon. A very large one with dark hair."

"Really?" Evelyn attempted to hide the excitement in her voice.

"I think so. It was so fast I only saw fragments. Gah. What a useless talent."

Eden wrapped an arm around Nora. "Perhaps not. Some information is better than none."

"I'm not so sure."

"Well, did you get a threatening feeling, like the demon was dangerous? Like it was a warning?"

"No. It was nothing like that. In fact, it was quite the opposite. He was almost ... I don't know. It's so jumbled."

"Then trust your gut. If you ever see this demon, you'll likely remember the vision and the feeling will come back. You'll be the one to know whether or not he's a threat. Maybe it's not control of an element, but your visions could be extremely important."

"Doubtful, but I'll take it under advisement."

"Good. Come now, let's let Evie rest."

Nora bent down to her sister in an awkward hug. "Sorry about your face."

"Sorry about yours, as well," Evelyn retorted and Nora huffed in good humor.

Eden put out the lamp and led Nora through the door. "Call for me if you need anything," she said in that mothering way of hers.

"I will."

The door closed and Evelyn turned to her side, trying to get more comfortable. Relaxing, she drifted off.

* * *

Evelyn opened her eyes and found herself in the clearing. She sagged in disappointment. She was almost looking forward to the nothingness she'd been feeling this last week after she drifted off.

The elixir had done its job in making her drowsy. She'd mistakenly believed it would also prevent her from dreaming. In addition, it didn't prevent her from feeling the ache of her wound in the dreamworld.

"It's about bloody damn time," a voice grumbled behind her.

Startled, but unafraid, Evelyn turned her head, looking over her shoulder. Her hair slid across the side of her face, cool against her tender skin—a safety blanket she hid behind. She feared her blemished appearance would act as a repellent to the one person's attention she desired.

Sitting on the ground, leisurely leaning against the trunk of the nearest tree like he didn't have a care in the world, was Marrok. The quiet hum of his power radiated into the night air. Her breath caught in her throat.

One long leg stretched before him. The other was bent and his arm rested atop his knee. The shadows hid part of his face, but she knew it was him. She would know this male anywhere.

Evelyn allowed herself a moment of scrutinizing his form before her brain registered his complaint. His terse indictment diminished her excitement to see him. Two years of anticipation fizzled and died faster than it took to get her breath back.

Bristling, she replied, "I'm sorry, I didn't realize we had an appointment."

He leaned forward, the sharp angles of his face emerged from the dark, more pronounced by the moonlight. "I don't appreciate your sarcasm. You pulled me here, then were nowhere to be found. I've been stuck in your woods for hours."

"Impossible. I've only just fallen asleep. And I did *not* pull you here. *I* get pulled here nightly. Something else is doing the pulling. I am not the puller. I don't even know how to do such things. And why were you even asleep before dark? The only males I know who sleep in the early evening are drunkards. Are you drunk? Or a drunkard? I don't associate with drunkards. Do you think ..."

The more she ranted the more animated she became. Marrok stared at the odd female as she prattled on, his stiff posture loosening. *Confounding little witch.* Surely, she'd run out of oxygen soon.

"Are you even listening to me?" She took a step towards him with clenched fists.

"No."

He could smell a trace of magic wafting off her, spiced with indignation. Did the little female think to attack him? The corner of his mouth lifted.

Her pursed lips demanded his attention as she raised her chin and flipped her dark red hair in a huff. The counterfeit night sky's soft blue rays fell upon the right side of her face. He jumped to his feet, snarling.

Evelyn recoiled so fast she fell to her bottom. She instinctively threw up her hands, reinforcing the magical barrier between the forest and the clearing.

Though her torso rose and fell with the deep breaths she was sucking in, she did not fear he would truly harm her. He'd surprised her, was all. Evelyn simply hadn't been prepared for his abrupt change in demeanor. It wasn't everyday a large demon pounced in her direction.

Marrok's gaze dropped to her chest, transfixed for a moment before he comprehended what he was doing. He refused to ogle the teenager, and snapped his focus back to her face.

"Who hurt you?" His voice came out far more gravelly than normal, traces of his power escaping without his permission.

All demons spoke in low tones. Severe emotions tightened their bodies to the point even their vocals were affected.

Demons who went rogue, who committed horrific acts in order to gain power, always spoke in this way. It was how his uncle had sounded right before Marrok killed him.

He knew his eyes were black. He was dangerously close to either breaking through the barrier or compelling Evelyn to lower it so he could reach her. He also knew both were terrible ideas.

Marrok couldn't help that he wanted to comfort her, to assure himself she was alright. Instinct was driving him to protect, to destroy any threat to her. He may not be able to properly claim Evelyn, but he'd be damned if he allowed another to harm his mate and get away with it.

At his sides, his thumbs rubbed against his fingertips. His hands itched to feel her fragile skin, to take away her pain. Maybe if he had the name of her assailant he could focus on him instead. Make a plan. Invade the male's dreams. Remove his heart. *Avenge her*, his demon hissed.

He needed a name, and an image of the culprit's visage. "Answer me, Evelyn."

"What is wrong with you?"

"Nothing." *Everything.* Things in the Southland had only gotten worse. The weight he'd been carrying for decades, the one he used to be able to easily shoulder, was becoming a burden.

Worse, his mate had apparently been attacked and he hadn't been here to protect her. She was supposed to be safe in Gwydion. Elementals were a peaceful people, not known for attacking innocents.

For the first time in two years, Marrok felt his inner demon push forcefully against his mind, demanding he do his duty to Evelyn. The band of tension, the one pressing in on him since the night he'd chosen to walk away from his mate, tightened.

He hadn't chosen to *gandeste*, to decisively break into the dream of another. Only the most powerful of demons could manage it. Even then it wasn't an exact science. There could be both physical and mental tolls to pay for such exertions. Yet, his saatus seemed to have done it with ease, repetitively drawing him to her in sleep.

Marrok knew he'd taken a huge gamble trying to deny the mating bond, or, at the very least, prolong it as long as possible. He should know better than to foolishly believe he could outplay the powers of the universe.

If Evelyn hadn't been the one who summoned him, then other forces were at work. Fate introduced them over a decade ago. He'd been forced to return just two years past. Ignoring the third calling was asking for trouble from the Goddess.

Marrok was tired. So tired he was close to making a decision he might regret. *Was it so bad to want to protect his mate*?

As one half of his mind focused on things out of his control, the other half took in the damage done to Evelyn. Now that her face was in full view, he also noticed she was lacking an eyebrow. The skin where it used to be was pink, as though it had been scorched away.

She'd been struck *and* burned? His hands formed fists, wondering what other injuries she'd endured. What sort of monster put his brutal hands on his female?

"Last chance before I tear through your shield."

She laughed, the musical notes both attracting and inciting him. *The little minx actually had the gall to laugh at The King of Sundari?* His carefully constructed control slipped until it was hanging by a thread. He would tend to her whether she wanted it or not.

"Have it your way." Marrok opened his mental flow of energies and directed them towards the barrier.

Evelyn watched in awe as white and silver threads of light shot out from Marrok's eyes. They hit her shield with such force, she was sure the light would reflect back to him. Instead, the elements making up her barricade absorbed his energies.

Marrok had expected to tear through the barrier easily, or at the very least, chip it away. Astonished, neither occurred. He marveled at how much stronger her protective magics were than the last time he'd felt them. Not only that, they seemed to grab ahold of his stream of power and siphon it greedily.

His mate's demon iris glowed, somehow connecting them without touching. Marrok slowed the flow, afraid cutting it off abruptly would do damage to one of them.

Evelyn gasped as Marrok's power was channeled into her, spreading through every cell in her body. Euphoria swamped her system. She wasn't even in direct contact with the wall of mixed magics, yet somehow, she could feel what he was doing.

"Damnit!" he cursed, reining in his assault until it stopped completely. He wouldn't have attacked the shield if he'd known the power would fuse with his mate.

Evelyn stood on shaky legs, feeling more energized than she had in years. She wiggled her fingers in front of her face. "You should bottle this up and sell it in the market."

Marrok watched in awe as she marveled over the power coursing through her veins. An elemental absorbing a demon's magics was usually a death sentence. Evelyn acted like it tickled.

His saatus was strong. Formidable. Able to take his power and contain it within her body, a feat few could have managed.

A piece of Marrok swelled with pride, celebrating the fact Fate had created a mate for him who possessed remarkable abilities. *Claim her,* his demon hissed. *Stop punishing us and take her.*

He ignored it. The female was only seventeen or eighteen at the most. He would not complete the saatus bond with one so young.

Evelyn giggled. She looked like she was drunk—on his powers. It would be so easy to compel her now his essence coursed through her limbs. It would also violate something between them. Instead of bending her to his will, he decided on a different approach.

"Lower your shield. I only want to check your injuries, *moj draga.*"

Evelyn chewed the inside of her mouth, focusing more on the endearment and what it might mean. *Moj* was the word for *my* in the old language. She didn't know what *draga* meant, but he'd claimed her as his something. Her face flushed and she looked away.

Nervously, she considered his request. The barrier was always up. Since the day Brennen first invaded her dreams, she'd kept it in place. She didn't know if others would be able to enter as Brennen had, so she'd never considered dropping her protection.

What would Marrok do if she lowered it? There was only one way to find out.

Chapter 4

Evelyn slid the elements apart, allowing enough space for Marrok to pass through. His lips separated, seemingly surprised she acquiesced.

Marrok stepped across and the wall of magic closed behind him. Immediately, her aroma assaulted his senses. Images of a desert garden in a summer storm came to mind. Her scent embodied what she was—a precious rose in the path of a fast-approaching tempest.

He was thankful he could detect the traces of youth, reminding him she was still too young for the likes of him.

He moved close and Evelyn's spine straightened, wondering what he intended. He lifted his hand towards her, hesitating briefly. Gently, oh so gently, his fingers clasped her chin, tilting it up and to the side.

Tiny zaps of power shocked his skin, far too faint to rouse the urge to mate. Something deep within Marrok clicked, like a lock being turned. His spirit settled and his demon hummed in satisfaction. His mind cleared and he felt ... peace.

He inhaled sharply. Touch was the catalyst for the mating frenzy, forcing a pair to physically join and complete the bond. Either the dreamworld or the fact she hadn't reached full adulthood prevented the frenzy. He suspected it was both.

The feel of her soft skin didn't provoke his libido. Instead, it soothed his spirit, lulling his demon into a calm contentedness.

Goddess above, how he'd missed the serenity he once held in his soul. This is what a saatus did for a demon—settled his spirit and, thus, cleared his mind.

Marrok had been losing bits of himself for years, right along with his brethren. Sometimes his thought process muddied and he couldn't see past the haze for a moment. It wasn't as severe as what the rogues experienced, but it was there.

The haze always cleared, but the older he got, the greater his risk became. The longer a demon lived, the more likely madness would ensue.

Power-hungry demons succumbed to the illness much earlier in life. There were twisted ways to increase one's magics. The price a demon paid for committing such atrocities was to risk his or her sanity.

Only mated pairs seemed to be immune to turning rogue. Bonding to Evelyn would keep him sane. *But at what cost to her?*

The image of lustrous midnight hair and a seductive smile flashed across his mind. His jaw clenched.

He'd been through one mating before, to a female who wasn't his saatus. He'd barely survived it, emotionally at least. Judging by his reaction to the marks upon Evelyn's face, he knew it would be far worse if his true mate suffered a similar fate.

His fear reaffirmed his vow to never love another. Marrok shook his head, dissolving the contemplation. There was a lot of space between love and companionship. Maybe the Goddess gifted him with Evelyn to anchor his demon soul. He didn't have to fall in love with her.

The bond linked two souls—making the subsequent relationship work was up to the couple. Of course, a mated pair was always drawn to one another, would always protect one another. There was comfort in knowing he did not have to walk through eternity alone.

Marrok fixated on the beauty in his hand, pondering the possibility of an intimate relationship, of once again having someone to share his life. Fate picked Evelyn for a reason. Only time would reveal why she was deemed to be his match.

It was too late for him to pick any other course. Too late for them both. For better or for worse, he had to come to terms with his destiny. He would never come out the victor against it.

His eyes roamed the right side of her head, from nose to temple to brow. He marked every broken blood vessel, every point of swelling, every scrape. With his opposite hand, as lightly as he could, he placed his palm upon her injured cheek.

Evelyn's mouth pressed tight. Her skin was tender. The place he was touching quickly heated. She waited for the pain that didn't come. Energies flowed out of her and she closed her eyes, sighing contentedly.

After a few seconds, he lifted his palm away. The thumb of the hand still holding her chin lightly brushed across her bottom lip and her eyes popped open.

Marrok let go and took a small step back. Evelyn blinked, assessing. It was gone. The discomfort, the hurt, all gone.

"You healed me?"

"Not quite."

"What did you do?"

"I took away your pain and siphoned some of the magic you absorbed."

Evelyn lifted her hand and patted the side of her face. "It's still swollen."

"I'm not a healer. As I said, I took away your pain."

"How?"

"Does it matter?"

"To me, it does. Please, I'd like to know. If it's something that can be replicated, I'd very much like to know how. Such a power could be very useful to others.

I could help the midwives, or ... people who are suffering."

Marrok's look softened. Not only was she powerful, she was compassionate. Unfortunately, she would not be able to reproduce the power with anyone other than him.

"I pulled your pain out and absorbed it into my body."

"That's amazing. Is it possible for me to do that?"

"I'm sorry, but no," he lied. Technically, a saatus could, but only with his or her mate. It was abhorrent to him to even consider allowing her to feel his pain.

Her eyes moved to his cheek. "Does it hurt you? Like it did me?"

A heartbeat passed. Two.

"Yes. Enough that I'm surprised you were handling it so well."

"I am not weak."

"I didn't say you were. You took quite an impact, as well as a burn?" his chin lifted towards her brow.

Her lopsided grin hit him square in the chest.

"Noticed the missing eyebrow, did you? Any chance you know how to grow it back? Immediately?"

Marrok shook his head.

"Well, that's unfortunate."

"Who did this to you, Evelyn?"

Her nose crinkled. "Well, it was actually two separate incidents."

"You were attacked not once, but *twice*?" he seethed.

"Well, no. I wasn't attacked, exactly. I appreciate your concern, but it's not what you think. My sister, Eden, took the eyebrow in retaliation for me using my powers when we were sparring—"

"Your father allows you and your sister to *fight*?"

"Understatement of the century. He makes us. And it's sisters, plural. All three of us receive training."

Marrok crossed his arms, scowling. "Why in the Goddess' name would the King of Gwydion force his daughters into combat?"

"Why wouldn't he? He'd never let us grow up to be vulnerable. I, for one, am thankful I know how to protect myself with more than just the elements I command. Especially considering my family's history. Father thinks we have targets painted on our backs simply because of who birthed us."

Evelyn's tone was level, her speech came out as a matter of fact. Marrok could guess it had been ingrained in her and her sisters since their mother's murder.

He scratched his head, thinking King Edward may be onto something. If Marrok had a daughter, he would not want her to feel defenseless. At the thought of progeny, his claws scratched his chest.

"Wait, how do you know who my father is?"

His gaze moved over her shoulder to the manor house. "The royal residence is behind you. I was here once, long ago. I've also met your father a number of times at the Temple of Sanctus Femina. He brags about his daughters, Eden, Evelyn, and Nora."

"Oh."

"And this?" his knuckle grazed her temple, gliding along her enflamed skin.

Evelyn folded her lips over her teeth, a tad embarrassed. She didn't want to come across as the clumsy female she'd always been. Not with Marrok.

"I can pull the memory from your mind, but I'd prefer it if you told me."

"And what King Marrok wants, King Marrok gets?"

His eyes crinkled and one shoulder lifted. "Usually. Not always."

Evelyn liked the way he responded, almost playfully. During their sparse encounters, he was always so focused and severe. She hadn't expected his candid jest.

She released the tension from her lips and said, "I did it."

"You did it."

She looked away. "Basically."

"Explain."

Evelyn met his glare and lifted an eyebrow, the one still attached.

"Please," he amended, wanting her to volunteer so he didn't have to pull it from her mind.

"I fell."

"Onto your face?"

"Basically."

The heavens help him, she was beyond vexing. He reached deep for patience and waited her out. She must have felt his annoyance because she started talking.

"I was at the stream, not far into the woods over there," she pointed. "There's a set of boulders in one of the bends that I like to climb. I go there to meditate sometimes. Do you meditate?"

"No."

"Hmm. Well, I was on top of the boulder. Jasper was sitting with me."

"Jasper?" Marrok's pupils expanded just as the inherently masculine name slid off his tongue in repugnance.

"He's a male from town, one who recently joined my father's army. I've known him since I was very young. We're ... friends."

She waited for the amber to return to his irises. It didn't.

"Continue."

"Right. Well, we were chatting and he leaned towards me—"

"Leaned?" he growled.

"Um, yes. Really, it happened so fast I'm not completely sure how I managed to tip backwards like that. One second his face was moving towards mine and the next my face was crashing onto one of the smaller boulders below me."

Marrok took a step towards her, their fronts a breath apart. "He meant to kiss you?"

"I think so."

"No lies, Evelyn. I can feel even a half-truth grate upon my skin."

"Really?"

"Really."

"How inconvenient for others. They must talk in riddles around you. Is this just you or can all demons do this?"

"Evelyn."

"Alright, alright. Yes, I believe he meant to plant his mouth upon mine."

His eyes bled completely black, covering even the whites. Evelyn swallowed. Marrok didn't like the thought of Jasper kissing her. Her body grew tingly all over. She felt his jealousy, innately knew that was what he was experiencing.

"Where might I find this *Jasper*?"

"That, I will not tell you."

"You are but a child, Evelyn. This male should not be attempting you. His actions caused you harm and I will seek retribution."

Her excited tingling quickly turned cold.

"I am *not* a child. I am a half year past eighteen now. Old enough to marry. Old enough for ... other things."

The black shrunk, making him look less demonic. Amber burned bright along the edges of his still-large pupils. So bright, she wondered if it reflected upon her skin.

"Just what do you know of *other things*?" his voice rasped, seizing her with its power.

Instinctually, she arched towards him. "I—"

"No," he shook his head, knowing he was close to crossing a line. "Do not answer that. I am centuries older than you. I should never have asked such a thing."

He moved away and Evelyn had the urge to follow. "I don't mind, Marrok. Shouldn't we be able to speak freely with one another?"

The dumbfounded look on his face made her want to laugh. Did he think she knew nothing of coupling?

Marrok cleared his throat. "You hardly know me well enough to have such conversations, little one."

Evelyn clasped her hands, trying not to fidget. Theron had whispered a single word to her two years ago. *Saatus.* Mate. She'd felt the truth of it. Surely, Marrok knew it as well.

"While it is true I don't know you very well," she conceded, "I also think it is true that, at some point, I *will* know you. Very well. How else can I explain your return to this place?"

She bit her lip. A lifetime of insecurities bubbled up. She didn't have feminine wiles to throw at him. All she had was her honesty and faith in their destiny.

Evelyn dug deep for courage. She worried she may not have many more chances to speak to him, especially if they went years without being in the same dream. "Am I not—do you not know what I am to you?"

Marrok cocked his head. "Of course, I know what you are to me. I knew it the first time you pulled me here. I'm wondering how it is you came to know."

"Theron. The last time you were here, he, well, communicated with me."

"Ah, of course. The meddling priest."

"Why ... why have you not come for me?" Evelyn couldn't hide the tremor of her voice. Wasn't finding one's destined mate something magical? Wonderful? A blessed gift to be cherished? He was acting so cavalier about it.

She understood she was still a teenager. She didn't understand why he had not taken steps to ensure he would have her once he considered her an adult.

Marrok could hear the disappointment in her tone. She wanted him to come to Gwydion and claim her? Goddess help him.

Marrok could skirt the issue or he could be truthful with his mate. He respected how bold and honest she was with him. He could only do the same in return—to a degree.

"You're too young."

"I am of age."

"Eighteen is still too young, Evelyn."

"My sister is to be married at age twenty. It is commonplace for females in Imperium to be married by then."

He hid his wince at the mention of marriage while his demon perked up. His palms scrubbed his face.

"It is not so simple."

"Isn't it?"

"No. Things in Imperium are not as they were. Each faction is facing its own difficulties." His intricate network of merchants and spies kept him abreast of the happenings in their world, and what was happening wasn't good.

"I'm aware of the Northland's dying forest."

"Many are. What do you know of the Eastland? Or of the Southland?"

"The vampires are secretive. They do not readily share information. Everyone knows that. I've not heard of anything amiss in Sundari."

It was true. The vampires, who lived in the Eastland, in the Kingdom of Prajna, kept to themselves for the most part. Though, just like the other factions in Imperium, they did do business from time to time across their borders.

Tricky demons in the Southland were awfully nosy and had ways to extricate information. They were, quite literally, mind readers. Beings without strong mental shields were easy prey to the demons.

Marrok took news of the Burghard's dying forest in stride. He'd even palleted the reports of Gwydion's draining magics.

When the details of the Prajna's lack of matings and zero birth rate hit his ears, he knew. He knew beyond all doubt the sufferings around Imperium weren't isolated. He simply didn't know what to do about it.

"What's going on in the Sundari Kingdom?"

"Nothing for you to worry about."

"Let me guess, you have it under control?" she huffed.

"No, not yet."

She was surprised at his admission. Both because she believed he was more than capable of handling his kingdom and also because she hadn't expected him to admit he didn't have control over things. Yet he was still holding something back.

"You're not going to tell me the details, are you? You can trust me, Marrok."

A flaring pain cut across his forearm. He lifted it and saw blood swell to the surface.

"Not tonight. I must return. Immediately, it seems."

Evelyn gasped. "What's happening?"

"Someone's trying to wake me."

"By cutting you?!" she screeched.

"Drawing blood is sometimes the only way to be released from dreamwalking."

"That's so barbaric."

"Says the female holding me hostage."

The corners of her mouth turned down. "If I'm holding you here, I'm not doing it purposefully."

Marrok reached out and stroked her cheek. "I believe you."

The contact, as fleeting as it was, reinforced his control. The transitory snippets of madness had been gone since he'd cusped her chin.

See? She is the answer. Marrok ignored his demon spirit. It wasn't the time to claim his mate, but maybe she could keep him centered, help staunch the spreading sickness inside him long enough for him to find the solution for his people.

If he could dreamwalk to her at will, touch her skin when he did, it might work. His saatus might be able to buy him enough time. It would be easiest to gandeste if she willed him to her while he did the same.

Another cut appeared next to the first. He could feel himself slipping away.

"Marrok?" she whispered.

He opened his mouth to tell her to try calling for him in a few nights, but no sound came out. He blinked and the ceiling of his chambers came into view.

The outlines of four large heads focused above him. Favin and Petr on his left, Danil and Lazlo on his right. These were the only males he'd ever thought of as brothers.

His face stung, and not from absorbing Evelyn's negative energies. He worked his jaw, making sure they hadn't broken it.

"Who cut me?" he demanded of his men, pushing himself into a sitting position.

Favin lifted the blade in his hand. "I did, Sire."

"I assume this was because the blow to the side of my face failed to rouse me?"

"Yes, Sire."

The soldiers all shared a look.

"And?" Marrok's head swung to each them, landing on Danil, the most verbose of the four, and the only one of them with a white head of hair.

"You were talking in your sleep. Talking nonsense. Nothing was working and we feared ..." Danil gulped, diverting his eyes.

"You thought I might have succumb?"

Favin sheathed his blade, answering when Danil couldn't. "Yes, Sire."

"I was dreamwalking. Nothing more, nothing less. Understood?"

All the men gave curt nods and he commanded, "Now tell me, Favin, what has the four of you in my chambers at this hour."

"Rogues. A group of them breached the perimeter walls."

"Did they reach the fortress?"

"No, Sire. They didn't even try to."

"Then where did they go?"

Again, they exchanged a look.

"Where?" Marrok barked.

"They went straight to the tombs."

The tombs? There was nothing there but earth and stone and the bodies of the dead. Only a handful of guards would have been anywhere near there.

"Were there any casualties?"

"No, but they desecrated one of the crypts. Broke it wide open. They—they removed the body and left it in the courtyard. It's why we woke you."

Marrok froze. "Whose tomb?"

Favin faltered.

Marrok's rage came fast this time, faster than Favin could say, "Your wife's."

* * *

Evelyn awoke, filled with a fury that was not her own. Clutching the chain around her neck. She dropped to her knees beside the bed and prayed for Marrok's safety.

Chapter 5

Evelyn, Age 20

"No? What do you mean he said *no*?" There was no hiding the disbelief in Evelyn's voice.

"Hush! Nora will hear you," Eden chastised. "Do not make me regret telling you."

"Nora is out in the woods replenishing her energies. Unless she's recently developed a wolf's acute hearing, she'll know nothing of this."

Eden went to the window. Nora always returned on the same path and would be easily visible if she emerged. She had just informed Evelyn that, a week ago, their father invited King Kellan for a visit in order to get to know Nora a little better. She was now eighteen and the wedding was less than two years away.

It was the same offer he'd made when Eden turned eighteen. The Wolf King had accepted the invite to meet

Eden. In contrast, this time around, he rejected the offer to spend some time with Nora, his true mate.

Evelyn found it unsettling and she wanted to know why he declined. It went against what she knew of wolves, of how connected they needed to be to their lifemates.

She stood and walked over to Eden, keeping her voice low. It was more for Eden's benefit. Evelyn herself had seen Nora run off less than ten minutes ago. She'd be gone for at least another hour

"Did Father demand Kellan come for a visit or was it a request?" Evelyn inquired.

"I did not read the missive. We only spoke of it in passing. He wanted to make sure I was okay with my betrothed returning to our home to get know my youngest sister."

"*Ex*-betrothed," Evelyn stressed.

Eden sighed. "Yes, ex-betrothed. I assured Father I had no personal feelings towards the male. I mean, I only met him once. It was hardly enough time to become attached."

"True, though, you were engaged to him for your entire life. Right up until Nora walked in the door that day. Father was right to ask you."

Eden looked at her sister and grinned. "That was sweet of you to say, Evie."

"That's me, Sweetie Evie."

Eden laughed. "Right."

"So back to the Wolf-Man's refusal."

"You really should stop calling him that."

"Fine. *Kellan* refused to visit his mate. His true mate, the one the Goddess created just for him. The other half of his whole. The one single creature alive who would complete him. I didn't know it was possible to stay away like that."

Only, Evelyn *did* know, she just didn't understand it. Marrok hadn't been in one of her dreams since the night he'd touched her bruised skin. Nor had he come to Gwydion to speak to her father.

When he'd vanished with those cuts, she feared something terrible was happening to him. She tried to awaken, but the dreamworld wouldn't relinquish its hold until it was good and ready.

Sitting in the clearing that night, hoping he'd come back into the dream, she considered broaching the subject with her father when she woke. He wouldn't be happy about it, but he would understand the ramifications of dodging Fate.

Just as she'd come to the decision to confess her entire dreamlife to her father, Theron appeared in the forest and whispered in her mind. *Patience.*

The next thing she knew, she was out of bed and filled with rage—Marrok's rage. Evelyn knew it down into her very bones. She'd prayed every night since for his well-being.

Every once in a while, she would feel random bouts of anger or mania. Not enough to affect her, thankfully, just enough to make her aware.

Since the moment he touched her, they'd established some sort of feeble mental connection. She wondered if he could feel her emotions. If he could, he would know how she longed for him to come for her. She was his mate. What would keep him away?

This was the question that had bothered her for years now. She could admit to herself it was why she was upset on Nora's behalf. Hence her current interrogation of Eden.

"He is King, Evelyn. I'm sure he is tasked with many things and his time is sparse."

"He was King when he came to visit you and you weren't even his mate."

"I know," Eden's soft voice acknowledged on an exhale. "I'm sure he has good reason. Besides, it's not like Nora has any expectation to see him."

"How do you know? Did you ask her?"

Eden looked nonplussed. "Well, no."

"Then how do you know she has no expectation to see him? Perhaps she would like to meet him again, this time as an adult. To know him or, at least, have some sense of him prior to matrimony. It's not unreasonable."

"No, it's not unreasonable. However, she's never voiced it so I propose we say nothing of his refusal. There's no sense in chancing any amount of anxiety or disappointment. She'll have a hard enough time of it as it is."

Evelyn chewed the inside of her cheek. Eden was right. Nora might not know Kellan, but there would only be negative emotional consequences if she knew he would not come to her when invited.

This much Evelyn knew for certain. She felt it every night when she laid her head upon her pillow and sought out the male who had taken over her thoughts. Searching, always searching the only space her dreams allowed her to visit.

Marrok hadn't returned to her dreamworld. Try as she might to summon him, he never came. Her faith in Fate was being tested. Evelyn would not lay such disappointment at Nora's feet.

She squeezed Eden's shoulder and nodded silently.

* * *

Evelyn felt the change before she opened her eyes. Her stance widened and her hands flexed with her magics.

No calm breeze brushed across the clearing. Tonight, a blistering wind struck her form, its howling whistle bounced irritatingly off her eardrums.

Instead of soft blues and purples, the moon was giving off shades of red and orange. Flames crackled and licked the trees of the forest, but nothing was burning. The dreamworld, or something in it, was irritated.

Slowly, she rotated, seeking information, waiting for the elements to speak. They buzzed, drawing her attention to one of the paths connecting the clearing to the woods.

The fire split into columns on either side of the trail and a form emerged from within the inferno. Tall, with broad shoulders and a lean trunk, the male stalked forward.

Blackened eyes locked on hers, so intense she felt them in her core. Long, predatory strides moved him directly in her path. Without thought, Evelyn opened the barrier and he stepped into the clearing.

The wind screamed and the only other sound she could hear was the boom of her thundering heart. He advanced swiftly, everything about his approach screamed he was a man possessed. His intent couldn't be clearer.

In two seconds she was in his arms, his mouth slamming into hers. This first kiss—the first she'd ever experienced—was hard and unyielding. It was nothing like she had imagined, and almost more than she was prepared to receive. This wasn't the kiss of a lover. It was a punishment.

Evelyn gasped and Marrok took advantage of her parted lips, driving his tongue into her mouth. Her fingers clenched the fabric on his shoulders as she trembled in his embrace, struggling to stay on her feet.

Her veins throbbed, her heated blood reaching a rapid boil. His arms tightened and she knew he'd never let her fall.

Evelyn felt him everywhere. His powers slid up and down her skin, caressing, inciting. Their shared breaths depleted her of oxygen and tiny pinpoints of light burst from behind her eyelids.

The high-pitched winds built into a crescendo and the blazes roared. Higher and higher until the dreamworld exploded with a blinding radiance, bathing their bodies in the white of their magics before returning once more to muted colors and a calm breeze. The forest was once again covered in purple and blue moonbeams.

The world settled, along with Marrok's spirit. He'd been on the verge of something terrible. He'd gotten worse every day without his saatus. Another two years without her was out of the question.

Feeling once more in control of himself, he slowed the kiss, bringing a hand up to palm the back of her head. His lips drifted to the corner of her mouth, then to her temple, before dropping to her ear.

"Never again, *moj draga*," he warned, biting her earlobe.

She shivered. "P-pardon?"

"You'll never again wait so long to summon me." He failed to mention his own unsuccessful attempts to enter her world.

Evelyn, still reeling from his arduous assault, took a moment to process. He was upset she hadn't pulled him into her dreams. She smiled against his chest, then tipped her head back.

"Missed me, did you?"

"Don't tease."

"I'm not. I just wanted to hear you say it."

"I don't know you well enough to *miss* you. But I never imagined, little mate, once I'd confirmed for you that you were my saatus, you'd wait so long."

Evelyn attempted to free herself from his arms. He didn't budge and she glared up at him. "And I didn't think, once you confirmed for me that I was your saatus, you'd do absolutely nothing to find me."

He let go and she felt oddly bereft when he put space between them.

"So you didn't call for me out of some sort of revenge?" he snapped, trying to let go of the last of his frustration.

"What? Of course not. And what makes you think I didn't call for you?"

A muscle in his jaw ticked. He glared at his gorgeous mate, who had physically matured greatly these last two years. Evelyn would be twenty-one by the next solstice, which meant she'd reached full physical maturity during their time apart.

Her cheekbones were more pronounced, giving off a regal countenance. Her small nose pointed to two full, pouty lips, still swollen from their shared passion.

Her breasts were larger, rounder, making her waist appear tiny. Maybe it was tiny. He was having trouble concentrating, caught between spanking her arse and kissing her senseless again.

"I think you didn't call for me because I haven't seen you in almost two and a half years, Evelyn."

A thrill shot through her. Marrok really was upset about being away from her. He must have missed her greatly. "I'll remind you I have no idea how you come to me in my dreams. Besides, I thought demons could break into the dreams of others, if they chose."

His arms crossed, not liking the reminder. He, too, had tried everything he knew of to enter her dreamworld. For more than two years he'd desperately hunted her in his sleep, needing the touch of her skin to sooth his mind. With every attempt, he came up against a barrier he could not breach.

He'd come close to riding into Gwydion to retrieve her. When he'd last left, she'd been battered and bruised. He wanted to know of her health, to look upon her with his own eyes. The dreamworld was the only safe place to do so.

Several more attempts had been made by the rogues to breach the walls of the Terenuskit Fortress, the building he called home. Only the constant fighting kept him away from his mate. It reinforced the fact she would not be safe in Sundari.

Marrok was the strongest of his species. It was too risky for him to travel to the Westland and leave his people vulnerable. Or, worse, risk rogue demons following him. He was loath to bring her to the Southland. What was he to do? He felt like he was fighting on every front of his existence.

Evelyn licked her lips and he fixated on the reddened skin. He hadn't intended to be so rough and he certainly hadn't expected her to return with equal fervor. His trousers had grown uncomfortably tight, a direct result of her enthusiasm.

"If it means anything," she said, "I did try reaching out to you. I've tried every night since. I was afraid you wouldn't come for me so I tried to pull you here. I thought ... I was afraid something had happened to you. They cut you." Her voice whispered the last part sadly.

Marrok lost some of the fight in him. His mate had worried he'd been harmed. He reached for Evelyn and she didn't resist his embrace.

Resting his chin atop her head, he told her, "I tried, as well. Dreamwalking is tricky business and, obviously, I was just as unsuccessful."

"Why didn't you come for me? To Gwydion?"

"My kingdom is not a safe place to be. I'm not inclined to endanger you."

"Then don't bring me to Sundari. You can still come to see me, to visit, maybe speak to my father?" she added hopefully.

Marrok exhaled. "Walk with me."

83

C.A. Worley

He spoke with no emotion and Evelyn's heart plummeted. He wasn't going to come for her.

Chapter 6

Marrok's hand drifted to Evelyn's as he released her from his arms. He tugged her alongside and started strolling the tree line.

The little zaps of power flowing through their touch were stronger than the last time, but not as strong as they would be if they were together when awake.

He held up their joined hands. "Do you feel this?"

"Yes. When our skin meets, it's like our energies increase tenfold at the point of contact."

"Exactly. This is us touching without truly touching. We are in the dreamworld, Evelyn. We are not actually together. Things are muted here. Subdued."

"Hmm."

"What do you mean *hmm*?"

"I thought things were rather exhilarating back there."

"You would if you'd never been handled as such."

"Handled?" she sniffed, trying to extricate her hand. "Wonderful. I suppose it wasn't quite as earth-shattering for you as it was for me."

Marrok refused to let go, amused by her defiance. "Let me clarify. What we just shared? It was powerful. Exhilarating. Life-altering. As awe-inspiring as it was, it was only a fraction of what we would feel if my skin came into contact with yours outside of a dream."

"Oh," her brows drew close then quickly lifted towards her hairline. "*Oh.*"

"Yes. *Oh,*" he mimicked her voice and she laughed. His demon chuckled, liking the sound.

"Well, that certainly makes shaking hands a complicated task when first meeting your saatus."

"It does, indeed."

"Is it always like that? Every time mates touch?"

"No. The first contact sparks what we call the *bjesnilo*—the mating frenzy. It lasts as long as it takes to complete the bond."

"How do you complete the bond?"

His incisors, smaller than a vampire's, but larger than an elemental's, stretched. "First is to simply touch. Initially, it does something to connect our spirits on a superficial level. Sometimes mates feel each other's emotions even when they are apart."

"Yes, I've felt a few moments of your anger."

Marrok stopped walking, staring down at her. "You shouldn't have been able to. By superficial, I meant when we touch, my spirit calms in reaction to yours and you can pick up on it. How do you know you were sensing my emotions and not your own?"

Evelyn shrugged. "I just know. The first time was the night you were cut. Not very long after you awoke, I did, too. I nearly went blind with the rage coursing through me. Instinct told me it was yours. I assumed you were about to tan the hide of whomever cut your arm."

The image of coming upon his long-dead wife's shattered tomb flashed in his mind. Evelyn squeezed his hand.

"I just felt it again. Should I not have told you?"

"No, you will always tell me the truth, whether or not I want to hear it."

Evelyn nodded and squeezed his hand again. She sensed he wasn't prepared to talk about whatever it was that had ignited his fury.

"What happens after the initial touch?" she asked.

"Sex."

Evelyn coughed and Marrok smirked. "Mating frenzy," he clarified. "It spurs the drive to couple."

"So, intercourse completes the bond?"

"No, an exchange of blood will complete the bond. Some argue the consumption of blood is more palatable when in the throes of passion, so the powers that be

87

added in the irresistible draw between mates to make sure it is carried out."

Marrok's earlier anger was now long gone, replaced with something far more tantalizing. He licked his teeth, imagining himself driving into his mate's heat as he consumed her lifeblood.

"I'm thinking I wouldn't have to be buried inside you to desire a taste."

Evelyn swallowed. Her nipples pebbled and her center turned warm again. No male had ever spoken so crassly to her before. She liked it.

"You're very direct," she told him.

His nostrils flared, filled with the sweet aroma of Evelyn's arousal. His mate liked his directness, which was fitting since he thoroughly enjoyed hers.

"And you aren't?" he returned. "I seem to recall being accused of being a drunkard ten seconds into our first real conversation."

"That was over four years ago."

"And yet I remember it as if it was yesterday."

Marrok allowed his magics back into his voice. Holding them back every time they spoke was tiresome. He watched intently as her skin flushed, heating as though he was stroking her.

"You're doing it again. Your voice, it's doing something to me."

"It is my nature. I am a demon, Evelyn."

"This happens when you're around others? Around other females?" A heavy dose of jealousy rankled her senses, thinking of the she-demons on the receiving end of his demonic tone.

"Of course, but demons don't feel it quite the same. It affects mates differently—to a saatus it can be highly arousing. To demons who are not mates, it's more like a pleasant tone of voice conveying friendliness. It also helps get other beings to, shall we say, do business with us?"

"You compel others during business transactions?"

"No. It just makes us more likeable. Compulsion, true compulsion where one's will is taken, takes an immense amount of power. Few have such an ability."

"I've heard rumors of demons amassing power."

His pupils expanded. "From whom?"

"My father. Before you ask, I don't know where he gets his information. Most likely, it came from Theron."

Meddling priest, Marrok grumbled to himself.

"I'm guessing it's related to your statement of the Southland not being safe?" she guessed.

"You'd be correct."

Evelyn looked towards her feet, her mouth twisting. Then she met his gaze and asked, "Are you planning to come for me? Ever?"

"If it was safe, you would be asleep in our bed this night."

C.A. Worley

Our. He'd said *our* bed and Evelyn's pulse spiked.

Marrok cupped her face. "My mate likes this idea."

"She does. So she will demand you make it safe for her. Immediately."

Marrok howled with laughter at her command. His little saatus, as innocent as a spring flower, was demanding access to his bed. His demon pressed forward. *We will give her this, then we can have her. Forever.*

He wanted to assure her it would be done, but he wouldn't lie to her. "I'm doing my best, *moj draga.*"

Evelyn's mouth turned down at the hint of sadness in his voice. Things must be truly grave in Sundari.

"I believe you."

Evelyn lifted her hands to his chest. Bravely. Confidently. Pretending she was both. "I don't want to wait another two years to see you."

Marrok tilted his head. His hands lowered to her sides. "As I stated earlier, never again."

"If you cannot come for me, what do we do?"

"We could try to complete the blood bond. It probably won't be the same as if we were awake, but it might connect us on this plane, making it easier for me to enter your dreams or for you to summon me."

"You mean ..." Her eyes grew big.

"Blood exchange," he said at the same time she asked, "Sex?"

His muscles flexed with restraint. The temptation to rip off her dress and take her on the ground was great. Already, her arousal taunted both he and his demon.

He could easily seduce her, but his saatus deserved more from him than a tumble on the grass when they hadn't seen one another in two years. Handing him her innocence, even in the dreamworld, was something he should cherish.

"I'm not sure you're ready for both, little mate. Let's start with one then we'll see about the other."

"It wasn't an offer, Demon."

His body shook and he didn't know if he wanted to laugh or take her mouth again and force her to be quiet.

"Very well." He removed one hand from her side and unsheathed a claw.

Evelyn eyed it warily. "You're not going to bite me on the neck or something?"

Marrok shook his head. Slowly, seductively, he slid the talon across his lower lip. His dark blood welled to the surface. Evelyn could smell a hint of savory spice and her mouth watered. It should have repelled her, but she found herself leaning towards him.

"Kiss me, Evelyn."

"What about—"

He cut her off by pressing his mouth to hers. He felt the moment her body relaxed into his and her lips parted to receive his blood kiss. Languidly, his tongue brushed hers before retreating. She chased it with her own, licking at the blood on his bottom lip.

Evelyn sighed, the tangy flavor of his essence was heaven on her tongue. She dipped further into his mouth and accidentally nicked the tip on one of his small fangs hard enough to draw blood.

When their lifeblood mixed, her heart stopped, gripped by the shared power. She felt the presence of another, felt it reach into her chest and draw out her soul.

Marrok felt her panic and shifted his hand to her breast, stroking her hardened nipple through the fabric of her shirt, distracting her back into their kiss and increasing her pulse. His cock strained to be freed but he made no further advance. He would not take her fully. Not yet.

His demon spirit lovingly tasted her soul, connecting them further but not fully merging. He'd been right about things being subdued on this plane. Still, the kiss was explosive and he worried what would happen if and when they really touched.

Evelyn arched into Marrok's hand, fevered with desire. She rubbed her lower body against his thigh, seeking relief. She felt his other hand drop to her behind and clutch her closer. His mouth drifted to her ear, forcing goosebumps upon her flesh.

"Do you want me to touch you, Evelyn?"

"You are touching me." Oh, how he was touching her! Her backside. Her breast. Her core was pressed tight to his thigh. She could feel his erection against her belly and for a second she wished she was taller.

"No, little mate. Do you want me to *touch* you?" His hand abandoned her breast and his knuckles brushed the sensitive apex of her thighs. "Here?" Even through her clothing he could feel the heat of her skin.

"Y-yes," Evelyn whimpered. Everything in her wanted his touch.

Marrok took her mouth again while simultaneously pulling up the bottom of her long skirt. Normally, he would command her to do it. Either that or destroy the garment.

He wasn't known for his patience. Yet he believed Evelyn's lack of experience warranted his seduction. He'd never been with a virgin and he wanted to make sure she was prepared. He would give her whatever she needed, and he would teach her to ask for what she wanted.

He used their bodies to pin the material between them before slowly gliding his fingers along the skin of her leg. He inched leisurely across to her inner thigh, then up.

His fingers touched lace and he thought he'd spend in his trousers. He wanted to drop to his knees and see her underthings. His demon agreed wholeheartedly and Marrok threw him back in his cage.

This was about Evelyn, not about him. Tonight, she'd not be teased. She would be rewarded for her acceptance of their bond.

Marrok cupped her center and her hips jerked. He pressed harder and she did it again. Goddess above, she was responsive.

"Please," she breathed into his mouth. Her thoughts were muddled, her only focus was soothing the growing ache between her thighs.

Evelyn's plea was more than he could stand. Marrok used a claw with delicate precision to tear apart the lace. He yanked it from her hips and hastily stuffed it in his pocket. Now that he had full access, he retracted his claws and used his middle finger to stroke her folds.

His mate was wet. For him. He shifted and ground his erection into her upper hip.

He stroked her folds again and then circled her hardened nub. Evelyn's sharp intake told him all he needed to know, giving away exactly how and where she wanted him most. He repeated the action. Once, twice, three times.

Her body started to tremble and he increased the speed of his hand's movements. When his finger dipped inside and his thumb pressed on her clitoris, Evelyn broke the kiss and bit into his pectoral. Her muffled yell vibrated across his chest.

Marrok secured her to him with his left arm while his right hand worked to draw out her orgasm. He could feel her spasms against his fingertips and he longed to feel them while he thrust between her legs.

Soon, his demon promised.

She was still coming when she dissolved in his arms, sighing his name.

* * *

Evelyn came to, panting and gripping her sheets tightly. Her body was still pulsing from her pleasure, the phantom touch of her male a whisper upon her skin.

She slid her hand down to cover her mound, trying in vain to duplicate the contact. She couldn't.

She also couldn't feel her underwear.

* * *

Marrok awoke to the sound of his own shouts as he stroked his shaft to completion. He couldn't remember the last time he'd touched himself and been so sensitive.

Breathless, he looked down at the mess he'd made and frowned. Wrapped around his cock, covered in his semen, was a swatch of torn white lace.

Chapter 7

She was hot. Too hot. Though she'd found release at the hands of her handsome male, Evelyn was having difficulty cooling off. If anything, she hungered for more.

She'd removed her nightgown and turned down all the bedding aside from the sheet. She liked the feel of the cool material upon her skin. She even rose to open the window, hoping for a draft of fresh air.

For the past hour, she had been replaying the dream, reliving every moment. She'd gone as far as attempting to reenact it with her own hand this time. Her attempts were clumsy and unsatisfactory.

Evelyn had never brought herself to climax before. Nothing in her education on intercourse had prepared her for the sensations Marrok had wrought in her dream. No, she'd been informed many females found coupling to be *satisfactory* or *pleasant*.

A full belly was satisfactory. Eating a half-stale pastry could be pleasant. There was no word for what Marrok made her feel. Consumed? Frenzied?

Wanton. Yes, that was a better word. Her lust had obliterated any sense of propriety she may have possessed. Marrok, like most males, she supposed, didn't mind her licentious behavior.

Goddess, how she fixated on that demon. She needed to think of something else. She was starting to obsess and she'd never get back to sleep if she didn't unwind.

Giving up on the sheet, she tugged it off and turned to her side. The muted light from the full moon had crept further across her floor since she'd awoken and opened the window.

She watched the rays, picturing the soft colors of her dreamworld's moon. Gradually, Evelyn's fixation slackened, staring at the light. Her body started to relax and she felt the first tendrils of sleep wrap around her.

She drifted, floating in nothingness. She waited to be planted in the clearing. Her body jolted forward and she felt like she was flying.

The blackness gave way to something down below. She was zooming towards it. As she drew closer, she could make out the top of a building sitting next to a clearing. Just beyond was a huge expanse of forest, and she was headed right for it at break-neck speed.

She braced for impact, thinking her body was about to be broken. It never came. Sounds of limbs and leaves echoed, but she felt nothing. When she opened her eyes, she scented the air and growled.

Growled? Evelyn didn't growl.

Brennen came crashing through the foliage. She could scent him before she saw him. Decades' old rage and disgust surfaced. This was how they'd finally war? In a dream?

The whirlwind of foreign thoughts felt intrusive. Before she could think on her reaction, she was being tackled to the ground.

Her body fought back. Scratched. Punched. Kicked. She wasn't controlling the movements, nor could she feel the impact of his strikes.

"You've gone too far, Uncle!" a voice roared so closely she could feel the vibration of it from within.

"No, I haven't gone far enough! You'll never be King, Marrok. Over my dead body will you take this throne from me."

"I didn't want the bloody throne, Brennen. Now you've left me no choice," the deep voice threatened as she charged towards the vindictive demon.

When her fist landed a blow hard enough to stun Brennen, she clamped both hands around his throat. Only, those weren't her hands.

Evelyn couldn't control her eye movement, so she concentrated on what she could see. Long, strong arms. Tanned skin. Definitely male.

Brennen groped blindly at anything. He managed to get ahold of her necklace and rip it away.

No! a voice echoed in her head.

The hesitation allowed Brennen to gain purchase. Roaring, he threw her through the air. Evelyn crashed into something and dropped to the ground.

Rising to her feet, she noticed a youngling standing beyond the barrier she'd just slammed into. Dark red hair. Bronzed skin. Mismatched eyes. It was like looking into a mirror—fourteen years ago.

Saatus the voice whispered in her head.

Marrok's voice. She was reliving Marrok's fight with his uncle, from inside his body.

Evelyn held the stare of her younger self for a moment. *Ah, Goddess no.* Marrok's thoughts jeered, laced with frustration instead of worry.

Before she could think on his dismay, young Evelyn shouted, "Look out!" The large body she was inhabiting spun around in time to see Brennen's twisted magic coming towards her.

She dove sideways, narrowly escaping the wisps of smoke-like power. The perverse magic screamed when it pounded against Evelyn's shield.

"You'll never get to her," Marrok promised. Evelyn could feel his wrath building. There would be no mercy for Uncle Brennen.

"Then neither shall you."

Brennen jumped into view, his black magic swirling and sullying the air with its stench. She turned, commanding the girl to run. Then faced the foul demon coming closer.

This is where it ends, Marrok's thought vowed, circling the King of Sundari. He was going to have to kill Brennen.

Yes, then we'll take our mate, a second voice invaded her skull.

No. We'll never take the witch.

Evelyn flinched internally. Calling an elemental a witch was a grave insult. Was that the true reason he hadn't come for her, because she was born an elemental?

The demon within screamed as Marrok flew towards his enemy, landing a punch powerful enough to puncture his chest. The last thing she saw before she awoke was Brennen's heart, still beating in her hand.

* * *

Marrok stepped out of the bath, toweling himself quickly and efficiently. He needed to dress and go find Favin.

After his bellowing in the middle of the night, awaking to his shaft in hand, his guards burst through the door. They'd thought he'd been under attack.

Lazlo and Danil were right to enter if they suspected he was in peril, but he wasn't fond of them catching him in a private moment. He snapped something about allowing a male his privacy and sent them back into the hall.

Danil was the only one who hesitated. He looked right at Marrok, assessing. "Carry on, then," he'd finally said with a chuckle, knowing exactly what his king had been doing. Marrok's snarl didn't appear to affect the guard in the least.

Marrok didn't go back to sleep. He couldn't. His mind wouldn't shut off long enough to relax. It was too preoccupied with the implications of what he could do when he dreamwalked. More specifically, what he could do with Evelyn.

It had felt so real. Despite the dampening of the mating effects as a result of being in the dreamworld, it had been one of the most invigorating encounters of his long life.

Such was the way with true mates. He'd heard of it. He hadn't experienced it, hadn't truly believed it could be so overpowering.

Marrok had known love. Had known what it was to both give and receive romantic love. He had that with Melena, before she'd selfishly taken it away. He'd always believed nothing could have come close to the desire he felt for his wife. He'd presumed it was their love that powered that desire.

Last night proved him wrong. He didn't know Evelyn well enough to love her in the way he'd loved Melena, but he could not deny the craving he felt for his mate. Physically, nothing would ever compare. He hadn't been inside her and yet he still knew the truth of it.

After Melena's death, he'd vowed to never love again. He'd chosen to guard his heart against the risk of another heartbreak. Severe distress made the Sundari more susceptible to turning rogue. It wasn't worth it.

With his strong demon sex drive, he eventually found his way back to coupling. He enjoyed many females and enjoyed them often. He couldn't recount a single encounter that came close to the pleasure he'd borne with Evelyn quivering in his embrace.

Phantom traces of her heat still warmed his fingers. Her scent still tickled his nostrils. There was magic in his memory, enough where his body swore she could have been only inches away. Though wary at first, he liked the connection to another.

On top of everything, he wanted to feel the calming influence only a saatus could provide. He wanted to feel it often, just as he wanted to take and give pleasure. Marrok might not be ready to completely share his heart, but he was more than willing to share his body.

He reluctantly admitted he was also drawn to her humor and brash personality, not just her physical form. He'd never met anyone like her. Marrok couldn't remember the last time he'd laughed as he did during their encounters.

He'd taken a gamble exchanging blood with her. There was no way to know if it would help either of them get back to the same place at the same time.

Often times, bonded mates could gandeste to one another. It was how they dealt with any amount of time apart. Though, these mates would have bonded while awake, not in the dreamworld. He had no real way of knowing the effect of their exchange until he tried. He'd figure it out whenever he next slept.

His eyes darted to the tiny ball of fabric still lying on his bed. He'd taken the lace from her last night and awoken with it in his hand.

Yes, dreamwalking was tricky business, indeed. He didn't understand the magic behind it, but he assuredly understood the implications.

Pulling on his boots, he wrestled with how much to reveal to Favin. The male was his Second and Marrok trusted him with not only his own life, but with the life of his mate. He would listen to his comrade's counsel.

* * *

"Repeat that."

Favin didn't bother with formal address. He typically only called the King 'Sire' when others might overhear.

"I woke up with that in my hand." Marrok nodded to the white lace lying on his desk. He was sorely tempted to hide it away from Favin's eyes, but he felt obligated to present irrefutable proof.

The pair were sitting in his study. He'd just confessed to his Second, revealing the series of dreams he'd had and his discovery of his saatus in those dreams.

Marrok started from the beginning, from the night he'd killed Brennen, and ended with how he awoke just hours ago, having somehow brought the material back with him.

He left out the part where his hand had also been holding the fabric around his engorged member. Favin could surely pick up the scents of both Marrok and Evelyn. Close as he was to Favin, Marrok would never discuss intimacies between he and his saatus.

Favin and the other men already knew he had dreamwalked to Brennen all those years ago and it was in the dreamworld he'd taken his uncle's life. Marrok had kept quiet about Evelyn, preferring, at the time, not to deal with the fallout from his warriors knowing he had no intention of claiming his mate.

Now, with his decision to keep Evelyn, he'd have to explain how he came about the knowledge he had a saatus living in the Kingdom of Gwydion—the king's daughter, no less.

Favin's shields were up, his face blank. He was good at hiding his emotions, maybe even better than Marrok. His Second only employed these mechanisms when he was truly upset with Marrok.

"You've known, all this time, that not only you had a saatus, but exactly where she was?"

"Yes."

"And you did nothing about it?"

"She was a child the night we met."

"That was almost fifteen years ago, Marrok. It's been long enough. You know better than to deny the wishes of the Goddess. What if our troubles were because of your refusal to claim your mate?"

"I do not believe I caused anything. The rogue problem began long before the night I killed Brennen."

"That may be, yet it hasn't gone away. In fact, it's gotten worse."

"Which is exactly why I kept my distance."

"You deny Fate thinking there would be no consequence for it? Damnit, Marrok."

"I avoided her because it is not safe for her in the Southland. She's twenty years old, Favin. Barely an adult. Do you think she could protect her mind from the strength of a rogue? Even if I'd planned to retrieve her, where would I take her? Do you think I would ever put her life in jeopardy? Do you think it would be fair to lock her away for her own safety? Trust me, I did not make this decision lightly. I know denying the bond would take a toll. I just didn't see any other way."

Favin nodded at the undergarment. "Judging from the scent of things, I'm guessing something—or some*body*—changed your mind."

Marrok growled, snatching the lace and burying it deep in his pocket. He pointed a finger in his Second's face. "You'll not speak of her *scent*, Favin. Not ever again."

Favin could feel his friend's unstable power dancing across the space between them. It wasn't because he was succumbing to madness. No, Favin had provoked the King's jealousy. He smirked.

"As you wish, my lord."

Marrok's posture relaxed. "My reasons are my own. What matters now is that I've found her and I've come to terms with the fact I need to keep her. I want to keep her."

Evelyn was the key to maintaining his sanity. He'd made peace with his reality, accepting his attraction to both her body and mind as ways to stave off the aloneness in his life.

"I'm happy for you."

"Don't, Favin. I don't know how to make this work where she doesn't end up harmed in some way. I only showed you her ... the garment because I needed you to know I was being truthful about finding her and about being able to pull something tangible through the dreamworld."

"I would have believed you. When have I ever not taken your word?"

Marrok's gaze dropped to the desk. "I didn't want you think I was losing my mind. All demons know our bodies can be vulnerable during a dreamwalk. I've never heard of anyone taking something and waking up with it."

Favin shrugged. "Being that only a handful of demons are powerful enough to dreamwalk to anyone other than their mate, and, thus, powerful enough to, say, remove a heart while doing so? I don't think coming away with a small token from a dream is entirely outside of the realm of possibilities. Besides, she's an elemental. It could have something to do with her powers, as well."

"Perhaps."

"The bigger question is, what else might you find in your bed the next time you wake?"

Marrok's abdominals tightened, picturing himself awakening with Evelyn in his arms. Whether it was out of excitement or dread, he wasn't sure.

"I don't want her arrival to the fortress to be accidental. I'll want every precaution in place for her safety. Even then ..." Marrok trailed off, wrestling with his decision.

"She is young still. There is time. Let us secure the Southland and then we will welcome your mate."

"Favin, we've been trying to secure Sundari for decades "

"Yes, but that was before you found your mate. Not only will you be stronger because of it, your spirit should be settled. Logical. Also, what better motivation could you possibly have?"

Marrok recalled the elation he'd felt last night. Touching Evelyn, feeling her shudder against him as he'd held her close and stroked between her thighs. He'd felt truly linked to someone for the first time in a long time. He didn't want to give that up.

Favin was right. Selfishly, there was no better motivation to bring peace to his land.

"I would advise sharing the fact you've found your saatus with your people."

"No. I'll not risk Evelyn becoming a target or even an accidental casualty."

Favin sighed. "Fair enough. If not the kingdom at large, then at least tell your men."

"Why?"

"Do you not think they yearn for the same?"

Favin's question gave Marrok pause. He had not yearned to meet his saatus. He'd been too caught up in his grief after losing his wife, then in dealing with Brennen and the rogues.

Thoughtlessly, he hadn't considered his soldier's desires. He'd callously believed their combined focus to end their troubles to be their only focus, that the mating bond would come second to their duties, that it was something to think about in the future. He pondered if he would have felt the same had his wife not ripped his heart out of his chest.

"I've been remiss in my duties to my men, it seems."

"I wouldn't go that far, Marrok. There's a reason we all follow you."

Favin's words touched a dark place inside Marrok. Sometimes he wondered what he'd done to deserve such loyalty. He cleared his throat and continued his assertion he'd let them down.

"Still, I hadn't given much thought to anyone in the ranks actively seeking their mate, not with the way things are. I'll tell them soon. I'll need their cooperation anyway if I'm able to bring Evelyn here."

Favin dropped his shields, his pleasure obvious. "It will be a gift to them."

"A gift?" Marrok mused. "Of what?"

"Hope."

Chapter 8

Marrok returned to his chambers earlier than normal. He was tired and looking forward to testing his connection to his saatus. He took his time undressing and reminiscing over the day's revelations.

He and Favin had spent the morning and afternoon talking out new plans to deal with the rogues. What they'd been doing obviously wasn't working.

Most of the rogues were still contained on the peninsula. The last twenty or so who popped up elsewhere, or escaped from the containment area, were destroyed. It wasn't Marrok's preference, but some were too dangerous to simply put back into confinement.

Exterminating the entire population of rogues was out of the question. They were his people, many of whom he'd known for years. For the bulk of them, their affliction was an illness.

Sadly, there were some who slipped into madness out of their hunger for power. If he could read into their minds any memories of committing detestable acts against others to increase power, those he put down without question. They were corrupt prior to going mad.

Favin helped Marrok see they'd been merely performing triage by rounding up rogues and sending them to the colony they'd built on the peninsula. They weren't addressing the disease.

No one could uncorrupt a demon with the proclivity to perform nefarious deeds. But there was one thing they knew did lessen the likelihood of going mad—finding a mate. They needed their people to find their mates.

How to make that happen was another matter. When he'd left his study, however, Marrok felt lighter. Maybe there was a reason for him to hope after all. They didn't have a foolproof answer, but they had a place to start.

Before removing his trousers, he reached into his pocket and pulled out the small white bundle he'd left there the entire day. Marrok tossed it on the bed and finished undressing.

He extinguished the lamp and slid under the covers. Reaching across, he pulled the lace closer so he could better smell Evelyn's sweet fragrance. The heady scent had him hard as granite.

Controlling his desire to take her would be a challenge. He had already decided to try to take things slow with her. His demon wasn't happy about it and made the weak argument the dreamworld wasn't real, so making love to her would have no consequences.

To Marrok, being in the dreamworld was irrelevant. It would feel real and he should be mindful of her inexperience, no matter how responsive she was. She deserved to be courted, as was the custom in Gwydion. This much he could try to give her.

He closed his eyes and waited for his mate.

* * *

Marrok came out from the foliage, his eyes landing on the beautiful creature just beyond the edge of the trees. Flickers of anticipation danced under his skin. Evelyn lifted her arms and the magical barrier parted enough for him to enter the clearing.

As he stepped through, he could feel small sparks of power, different than he'd felt here before. The coloring of the night's moon was off, as well, similar to when he'd entered the dream in a rage, furious she'd waited two years.

This wasn't anywhere near as severe, but he could tell something was amiss. Marrok offered a gentle smile, one his mate did not return. Sensing she wasn't quite as happy to see him as he assumed she would be, he halted two steps in front of her. His arms remained at his sides despite his urge to reach out.

"I had no trouble entering, this night. I think this will be easier from here on out," he said. He'd only had to think of her and he'd entered this night's dream in her forest.

"Yes, so it seems."

Her voice was flat. Marrok studied her face. She was avoiding eye contact, looking over his ear.

"I thought this would be pleasing to my mate, especially since she demanded I make it safe for her to be claimed and brought to my kingdom."

"I am. I would rather have this than nothing at all from you," she begrudgingly acknowledged.

Marrok frowned. "What's wrong?"

Evelyn's eyes flashed to his. "I dreamt of you. After I awoke, I dozed off again and returned to the dreamworld. To the night you fought the other demon."

"Brennen."

"Yes, Brennen."

"Did you see me kill him? Is that what is bothering you?"

"Partly. That night, I awoke before you. I didn't realize ... I suppose I didn't piece it all together. That you removed his heart and that it meant ..." her stomach turned, remembering the image of the blackened heart outside his chest.

"That it meant he'd die? In reality."

She nodded.

"Dreamwalking is more real than most know, Evelyn."

"Yes, I've learned that. My father doesn't definitively know what happened to the previous king. I was always too afraid to tell him what happened here. Besides, I knew Brennen was not a good male. The first time he broke through I tested his magic. It was twisted. I'd never felt anything like it. So when news arrived he'd passed away, I figured it was best to keep my mouth shut. Father tends to worry and my instincts told me to keep quiet."

"I understand. For what it's worth, Brennen deserved far worse than he got. He was a scourge on this world."

"I can see how he could be." She motioned towards the barrier. "He tried to reach into my mind so I added the extra protection."

"Are you saying you were strong enough to keep a rogue out of your head? Even in the dreamworld this would be almost impossible," his tone held a hint of his skepticism.

"He was rogue?"

"He was. It's why he felt wrong to you. Evelyn, you were six years old. There's no way that should have been possible."

She shrugged, looking down at her feet. "Possible or not, he didn't get past my shields. The one in my head or the one I constructed around the clearing."

He caught her chin with his knuckle and nudged it upward, forcing her to look at him. "I'm not saying I don't believe you. I'm saying it's implausible. Incredible, really. Few demons were ever strong enough to resist him. Once he'd crossed boundaries no one should ever cross, he grew in power—and let's just say he crossed an awful lot of boundaries. You were lucky he wasn't here long."

"Not here long? He came every night for a week, taunted me for hours on end. I ignored him as best I could. I knew he had tremendous magics and I was terrified he'd get to me eventually. The night before you arrived I prayed to the Goddess to either send him away or give me the power to make him disappear forever."

"I'd say She heard your prayer, little mate. She gave you the ability to pull me here. Either that, or She intervened. It's irrelevant, however."

He cupped her face with both hands. "I came to you and now there's no going back. You're my mate. The saatus bond has begun."

Evelyn's eyes filled and she blinked to keep the tears at bay. "But you don't want to bond with me. Not really."

She thought back to his internal dialogue. *Yes, then we'll have our mate,* the demon spirit had rejoiced. *No,* Marrok insisted. *We'll never take the witch.*

He'd called her a witch and Evelyn questioned his ability to accept what she was. Calling an elemental a witch was the height of insult. It implied sorcery that manipulated nature against its will, when elementals had a cohesive relationship with their elements.

"Of course I want it," he countered. "I explained why I did not come for you. Your safety is my principal concern. Where is this coming from?"

115

"I dreamt it."

"You dreamt of my fight with Brennen and took it to mean I didn't want you?"

"No. In the dream, I—I was you. Well, I was inside you, living out your actions. I could hear your thoughts, felt traces of your feelings. I even heard you argue with your inner demon."

Marrok crossed his arms, disconcerted and a little perplexed. Perhaps his powers were meshing with hers and she was able to read his mind. It wasn't uncommon with demons.

What was uncommon was dreaming someone else's dream, from their point of view. Though, nothing about their pairing was what he would consider normal. He worried what exchanges she'd overheard.

"What did you hear me say?"

"That you'd never take the *witch*. It wasn't just the words or the insult. I could feel your contempt. You were irate over it."

He reached for her hands, pleased she didn't stop him. "I apologize if the term I used insulted you. Factions outside of Gwydion do not see it as an insult. It's only a word. I'll not use it again if it bothers you so."

Marrok brushed a strand of hair away from her face. "As for my ire, you are right. I was furious. Furious with Brennen for daring to come near you. Furious he'd been able to figure out who you were and try to exploit that knowledge. Furious with Fate for bringing us together in that moment. I was also furious with myself there wasn't a damned thing I could do about claiming you. I was living in a cave with my soldiers, trying to figure out how to get to Brennen, how to stop the madness from spreading across Imperium. It was no place for you. Besides, you were a child."

"So you weren't upset your mate was an elemental?" Some of Evelyn's hurt diminished.

"No. Admittedly, I wondered how the Sundari would react, but I never considered it to be the reason to leave you in Gwydion."

"You could have spoken to my father. Arranged something for us for when I was older."

Marrok stepped forward, crowding her. He'd already addressed this concern once and he didn't like repeating himself. "I would never have arranged a betrothal without knowing beyond the shadow of a doubt the rogue infestation had been ended and you would be safe. As I've told you before, that is the reason we were not together once you were of age."

He purposefully left out the fact he hadn't wanted to find his saatus, not after losing Melena. It seemed unduly cruel to declare his desire to maintain his sanity, along with the fear of upsetting the Goddess, were part of what pushed him to pursue the bond.

Evelyn's lips curved upward. Like a moth to the flame, he couldn't resist leaning down and brushing his mouth across her plush flesh. Her sweet exhalation fanned across his mouth.

His little mate pressed closer, her arms reaching up and clasping behind his neck. She tried to deepen the kiss and Marrok slowed it down.

"Touch me again," she pleaded.

Marrok grinned. "Not tonight, *moj draga*."

It took a second for his refusal to register with Evelyn. She pulled her face back enough to look at him. "You don't want to?"

"Does this feel like I don't want to touch you?" Marrok grabbed her hand and placed it upon the front of his trousers. She gently squeezed the evidence of his arousal. His demon teemed with glee and it was oh-so-tempting to allow her to explore.

She didn't withdraw so he pulled her hand away, entwining their fingers. Any longer and she might learn how easily she could manipulate his body.

"Why did you stop me?"

"We will wait a little longer. Tonight, I want some time with my mate. I want to know you, Evelyn, and for you to know me."

"You want to wait? For how long?" she asked. She hadn't meant to sound so petulant.

"Slow is better. Trust me on this."

He chuckled again at the look on her face. Marrok brought her hand to his mouth and kissed it lightly. "Let's walk."

Evelyn groaned. "Always with the walking. Look around, there's no place to go."

"You could lift the barrier."

"It's not the barrier holding me in the clearing. I've never been able to get past the tree line, even before I'd erected it."

"Maybe things are different now. Try it."

Evelyn looked past him, to the nearly invisible wall of power. *It couldn't hurt to try*, she thought. She lowered the shield and took a step beyond its previous boundary. This was as far as she'd ever gotten.

Marrok squeezed her hand. "Go on. I'm right beside you."

"Pick a path," she suggested.

"You pick. This is your home, not mine."

Evelyn led him to her favorite trail, waiting for the dreamworld to poof her back to the clearing. It didn't. She took another step. Then another.

She laughed nervously. "It worked. I can't believe I can get through now."

Keeping stride with his mate, Marrok pulled her closer to his side, enjoying her warmth as they strolled the winding path. "I think you'll come to find having a mate does have its benefits."

Yes, it does, Marrok's demon agreed. *Soon, we'll know them all.*

119

Chapter 9

As they walked, Marrok explained how there had always been a handful of rogues in Sundari. Some grew ill because of their age and lack of a mate to stabilize them, not because they were corrupted by their appetite for power.

The corrupted demons were his main concern. They fed off of others' minds, often until their prey lost so much of themselves they couldn't even maintain a heartbeat.

"Brennen's leadership created the perfect breeding ground for demons to do as they pleased. In fact, he encouraged his army to follow in his footsteps, thinking the added power would better protect him. Many commoners took this as reinforcement they could do the same."

"Weren't you a part of his guard?"

"Sadly, yes, but the majority of us were appalled with Brennen's actions. We didn't stick around for long.

Technically, we were exiled for daring to question the King."

"So you packed your things and left?"

"Yes. I couldn't stand by and watch the kingdom fall apart. Power-hungry demons are the worst sort of beings. Sometimes, they incite violence to encourage severe mental distress. Something about the brainwaves when in such a state is extra powerful. They feed off of their victim's negative energies. Unfortunately, the preferred targets are typically females who can be physically subdued."

Evelyn found it utterly disgusting. At least she understood a little better why Marrok was so hesitant to bring her into his kingdom.

"The only thing that seems to prevent the madness is the saatus bond," he continued. "With the growing number of rogues, all of whom have to be confined, the odds of males finding their mates have been drastically reduced. It's taken a huge toll on everyone."

After his exile, he and the soldiers who couldn't stomach Brennen's ways spent years secretly fighting rogues and planning to remove Brennen from the throne. Marrok had been dealing with this catastrophe for decades now. The amount of rogues had risen steadily and he felt he'd hardly put a dent in the numbers.

The previous king had tainted everything he touched. Marrok even refused to live in the royal palace, which was situated in the town of Piatra, near the border to Sanctus Femina.

Instead, he took up residence in Terenuskit Fortress and used it as his base of operations while piecing the kingdom back together.

Evelyn could feel the sorrow rolling off of Marrok as he spoke of his people. He was a good male who only wanted to do right by them.

"With this new campaign," he told her, "we intend to end the rogues. Once and for all."

"Your going to kill them?" Evelyn couldn't hide her dismay at the thought of killing so many. He said there were now well over three thousand rogues.

Marrok scowled. "Not if I can help it. Some will have to be put down. Favin and I can read their memories, try to weed out the ones who contaminated their souls for a taste of more power. Those demons must pay for their actions. When we first started rounding them up, it was too chaotic to read them all. Concentrating like that would make us vulnerable, so we simply took everyone we could find. When we aren't outnumbered and have only a single rogue or two to deal with, we take the time to do it."

Evelyn pictured some of the crimes Marrok had told her were being committed. She understood his stance.

"And the others? The ones who came by their illness naturally?"

"We're hoping to find their mates. It won't be possible for all of them, but many have mates somewhere in the kingdom."

"How do you plan to do that? Sundari isn't a small place."

"No, it's not. It will take time. I don't have the exact logistics worked out yet. It's taken this long just to get the bulk of them confined."

He was willing to line them up, one by one, to try to find the matches. He knew it could take years so he'd tasked Favin with figuring out the most expedient way to go about bringing together rogues with possible mates, close enough to feel the bond, but safe enough to prevent any harm if they weren't fated.

"Can the saatus bond settle a demon, after he's turned?"

"Yes."

"So, if you went rogue, I could cure you? That's amazing!"

His mouth quirked. "It is indeed. Lucky for me, I won't be going rogue. We've already begun the process of bonding."

"Yes, you're one lucky demon," she quipped, earning one of his roguish grins.

He really was the most attractive male she'd ever met. Not classically handsome, like the vampire she'd seen in her dreams that night years ago. Marrok also lacked the boyishly good looks Jasper had.

She was attracted to Marrok's rugged appearance, how he carried himself with an intensity that screamed danger. His black hair, bronzed skin, and dark stubble made him look even more dangerous. She could easily picture him taking on a swarm of attackers and coming out unscathed.

"What will you do if you don't find their mates?"

Marrok wiped his mouth with the hand not holding hers. "Whatever I must."

His frame had stiffened with her question. A good leader always had a backup plan. Of course he had one. He didn't have to say aloud what it was.

Evelyn stopped in place and tugged on his hand. He looked down where they were joined. Slowly, his eyes trailed up her arm to her face. She could feel his inner turmoil.

"I don't like the thought of putting them down, Marrok, but I know you'll do what you think is right. That's all you can do. If you need me, I'm here." She stepped closer, cupping his masculine jaw. "Whatever it is, you'll not face it alone. Not anymore."

Marrok closed his eyes and nuzzled her palm. His demon spirit purred as it did whenever it felt the solace of her soul. His mate was getting to him, offering him comfort on the chance he might have to perform despicable acts.

Needing to change the subject, he reached into his pocket. "There is something else we need to discuss."

Evelyn watched him dig a white swath of material out from his jacket. He dangled the familiar lace in front of her eyes.

"Is that … where did you get those?" She reached to snag them away but he pulled them out of reach.

"Ah-ah, these are mine now."

Butterflies danced around in her tummy. He wanted to keep her undergarments? How sordid—and yet so very riveting.

"How did you get those?" she asked again.

"I woke up with them in my hand."

Her head tilted slightly, her thoughts buzzing around, trying to land on a logical reason he could have done such a thing.

Evelyn looked to the right, thinking. The bubbling brook was close and she thought about the day she'd fallen off the boulder. The trinket still hung around her neck, under her clothing. She rarely removed it.

"When dreamwalking, you can transfer material objects?" she queried.

"Few can manage to enter the dreams of others, though it can happen. Obviously. We can harm one another while dreamwalking. As you've learned, we can also bring pleasure." Marrok took a long inhale before tucking the lace back into his pocket. Evelyn blushed.

"However, I've never heard of being able to physically manipulate inanimate objects to the point they can be transferred from one place to another. I could, say, rip your clothing and when you awoke, it would be torn. But it would still be with you. Me taking anything of yours, and it being in my possession when I wake, should not be possible."

"Apparently it is."

"Apparently."

Evelyn slid her hand out from his and walked to the small embankment, close to her favorite meditation spot. She lifted a hand to the boulders. "This is where I meditate sometimes."

Marrok's eyes flicked to the large rocks. "This is where you fell?"

"Yes. I didn't consciously walk here, this was just my favorite walking path. I've wanted to show you—to tell you—something."

"You want to show me the place where another male harmed you?" his soft voice was counter to the rage he felt. Two years had done nothing to diminish his displeasure.

"No. Something else happened that day and I think it's important for you to know."

Marrok's claws sprung free, unwillingly, as his demon vaulted to the surface. Seeing Evelyn's step backwards, he was able to get control.

"What else did he do?" he gritted out.

"Jasper? Nothing. He's harmless. I'm not referring to him." Evelyn reached inside her shirt and gently extracted the chain. She pulled it over her head and extended her arm towards Marrok.

"This is what I wanted to show you."

Marrok's already rigid muscles contracted and pulled even tighter against his frame. Air did not come easy and he had to fight to maintain his composure.

"Where did you get that?" he snapped, watching the medallion swing hypnotically, back and forth.

"It was in the stream. I found it when I was awake, minutes after I fell."

"Impossible."

"Obviously not. Is it yours?"

"It was ... I had it around my neck that night with Brennen."

Evelyn nodded. "I thought so. When I saw the 'M' engraved, your face immediately came to mind."

They stood still, the necklace between them. Evelyn stretched closer so he could take it. Marrok didn't reach out. He just stared, as if in a trance.

"Take it," she insisted.

Marrok blinked, watching his dead wife's necklace sway in the hand of his mate. After he'd awoken those years ago, he'd been preoccupied with the implications of Brennen's death. He hadn't thought of the missing medallion until he rode on the palace, days later.

He should tell Evelyn the 'M' stood for Melena, not Marrok. He didn't.

Too many feelings were working their way through his system. Melena wasn't something he was ready to discuss tonight, so he held up his palm and allowed Evelyn to drop it into his hand. Marrok put the necklace in his pocket, the one opposite the place where he'd stowed Evelyn's underwear.

"Are you not going to wear it?"

"No."

"Is everything okay, Marrok?"

"It's fine."

His eyes met hers and he felt like he'd somehow let her down. "I have a lot on my mind. Do not be concerned."

Evelyn's mouth twisted back and forth, making her appear more childlike than she was. "If you say so," she grumbled.

Despite his ill mood, his mouth lifted. "Come here, *moj draga.*"

Evelyn stepped into his embrace, allowing his sturdy form to support hers. The tension drained away and she rested her cheek upon his chest, inhaling his masculine scent.

"What does that mean? *Moj draga?*" she asked, mimicking his Sundari accent.

"It's an endearment. Something along the lines of 'my darling' or 'my sweet.' Why? Do you not like it?"

"On the contrary, I think I like it very much."

His chest shook under her face. "Don't laugh at me," she chastised.

"I'm not."

She tilted her head back. "You are."

"Maybe just a little. I can't help it. You're very entertaining. You tell me exactly what's on your mind. No one does that. Not once have I felt compelled to search your thoughts."

"I see no reason to not be honest with you."

Marrok's grin slipped. He would have to tell her about Melena. Eventually.

Wanting a distraction, he leaned down and kissed her pliant lips. He kept the pace slow and his pressure light. Ever eager, his little mate tried to ravage his mouth but he didn't allow it. He did not intend to play with her in this dream.

When they broke apart, she sighed dreamily and he nestled his head against hers. Suddenly, she jerked backwards.

"I think I'm waking," she said.

"Don't panic, Evelyn. This isn't the end, remember?"

"Tomorrow night?"

"No, I'll need some time. If I'm out on campaign, I'll need to sleep lightly. I can't afford to be dreamwalking and dead to the world. Give me a month."

"A month?" she whined.

"'Tis only a moment for an immortal."

Evelyn dissolved before his eyes. Not ready to wake, he put his hands in his pockets, rubbing the fingers of one hand across cool metal, and the fingers of the other across silky lace.

Guilt burned hot in his gut, coming to terms with which he preferred to have in his grasp.

Chapter 10

One month later ...

"Thank you, sister dear," Evelyn chirped sincerely after Eden handed her the plate of biscuits. They were the only two currently at the breakfast table, having been the last in the family to come down for the morning meal.

"What's gotten into you?" Eden accused, disturbed by her sister's sudden bout of pleasantness. It was the second agreeable thing she'd said in as many minutes. Evelyn was not a morning person.

"What? I say thank you all the time."

"Yes, but you rarely mean it. Even rarer is your lack of sarcasm. So I'll ask again, what's gotten into you?"

Evelyn's face split into an enormous grin. She was powerless to stop it. She'd risen from bed full of anticipation for the coming night. This was the night she'd meet Marrok in her dreamworld. She hoped he'd made progress and she was closer to being with him in the waking world.

"Nothing. I'm content today."

"Sure you are."

Evelyn rolled her eyes. "Stop. I'm capable of playing nice. Don't make me feel bad about it."

Eden's astute intellect wouldn't let her drop it. "Something's going on with you."

Evelyn studiously buttered her biscuit then crammed it into her mouth. She couldn't speak if her mouth was full.

"Manners, Evie."

Evelyn sneered at her sister and continued chewing. She took a swig of water to wash it down, tempted to shove another down her gullet just to avoid talking to Eden. She wasn't ready to divulge the details of her dreams, not until she knew Marrok was ready to talk to her father.

"Maybe I'm looking forward to sparring today."

It was the truth. Since the blood exchange, she'd felt stronger. Physically, as well as magically. She hadn't felt exerted once these past few weeks during their hand-to-hand exercises. She was by no means as strong as Marrok or any other male warrior, but she was starting to hold her own for longer.

Eden eyed Evelyn, a sly grin spreading. "Is it because you-know-who is sparring with us today?"

Evelyn pursed her lips. "Who is you-know-who?"

"Come now, don't play coy. You know today some of the male soldiers are grappling with us."

Evelyn wiped her hands on her napkin and threw it on her plate. "I'm sure I don't know what you mean."

"Sure you don't."

"Seriously, Eden. Why are you nettling me?"

"Because it's working."

"What?"

"Now you're acting normal. I don't like the Sweetie Evie routine."

"You are so odd," Evelyn laughed.

"And you think you're normal?"

Evelyn laughed again. "I'm going to get changed. I'll see you out there."

"I'll make sure Jasper saves you a round."

Evelyn stopped in her tracks. Slowly, she turned back towards her sister. "Jasper's sparring today?"

"Like you don't already know."

She didn't know. Well, she knew, she just forgot. Still, it wasn't relevant. He was one of her father's men. They all took turns training the king's daughters. He hadn't been around lately, so he was due to take a turn.

Without a retort, Evelyn lumbered out of the kitchen and returned to her room. She couldn't help but think sparring with Jaspar was a bad idea. He hadn't come on to her since the incident, but he was a terrible flirt. An incredibly handsome one, too.

Evelyn doubted Marrok would appreciate her being so close to Jasper, yet she couldn't refuse to train.

Lifting her dress over her head, she looked at the new definition in her frame, at the shallow lines forming outlines of her muscles. She could see the curve of her biceps, the roundness in her shoulders. Her thighs, though lean, were firm, reminding her of all the running and jumping she'd done.

Evelyn felt strong, even more so now that she looked it. Vigorous training was finally paying off. Plus, she was convinced mixing blood with a demon had added to the effect. She would take any advantage she could get.

She slid her body into her sparring attire, feeling more confident than ever. She could handle Jasper—she *would* handle Jasper. All she had to do was outlast him and not allow him close enough to pin her.

Armed with nothing other than her plan, she ran down the stairs.

* * *

"You're serious?" Evelyn asked her grandfather, Flynn, who was also her father's Second in Command.

"Yes. The three of you have spent a lot of time in the sparring ring. Your skills are good. Now we're escalating things."

Her head swiveled back to the forest, where a group of soldiers stood nearby. She ignored the one trying to catch her eye.

Nora and Eden had already gone through the exercise in the woods and moved on to the next activity. They were rotating stations and now it was Evelyn's turn at this one.

"Who's chasing me?" she asked.

"It's not a chase, Evie. You'll be tracked and attacked. The goal is to either capture you or subdue you."

"Fine. Who is tracking me?"

"I am."

Evelyn didn't have to look to know which of the soldiers had replied. Sparring with Jasper in the ring was one thing. There she had some advantages, namely she could see his movements. In the forest, he wouldn't be coming from the front. The element of surprise was on his side.

She couldn't outrun him. She wasn't supposed to use her powers to take him down. The idea was to figure out how to survive when weakened or unable to call forth the elements.

Flynn nudged her towards the closest trail. "You'll have three minutes before I send him in."

"A full three minutes, huh?"

Her grandfather's eyes gleamed. "Yes, smart mouth. Now get to it." He two-hand pushed her and she stumbled onto the path.

Some girls had doting grandfathers who whittled them toys and told fond stories of their youth. Evelyn had a grandfather who preferred being called Flynn and loved 'toughening up his girls' as he often said.

Evelyn gave a small salute and sprinted off down the path. She waited until it curved and she was out of sight of the males before she darted off in a different direction.

She zigzagged back and forth, jumping over logs and rocks, touching as little foliage as she could manage. She knew a little bit of tracking and tried to avoid the things that would make it obvious in which direction she'd gone.

She half expected Jasper to jump out at any moment. She paused every minute to listen for his approach. Only the usual sounds of the forest drifted around her. He couldn't be far behind. He was one of the fastest in her father's regiment.

After what she thought must have been at least ten minutes, she started searching for places to hide. If she could evade him completely, she could win. She finally settled down between two enormous trees covered in Gwydion's thick, purple ivy. It was often used to make rope because it was malleable yet strong.

Squatting, making herself small but also holding a position where she could bolt, Evelyn used the surrounding vegetation to cover her body. She kept her breaths shallow and quiet, listening for Jasper's approach.

The minutes ticked by. A noise to her left had her frozen in place. Another sound—*a twig breaking?*—a little further away echoed under the canopy. If it was him, he was moving away from her.

Evelyn released the exhale she'd been holding.

"This is fun," a breath whispered across her right ear. Evelyn screamed and sprang forward. She didn't even make it a full step when large hands wrapped around her waist from behind, lifting her off the ground.

"Never took you for a screamer," he chuckled.

Blood filled her head. He was laughing at her. This kissing bandit who had all but knocked her off a boulder trying to attack her mouth was laughing at her?

Not for long. The moron had left her arms free. She was too far above him to use her elbows. Glancing down, she realized her feet were at the perfect height.

She extended one leg and brought her heel back as hard as she could. Jasper shifted his hold and was able to deflect enough so his man parts didn't take the blow.

Evelyn twisted and grabbed a handful of his hair, yanking his head back and forth like a rabid animal with prey in its mouth. It wasn't a combat move, but her sisters hated it when she'd tried it on them.

"Ow! Bloody hell, Evie!"

"Let go of me."

"No."

Jaspar squeezed her tighter and she grimaced at the severe pressure around her abdomen. Close to panicking, she started kicking back with both heels and pulling harder at his hair. Several small clumps came out by the roots and he yelped. If she could just get a little lower, or turned, she could punch his face or go for his eyes.

In the struggle, his grip slipped enough for her to be lowered a few inches. It was all she needed. Her dominant arm crossed in front of her, winding up to elbow him in the side of the head. She caught his temple and they dropped to the forest floor like a sack of potatoes.

Evelyn turned to her side and pushed herself to a sitting position. Jasper's big body was next to hers. He wasn't moving. *Uh-oh.*

She shifted him to his back and checked his breathing. His chest was rising and falling so she knew he wasn't dead. Evelyn sagged in relief. She'd only knocked him out.

Lifting to her knees, she leaned over his trunk, slapping him lightly on the face. "Jasper! Wake up."

Nothing happened so she did it again. Still, he didn't wake. Evelyn covered her face. "Damnit. Now I have to go get Flynn to help drag your big body out of this place. Thanks for nothing, moron," she grumbled.

A big hand knocked Evelyn to her back followed by an even bigger body. Jasper had her pinned to the ground, his hands holding down her wrists. Her eyes narrowed on his smiling face and he chuckled again.

"I can't believe you fell for that," he gloated.

"That's not funny, you giant miscreant! I thought I'd hurt you!"

"Nah. I'll have a bruise but it wasn't enough to kill me."

"I'll be sure to hit you harder next time."

His head lowered towards hers. His breath blew across her face as his chest pressed against her own. Her body sparked with interest, liking the feel of his weight. She cursed it, knowing her physical response was because she missed Marrok.

"Apologize for calling me a moron."

"What? No."

"Do it or I'll kiss you."

"Quit joking around, Jasper."

"I'm not joking, Evie," his nose grazed hers.

Her eyes grew big. Had he gone mad? She watched in slow motion as Jasper's mouth descended. By the Goddess, he really was going to do it! She tried to turn her head and he grabbed her by the chin.

"Jasper, don't—"

His lips cut off her threat. Warm and soft, they pressed into her own. Too stunned to react, she remained still, her traitorous body tingling all over. His tongue tried to breach her mouth and something inside her snapped.

Evelyn bit his lower lip and he grunted, rolling off to the side and freeing her from under him. She popped up to her feet, fueled by her anger towards him for daring to do something so stupid.

"You bit me!" he yelled.

"You deserved it!" she yelled back.

Jaspar's hand lowered. "Am I bleeding?"

"Unfortunately, no."

"Never took you for a biter, Evie."

Her mouth dropped open. She could not believe the gall of this male. Her hands lifted and the thick ivy wrapped across and around his body.

"Hey, what are you doing? No magic, remember?"

Evelyn ignored his whining and used the ivy to secure him to the base of the tree, with his hands bound behind his back. He wouldn't be able to call forth his power like that, not without harming the ivy. She trusted he wouldn't be foolish enough to damage one of her elements.

The longer she looked at him, the more aggravated she became. "Not one word, Jasper. My father is still upset with you over the last time you pulled a stunt like this. You say something asinine and I'll have him be the one to come retrieve you."

Jasper's face paled. "You'd tell him?"

"I should. Seriously, what is wrong with you?"

"Nothing. Is it so bad to want to kiss you? You're gorgeous. Every male in the kingdom would give his right arm to have you."

Evelyn was taken aback. No, that couldn't be right. Jasper must be teasing her. Even if it were true, he shouldn't have done it.

"I'm going to go tell my grandfather where you are. While you wait, you might want to sit here and think about your actions and why I might be upset with you."

"Evie—"

"No. I don't want to hear it. Keep your mouth to yourself, Jasper. If you don't, I might just remove it from your face."

She didn't wait for his reply.

Chapter 11

When Marrok opened his eyes, he was on the path he'd walked with Evelyn a month ago. He could scarcely believe he'd managed to keep away from his saatus for so long.

Thankfully, the blood exchange had been enough to help him with his focus and to remain clear-headed. Even in the dreamworld, their combined lifebloods held true power.

If this moment was indicative of their bond, he would now be able to enter her dreams easily. Some of his anxiety over being apart diminished believing he could reach her when he needed to.

His entire core flexed with every step, brimming with anticipation to be reunited with his mate. Rounding the small bend, the clearing came into view. He was surprised to see Evelyn's barrier was already down. Or, perhaps, she'd never bothered to put it back up.

His lovely mate was already there, scanning the tree line, presumably looking for his arrival. This night, she was clad in nothing but her white nightgown, sleeveless and hitting just above her knees. Marrok walked faster and her head jerked in his direction. When she smiled, Marrok ran.

He hauled Evelyn against his front as his mouth slanted down over hers. The prickling sensation from the saatus bond tickled his lips. He could hear her heartbeat quicken, matching his own frantic rhythm. He loved how he could affect her as much as she affected him.

Marrok allowed himself to get lost in their kiss, content in one of the simplest, albeit most intimate, acts between lovers. He reveled in the feel of her soft, pink lips touching his. He adored the tentative press of her tongue, exploring and curious.

Even more, he basked in the calm she brought to his demon spirit. Centering him. Soothing him. Reminding him nothing else existed in this moment.

The attachment he was forming to her was overwhelming. Each and every day, Marrok thought of his little mate constantly. Even when he was being attacked by rogues, she was there in the back of his mind, a reminder he must prevail.

"I've missed you," he admitted, rubbing his cheek along hers, as many demons did to show affection. Her small hands fisted the front of his shirt.

"You hardly know me well enough to miss me," she replied playfully, throwing his words from a month ago back at him without any real heat in her voice.

Evelyn could feel the stretch of his grin against her face. Puffs of warm air tickled her ear with his chortle. He planted a chaste kiss to her temple and drew away. She bit her lip, staring into his darkened eyes, rimmed with bright amber.

"Your keen memory could be problematic for my ability to remain in nothing less than your good graces."

"Then I suppose you'll have to hold your tongue."

Marrok's grin grew wider. "Cheeky female. I missed your playful barbs, as well."

Evelyn's face warmed and her lips rounded over her teeth, a habit of her nervousness. He was in such a good mood, she hated to ruin it with what she needed to tell him.

Her hands flattened against his chest, feeling the steady beat of his heart. Her eyes remained fixed on where her fingers pressed into the fabric of his shirt. Her hands flexed just before she pushed away. Marrok's hold on her tightened and she went nowhere.

"Why are you pulling away? I think I'd like to have you in my arms a little while longer."

"I need to tell you something. Personally, I don't think it's very important, but I think *you* might think it's very important, especially after how you reacted the last time, so I told myself I would honor your need to be knowledgeable of my time away from you and—" her voice cut off when his fingers pinched her lips shut.

Marrok couldn't take her rambling, not after her lie scraped across his skin and stabbed at his psyche.

Whatever she wanted to say *was* important to her in some way.

Movement over her shoulder had his head snapping up, his spine going ramrod straight. He spun Evelyn behind him, shielding her from the threat who had snuck up on them. *Fool!* he cursed himself, thinking he should have told her to leave up the barrier.

He could feel Evelyn try to move around him and he used both arms to keep her from being exposed. His blackened eyes stared down the figure across the way.

The light-haired male appeared to be young, possibly not much older than Evelyn. Marrok perused his body for weapons and found none. He wasn't even in an attacking position. In fact, the intruder stood in a relaxed pose, with his hands in his pockets.

He couldn't place why, but Marrok wanted to wipe the young male's knowing smile right off his face. Preferably with his claws.

The longer Marrok stared at the male, the less of a threat he knew him to be. Something about his form wasn't quite right. He wasn't a demon, so he couldn't be dreamwalking. The green eyes gave him away as a being of Gwydion.

Elementals couldn't break into dreams. No, he was part of Evelyn's subconscious, part of something on her mind. *I need to tell you something.* Yes, apparently she did.

Lowering his arms, he finally allowed his mate to move. She remained close, brushing his arm as she shifted next to him.

"This is Jasper, I presume?" he asked without looking away from the male.

"How could you possibly know that?"

"The only other time you've dared to not be truthful with me was when you spoke of him, the day he pushed you off the rocks."

"He didn't push me."

"It doesn't matter. It was his fault you fell."

Evelyn tilted her head and crossed her arms, looking dream Jasper up and down with contempt. Her animosity towards her alleged friend was still fresh. "You're right."

Marrok glanced down and her. "About what? The fact you lied to me or the fact your injury was his fault?"

"Both. Though, I don't know that I lied. This time, I mean. Which part did you find untruthful?"

"You *do*, personally, think it's important. Whatever it is you're getting ready to tell me is important to you."

"Huh. I didn't realize I wasn't being truthful. Maybe I just thought it wasn't important enough for you to react how I knew you would react," she admitted. "You can feel it even when it's something I'm being dishonest about with myself?"

"Yes."

"How?"

"Istina nikad ne umire. *The truth never dies.* It's not just a saying. It's a demon gift—or curse, at times. Words hold power. Something about our magics can always discern truth from lie, no matter what the person speaking believes."

"I would think that would be very useful."

"It can be."

No longer concerned with Jasper, he turned to face Evelyn and she reflected his stance. "Now, stop evading and start talking. Then I'll decide whether or not the male needs to die."

"I would laugh if I thought you weren't serious."

"I am serious. Talk."

"Fine," she conceded, just short of rolling her eyes.

As succinctly as she could, Evelyn relayed what happened during her morning training session. By the time she finished, he'd gone so still she wasn't sure he was breathing.

"Marrok?"

Ignoring her inquest, Marrok approached Jasper, who was still standing there with his hands in his pockets and his irritating little grin plastered across his face. The harmless male reminded Marrok of a statue, lifelike, yet somehow eerie in its near-perfect imitation.

Unfortunately for dream Jasper, he was the only place Marrok could put the rage roiling deep inside.

147

Holding out both hands, he summoned two short swords. An evil sneer appeared as he took a moment to test the weight of his weapons. Then he attacked.

Evelyn gasped when the two blades appeared out of thin air. Though she had conjured blankets and books a thousand times, she hadn't been expecting the swords. A punch to Jasper's face was a fitting penalty. Stabbing him seemed a bit much.

"Marrok, don't you think ..." She trailed off, watching in awe when he spun almost too fast for her to follow his movements.

He twirled and sliced, reminding her of a windmill gone out of control. His black hair swayed as gracefully as his actions.

The blades slid through Jasper over and over and over again. Unlike in reality, the cuts did nothing but glide through his body as though he were made of smoke. Evelyn waited for Marrok to slow. He didn't.

The less he was able to harm Jasper, the more worked up Marrok became. His exertions came faster, he struck harder. He was within a hair of trying to break into Jasper's dreams and inflict a great deal of pain. His demon spirit lunged forward and touched the apparition.

Dream Jasper dissolved immediately, floating away in particles on the breeze. Marrok watched them drift until they were completely gone. If the two ever met, he feared he would react in the exact same manner.

Out of breath, he drew air into his lungs, scrambling for some semblance of control before he dealt with his mate. *Be calm*, his demon warned. Marrok flung the swords to the ground and closed his eyes, concentrating on his inhalation. Once his pulse normalized, he turned to face Evelyn.

She opened her mouth to speak and he raised a hand to cut her off. "Don't."

Marrok sidled closer as he spoke. "You evaded him once and it damaged your face, but you evaded him. This time, you restrained him with your powers. Easily, yes?"

Afraid to verbalize a response, Evelyn nodded.

"Good. It is good your magics are strong. I like that your magics are strong. It makes me feel better when I know I cannot be with you in the way I want to be. While I'm out fighting to save Sundari, fighting to make it safe for you, I am comforted by the fact you can defend yourself. Unfortunately, you did not use your powers until he took something from you that belonged to only me."

Marrok was surprised by this acute bout of jealousy, of his excessive degree of possessiveness. He'd never felt such emotions with Melena, and she had meant the world to him. His mouth was working faster than his brain, yet he couldn't find any untruth in his words.

"We weren't supposed to use our magic during training," Evelyn told him.

"I do not care. If you can keep him from touching you, you will. With whatever force is necessary. Am I making myself clear?"

His tone aggravated her. "It's not like I wanted him to do it, Marrok."

"No?" he taunted, tucking a piece of hair behind her ear. "You weren't in need of attention? Missing your male after I forced us to be apart for an entire month? No part of your body longed for contact with someone who could make you feel?"

Evelyn uncrossed her arms, aghast he'd read her so effortlessly. Did he think her desperate? His accusation, though true, chafed.

"I—I can't help it! I was excited to see you. I go to sleep every night repeating the same thing, forcing myself not to call for you. This morning, I awoke happy, giddy even, knowing you would come to me tonight. Rejoicing in the fact I could see you. Touch you. I'll admit I was aroused but it wasn't because of Jasper. I've been that way since the moment you first touched me. So if you want to blame anyone for my hesitation, for my inability to think straight because I'm so desperate for your touch, then blame yourself!"

His black eyes shrunk and bright amber glowed around the edges of his large pupils. This was how he looked each time he kissed her. Evelyn's body pulsed in anticipation of his attentions.

Marrok's eyes roved her shape. Her hardened peaks pushed at the thin material covering the parts he most wanted to see. The alluring scent of her arousal was stronger than it ever had been. His plucky little mate had admitted she longed for him, needed his touch.

"Give me your underwear," he commanded.

Evelyn's breath hitched. "What?"

"I'll extract payment for your indiscretion. Now."

"You're serious."

"Yes."

At her sides, Evelyn's fingers clutched the silky sheath she had worn to bed. She hesitated and his lips pressed tight. She'd anticipated some sort of physical communion between them this night. This wasn't what she'd envisioned.

It was better. It was almost a dare. Yes, he'd demanded it of her, but he'd never take from her anything she wasn't willing to give him. Evelyn trusted Marrok, trusted him enough to do as he wanted her to do.

Marrok's eyes blazed when Evelyn reached under her gown and tucked her thumbs into the sides of her under garment. She shimmied the flimsy fabric down, stepping out of the leg holes and bringing herself upright.

Boldly, she'd kept her vision on his face the entire time. Then she promptly threw the underwear at his head.

Lost in her look, he almost missed the lavender silk flying towards his face. He snatched it from the air, his demon chuckling at Evelyn's impudence.

"Now what?" she goaded, her core heating. She could feel the dampness between her legs, excited by his naughty game.

"Now, tell me you missed me."

"I missed you."

Truth, his demon whispered, delighted by her admission. Marrok was pleased, as well. Stowing her silky underwear in his pocket, he conjured a thick blanket and several large pillows, spread out beside them.

"Lie down, Evelyn."

Evelyn stepped onto the blanket and lowered herself to her knees. His cock flexed knowing he'd experience much from her in that position soon enough.

She shifted to her bottom, trying to keep her lower half covered. Her legs stretched out before her and she held the hem of her gown as low as it could go before sinking back and resting her shoulders and head on one of the large pillows.

Marrok dropped to his knees, beside her legs, rubbing the flesh from her ankle to her knee. Sparks of sensations emitted from her skin everyplace his fingers touched. His hand inched up, just under the nightgown and stopped.

"You are so beautiful," he whispered reverently.

"Marrok," her throaty reply died when he bent and took her mouth.

He slid his body alongside hers, his hip next to her hip, his upper half leaning over her chest. Their tongues tangled and her fingers threaded his hair. Gone was his mate's tentativeness. She was now comfortable in their kiss, almost demanding.

His hand drifted atop her gown, sliding along her ribcage and settling on her breast. Her little moan encouraged him and he pinched her nipple through the fabric. Evelyn gasped and Marrok did it again.

He released her tight peak and tugged her nightgown up. When she stiffened, Marrok pulled back enough to look at her.

"Do you want me to stop?"

"No, I just, I've never—"

"Shh. I know, Evelyn. I'll be careful with you. Relax, this is not the night we will join that way."

"It's not?"

Instead of answering, Marrok nipped her bottom lip, then licked away the sting. He massaged her thigh, moving higher with each caress. His hand slid under her nightie and her restless body arched when he finally reached her breast again.

She turned towards him, hooking her leg over his hip. When she rocked forward, Marrok rolled her to her back with him on top. He nudged her legs apart, gently, allowing her to stop him if she chose.

Evelyn parted her thighs and he settled between them. The heat from her center radiated into his erection and he rolled his hips gently. They groaned in unison.

Marrok's mouth coasted across her jawline, kissing and nipping. He licked the column of her throat, feeling her pulse increase under the slight pressure.

Shifting his weight to his forearms and knees, he edged lower and lifted her nightgown higher. Her full breasts hit the night air and he took a moment to gaze upon his mate's perfection.

Evelyn held very still as Marrok took his time looking her over. The amber was the brightest she'd ever seen it. Minute scorches seared across her skin wherever the light from his irises fell. She could feel his gaze boring into her very pores.

Those bright orbs locked on hers, his face lowering to her chest. His tongue darted out and rasped across her nipple. Once. Twice. Three times.

Her wide eyes watched, captured in the erotic moment, unable to look away. When he sealed his mouth over her taut peak and sucked, Evelyn cried out. Her hands dove into his hair and held him to her chest.

While he lapped and laved with his mouth, his hand pulled and rolled her other nipple, just to the point of pain. Her hips bucked, seeking the friction her male wasn't giving.

"Please," she panted.

"Please what?" he asked, switching his mouth's attention to the opposite breast.

"Touch me."

"I am touching you. You'll have to be more specific."

"Marrok!" she complained.

"I promise to give you what you need, *moj draga*. All you have to do is tell me where, specifically, you want to be touched."

Evelyn huffed, her body a quivering mess of need. He knew what she wanted. Why was he forcing her to say it?

"Like last time," she finally said.

"Technically, we only kissed last time. Are you referring to the time before last? Tell me, Evelyn," he ordered, allowing his demon power out with his words.

Marrok's power snaked across her skin, leaving behind molten tracks of desire. She let out a hiss, swearing the magics concentrated at the juncture of her thighs.

She was starting to perspire, something that never happened in the dreamworld. The heart of her ached, needing, wanting. She could touch herself and it wouldn't be enough. It would never be enough.

Growing desperate, she grabbed his hand and drew it to her core. "Here. Touch me here."

Marrok rewarded her by grazing his thumb across her clitoris and she moaned. Unabashed, unashamed, she lifted her pelvis wanting more pressure.

"Do you want more of this, my sweet?"

"Yes."

"Say it."

"I want more."

Evelyn's eyes closed as she waited. Already she was close. A few strokes would be enough to send her over.

Marrok kissed her hard and quick, then lowered himself further. He could see the tremor in her legs. Whether from need or nervousness, he didn't know. His large hands pushed her thighs wide and he blew on the sensitive skin of her pinkened folds.

Evelyn's eyes flew open and she tried to take a breath. Everything in her was tight and tense. She was fevered, needing more than his breath upon her skin. As if he'd read her mind, she watched his tongue glide across her sensitive nub. Lightning crashed through her veins.

He retreated then did it again. He did it over and over, going faster with each stroke of pleasure he lashed against her burning core. It was all she could do to lie there and take it. When his mouth clamped around the bundle of nerves, she crested, screaming his name into the night sky.

Her chest rose and fell rapidly as she fought for air. If this was what subdued felt like, she may very well die from ecstasy when they touched in real life.

Chapter 12

Marrok crawled back up Evelyn's body, watching her intently. His engorged shaft was painfully throbbing against his trousers, out of room like he was out of patience.

Just as he thought it best to try to wake himself to take care if it, his mate's smoky eyes caught him in their trap. Her hand cupped the back of his neck and drew him into a kiss.

It was so tempting—too tempting—to have her under him like this. He jerked in surprise when he felt her grab his shirt at his sides and started pulling it up.

"I want to see you. Take it off."

"Evelyn."

"Don't fight me," she told him forcefully, pushing him back with his hands.

How could he refuse his mate? Kneeling in front of her, Marrok unbuttoned his shirt and slid it off. He didn't dare remove his pants.

Evelyn moved to her knees, mirroring his pose. She licked her lips, bringing her hands to his pectorals, surprised he had no chest hair. She journeyed down his arms, over the curves and dips of his muscles, then came back to his chest.

His nipples were much darker than hers, a dusky brown, several shades darker than his tanned skin. She wondered if they were sensitive like hers.

"I want to try something," she said.

His mouth felt dry when he replied, "Go ahead."

Evelyn leaned in and kissed the bronze skin on his chest. She allowed her tongue to peek out and circle his nipple. Imitating his earlier actions, she secured her mouth around it and sucked, having learned she liked it when he did the same.

Marrok grunted and she sucked harder. His hands fisted in her dark red locks, tilting her so he could take her mouth again. Her kiss alone was almost enough to do him in. He jerked her head with another tug, searching her eyes. One iris glowing, like his were sure to be.

"I wasn't done exploring," she complained.

"I'm not sure I can take much more, Evelyn."

"You don't want me to explore?"

"I don't want you to start something I'm not sure you can finish, not when I'm this close."

She wants us, his demon hissed. *Let her have us.*

"Something I can't finish?"

"I'm a razor's edge from release, Evelyn. I don't want to engage in something you're not ready for, so I need to wake myself and take care of it."

Evelyn's stare landed on the bulge at his crotch. Her mouth twisted, thinking. He was obviously turned on. She wanted to make him feel as good as he'd made her feel.

"You believe I'm not prepared to … repay in kind?"

"I have no expectation for you to do anything you're not ready to do, Evelyn." His fingers brushed her cheek. "We can go as slow as you need."

Evelyn's heart thumped hard. Her big, dark, warrior was giving her time, time he felt she needed.

"So, by going as slow as I need, can we go also go as fast as I need?"

Marrok's brow slanted. "As fast as you need?"

"Yes. I believe I told you I wasn't done exploring. I would like to continue. That's what I need from you right now."

"Evelyn, I love you touching me, but—"

"No, Marrok. Do you think I don't crave you just as much? I want to *touch* you, Marrok. To give you as much pleasure as you've given me. Do you understand what I'm saying?"

Marrok sucked in a breath. Surely, she wasn't saying she wanted to reciprocate in the same manner. Was she? His erection jerked, thinking of how it would feel to have her mouth on him.

Evelyn could sense the excitement she'd elicited in her demon. She saw the moment he made his decision. His hungry look told her he was hers.

"Undo my pants, Evelyn."

Evelyn's blood spiked with eagerness. She was surprised her hands weren't shaking after she popped the first button and got a peek of the dark hair underneath. She had trouble undoing the next.

His trousers were stretched so tight she was afraid to pull on the fabric. Carefully, she undid the next two, catching a glimpse of darkened skin under his curls. By the time she got the last button undone, his hands were in her hair again.

Evelyn pulled and tugged the material until his erection sprang free. Her eyes were glued to it, fascinated. Curiosity had her hand wrapping around him, giving a little squeeze.

His exhale came out hard and she looked up, worried she'd hurt him. She released him and he placed her hand back where it had been.

"Don't stop."

"Should I ...?" she squeezed again instead of voicing her question.

Though she and her sisters had been educated on sex, they'd not been taught what to do outside of coupling. Mara, their governess, had assured them their husbands would know what to do.

"Like this," he replied, laying his hand over hers and stroking up and down his length. After several strokes, he let go and put his hand in her hair again.

"I want to try something," she told him once more.

"Anything. You can do anything," he whispered, thrusting his hips slightly, meeting her strokes each time they reached the base of his cock.

Evelyn bent and pressed her lips to the broad crown. His hands tightened, her hair threading between his fingers. She opened her mouth and licked.

"Close your mouth around it, *moj draga*."

Trusting his direction, she did as Marrok asked. His taste was salted spice, similar to his scent. She hummed in satisfaction.

Gently, he pushed further inside her mouth. A loud groan broke the silence and her skin heated, thrilled she could do to him what he did to her.

She swirled her tongue, wanting more of his flavor. His hands fisted her hair and he held her head still. His shallow thrusts increased in speed and so she stroked him faster.

"I'm close. If you don't want me to spend in your mouth, pull away."

Evelyn refused to move. She wanted to taste all of him, to be the force to pull forth his seed. Her grip tightened and she felt him pulse in her hand. His molten essence surged into her mouth.

"Ah, Goddess," he sighed. "Swallow."

Evelyn had to swallow several times while Marrok peaked. He cried her name like a prayer to the heavens. Eventually he came down from his high and withdrew from her mouth.

"Come here, little mate."

Evelyn went into his arms and he lowered their bodies to the blanket so they were facing each other. He brushed her lips with his then ran his cheek across hers.

She noticed he made no attempt to cover his exposed manhood. She considered the merits of lying nude, skin to skin, with Marrok. Was she really so willing to take the next step?

"What are you thinking, my sweet?" the deep timber of his voice cocooned her in warmth while his hand rubbed her back.

"Nothing."

"I can smell your new arousal. Need I remind you that you cannot lie to me?"

"I was just picturing the future. I find I am rather impatient."

His hand paused. "Be patient with me, Evelyn. I'm fixing my world for you. It will take some time."

Her heart fluttered, feeling genuinely connected to him in this moment. Marrok was fighting a dangerous battle, fixing his world not just for his demons, but also for her.

She prayed he could make it happen before she aged into an old crow. The mates of wolves, vampires, and demons, once fully bonded, could live as long as their other halves did.

Evelyn had heard of a handful of Gwydions who had mated with demons. Allegedly, these elementals lived extremely long lives. Having shared blood in the dreamworld, she wasn't sure her aging would be halted.

She didn't want to give power to her concern so she focused on the details of Marrok's task. "Did you make any progress?" she asked.

"We have had much success. Logistically, I mean. We have what we want in place and are beginning introductions."

"Introductions?"

"Not in the traditional sense. We'll be providing exposure, allowing rogues to sense other demons, one by one. They'll be in a containment space and be able to see the visiting demons as they pass by. If we bring enough of them together, we think there's a good chance at mates finding one another."

Summons had gone out to unmated demons to appear in designated holding stations around the kingdom to begin these introductions. The idea was to expose each demon to as many other demons as they could, rogue or not. The more saatus bonds they could identify, the fewer demons who could fall prey to madness.

With any luck, they'd be able to match rogues with their fated mates and start the healing process on site. Marrok knew this would take years, especially if a rogue demon's saatus was very young or had yet to be born. At least it was a start.

"And the rogues who find their mates will return to normal?"

"That is my hope, yes. You'll be happy to know Petr, one of my soldiers—a friend, actually—stumbled across his own saatus. I sent him to a village he would never have gone to otherwise. He was there to communicate my plan with the local magistrate, who happened to be female—and his mate."

Evelyn smiled. "That's wonderful."

"It is. The first of many bonds, we hope."

Marrok explained some of what he and Favin had enacted, dividing Sundari into sections on a map and assigning those he trusted to command each sector. He'd spent too much time in the past trying to be everywhere at once. It was time to allocate his resources and move things along quickly.

"I need to wake soon," he told her, burying his head in her neck.

"When will I see you again?"

His tongue dipped into her ear and she squirmed, giggling.

"Another month."

"I hate that it has to be so long."

"I know, but I need to sleep light when I'm not in the fortress. It's difficult for anyone to wake me when I'm dreamwalking with you."

Brazenly, Evelyn reached down and took his hardened length in her hand. "Can't you stay, just a little longer?"

Marrok's amber irises brightened to the point he could see the golden sheen reflecting off her hair. His response to Evelyn was so intense, he contemplated holding onto her as he woke, possibly pulling her into his bed.

When she lovingly caressed him as he'd shown her how to do, he rolled atop her. "Maybe just a little longer."

Evelyn's giggles died when Marrok slunk down lower and put his mouth to her center once more.

Chapter 13

One week later ...

"I cut off his hand and threw it at his head ... that was after we all bet on the horses while they danced a jig."

Evelyn's brow furrowed, finally looking at her younger sister. "What?"

"You're distracted."

"I was listening," she lied.

Nora's story about the gathering in the dancehall the previous evening had been muted from Evelyn's brain the moment they passed the boulders beside the stream. Everything about the outdoors now reminded her of Marrok. It had been a week and she was missing him terribly.

"Really?"

"Of course."

"Then what did I just say?"

"You held hands and danced a jig. Maybe rode a horse?"

"Alright, you were half-listening," Nora conceded. "Want to talk about it?"

"Not particularly."

Nora debated how hard to press her sister. Evie was usually jovial company. Today she seemed almost sad.

"Is this about Jasper?" she hedged.

"No. Though, I wouldn't mind going another round with him in the ring after the stunt he pulled last week."

"I can tell. Was it not enough you conveniently forgot to tell Flynn you'd left Jasper tied to a tree somewhere in the forest?"

Evelyn smirked. "Not really."

"You're diabolical."

Evelyn laughed. "Says the master decapitator."

"We're a pair, aren't we?"

"I think Father would argue we're quite the trio. Eden might appear put together, but she can be just as wicked, as my eyebrow can attest."

"True. At least it grew back."

When they crossed the small bridge over the stream, Nora dared to ask what she'd been meaning to for days. "Is this ... sulking ... because of the demon?"

This got Evelyn's attention. "What demon?"

"The one in my vision."

Evelyn's heart pounded. She worried for Marrok's safety. His past was riddled with strife, his present not much better.

If Nora had seen something befalling him, Evelyn would summon Marrok this very night and warn him.

"The vision from two years ago? Or did you have another?" she probed.

"No, no new visions. Only ..."

"Only what?"

"I dreamt of him. With you."

Oh dear Goddess above, her cheeks flamed. Evelyn was almost afraid to ask. "Doing what?"

"Dancing. Same as the vision, but this time I could see you more clearly. You looked happy. He, ah, was looking at you rather intensely. It was not a platonic sort of look, or the look of a stranger. I think the two of you were *together*. A couple, possibly."

The strain on Evelyn's shoulders disappeared. A tiny jolt of excitement zapped her belly. It was unlikely Nora was having random dreams of Marrok. It had to be a vision of the future.

"You don't seem surprised, Evie. In fact, I think you look relieved."

"I am."

"Why?"

Evelyn wasn't ready to share the details of her nocturnal life. She trusted Nora would keep her secret, as would Eden. She lacked the heart, however, to put her sisters in a position to keep a secret from their father, who would only worry, or worse, intervene.

"Why wouldn't I be relieved? Demons can be dangerous. If he was courting me, then I have nothing to worry about now."

Nora's face said she wasn't convinced. Evelyn blew out the breath she'd been holding when her sister shrugged and let the discussion die.

* * *

"Step forward, Melena." Brennen's voice echoed across the stone floor.

Evelyn's mouth tightened. She hated his voice, how he allowed his dark magics to scrape against others. Brennen was a plague on the demon kingdom.

Her fingers itched, one thumb brushing against her scabbard. *Her scabbard?* She didn't carry a sword. She quickly realized she was dreaming, inside Marrok's head again, reliving his past.

Had he thought to draw his weapon in this moment? Such would be suicide here in the hall. He stood to the left of the king's throne, dozens of royal guards were positioned behind and to either side of Brennen. It looked like a room where the king would hold court or perform royal ceremonies.

Hundreds of demons stood below. Rows and rows of black and white heads of hair turned to the back, following a figure moving up the aisle.

A tall female moved forward, approaching the dais. Her silky white gown clung to her like a second skin. Evelyn couldn't help but notice the swell of her bosom and curve of her hips.

She's stunning, Marrok's thought whispered in her mind. Reluctantly, she had to agree with his reaction.

Evelyn didn't like the growing need within Marrok. He wanted to jump in front of the she-demon and shield her from Brennen.

When the female reached the bottom step, she kneeled, bowing her head. Her long, black hair, fluid as water, fell forward. Marrok wanted to touch its softness. He wanted to touch other things, as well, and Evelyn had to fight to keep his ruminations at bay.

She felt queasy. Why was she being forced to experience this part of his life? She didn't want to relive his attraction to others, or his time with past lovers.

"Well, then," Brennen hummed. "Your father was right. You are quite spectacular. He's boasted of your talents and beauty for so long I simply had to see for myself."

Marrok growled in Evelyn's head.

"Thank you, my lord," Melena replied to the floor.

"Where are my manners? Rise and let us gaze upon your splendor."

The female rose gracefully. Her bronzed skin stood out against the white of her dress. She held herself with poise, her movements regal.

Her chin lifted, meeting Brennen's stare with her large, almond eyes. They were the color of whiskey with sparkles of amber, shining like jewels on either side of her slender nose.

Evelyn would have thought the she-demon completely unaffected if not for the slight blush growing on her cheeks, visible despite her tanned complexion.

She could feel Marrok willing Melena to give nothing away. Brennen would prey on any weakness, any insecurity, and Marrok felt oddly protective of the female.

"Nephew, allow me to present your gift."

Marrok's head swiveled to Brennen. "Sire?"

"She's yours now."

"I'm not following."

"The Seer. Melena. She's your gift."

Marrok's eyes darted to Melena and Evelyn had no choice but to follow. The female didn't show any sign of distress at being referred to as his gift. Marrok wondered if Melena had known she was being given away, like chattel.

"You are giving me a Seer? For what purpose?"

171

Brennen's pupils dilated, covering his irises completely. His sarcastic grin sent tingles of warning up and down Marrok's body.

"You may use her for whatever purpose you choose, of course. Though, I know what I would do with her."

The King lasciviously licked his lips and Evelyn felt like gagging.

Despite Brennen's heinous insinuation, the tension fled Marrok's muscles. Evelyn could feel the relief replace his anxiety. His thoughts became chaotic, too fast for her to follow. Focusing, she was able to latch onto several.

Evelyn sensed his thankfulness that Brennen had no intention to use the female for his own purposes. Marrok also experienced confusion over why his uncle would want him to take on a Seer.

His instant attraction to Melena excited him despite the dismay of knowing Melena wasn't his saatus. Until this moment, no other female had stirred Marrok's blood as Melena had.

It was the last notion that sat heaviest on Evelyn's chest, making her feel the need to claw her way out. She had no physical presence during these dreams. She was like a ghost inhabiting his body. She wanted out.

Panicking, she struggled against the forces holding her there. She didn't want to see what happened next. She wanted out of this dream, away from Marrok's life in Brennen's court. Straining and pulling, she silently screamed in anguish.

She jolted awake, panting and trying to catch her breath. Tears streaked her face and she wiped them away, refusing to give in to her hurt.

Marrok was centuries old. She'd known he'd been with others. She might not have witnessed it, but her sixth sense told her Melena had become his lover at some point.

Rolling to her side, she couldn't help but feel sorry for Melena, to be treated as an object by someone so cruel. The she-demon was as much a victim as anyone who suffered under Brennen's rule.

Whatever happened after she'd been gifted, Melena didn't appear to still be in a relationship with Marrok. Evelyn was confident he wouldn't pursue the bond with her if he was still committed to another.

Then again, she wasn't in Sundari so she had no real way of knowing. Melena could currently be living under his roof, working as his Seer. It was possible Marrok hadn't acted on his attraction and merely kept Melena in his employment.

Tied up in knots, Evelyn tossed and turned the rest of the night while Marrok's memories kept coming.

Chapter 14

Three weeks later ...

The first thing Marrok noticed when he opened his eyes was the incandescent glow of soft yellows and whites dancing under the canopy. Before him, where the wide path gave way to the meadow, was a table with a pewter candelabra standing in the center.

He also saw a bottle of wine and two flutes, already filled. What he did not see was his mate. He concentrated, using his inner demon to sense if she was near. After the blood exchange, he should be able to detect her presence.

Evelyn was right behind him.

Grinning, he spun around and plucked her off her feet. He buried his face in her neck, hugging her harder than necessary. His demon purred. Meeting only once a month was taxing on his spirit.

"Miss me?" she laughed.

"Yes. I came close to dreamwalking a dozen times just to steal a kiss."

"You don't have to steal when it is so willingly given."

"Then I'll gladly take what you'll give, *moj draga*."

Their mouths met and Evelyn slid her arms around his neck, holding the back of his head. His kiss was tender and sweet, not the rushed passion she'd assumed he'd bestow. She couldn't decide which she preferred.

Evelyn kissed along his chin and around to his ear, playfully nipping his lobe. Skimming her nose along his neck, she inhaled deeply, loving his exotic scent.

"I missed you, as well." More than she wanted to say. With each passing night, she grew more and more restless. She prided herself on being strong, but her dreams were testing her will. She needed Marrok's reassurance.

"Good."

Slowly, Marrok lowered Evelyn to her feet. He brought her hand to his lips and kissed the back of it. Keeping it clasped, he led her to the table.

"Did you do this?" he asked, handing her one of the wine glasses.

She nodded, taking a timid sip of the sweet alcohol. "I've been practicing, seeing what I can make work here. It can get rather boring dreaming of the same place repetitively, so I figured I would try new things to pass the time. I thought we could try sharing a meal. Do you like it?" she asked, taking another sip.

"I would have preferred you conjured a bed."

Evelyn spit her wine out, right onto Marrok's chest, who in turn began a deep, rich belly laugh. Wide-eyed, she started wiping at his shirt, babbling an apology. If her sisters ever saw her act thusly, she'd never hear the end of it.

He took Evelyn's drink and sat it on the table, along with his. Marrok grabbed her hand, tilting her reddened face by her chin with his other. His eyes glimmered in the candlelight, full of amber with very little black.

The corners of her mouth turned down, resenting his bemusement a little. At least he had the manners not to make fun of her.

"After what we shared with one another last month, the mention of a bed shocks you?"

"A bed implies intercourse."

"I could have taken you on the blanket just as easily, Evelyn."

"I know. I was caught off guard, is all. Here I was thinking of *sitting* down with you and your mind was on *lying* down with me. You're the one who insisted on going slow."

"This is true. Though I hardly believe your inquisitive brain hasn't thought of lying with me. I was merely pointing out a bed would be a nice place to recline as opposed to a blanket on the ground. We may have jumped a bit further than I'd planned last time, but I'll not push you into anything, Evelyn."

"I know."

Marrok was an honorable male. She trusted him with her body, more than he knew. If not for the constant dreams of late, she probably would have conjured a bed.

She'd had quite a number of dreams centering around Marrok and Melena together. Luckily, she never saw them exploring the physical side of things. Watching the beginning of their relationship was torture enough.

With every stab of envy and resentfulness, Evelyn reminded herself that she was Marrok's saatus—not Melena—and he would have no other mate. It was preordained.

She had great faith in Fate. It was the only thing she could hold onto bearing witness to his prior pursuit of another. Though, she did question to what purpose she was being shown these particular memories.

She'd learned Marrok had moved Melena into his home immediately after Brennen *gifted* her. Evelyn still cringed at the baseness of treating a sentient being in such a way. Though she was jealous of the raven-haired beauty, Evelyn did have sympathy for her situation.

From the dreams, Evelyn knew Melena's room was across from Marrok's. The first night, he'd walked her to her quarters, cupped her face in both hands, and told her to knock on his door if she needed anything, no matter how inconsequential her need may be.

The female's eyes had flared and swirled, an odd reddish blue mixed with the amber. She moved her mouth in speech, though Evelyn heard no words. She'd felt a whisper of power skirt across Marrok's skin, followed by a surge of responsibility towards his new charge. He vowed to keep her away from Brennen and his uncle's mind games.

During these dreams, Evelyn watched Melena as Marrok had watched Melena. The she-demon was often the center of his attention. He stared at her when they shared meals. When she walked the garden below his balcony. When entertaining guests.

Melena had totally ensnared him.

The worst of it was Evelyn's having to endure his inner dialogue of attraction, of his plans to seduce Melena slowly. Was this what he typically did with lovers? What he was doing with Evelyn?

She didn't judge him for wanting Melena. She'd felt his loneliness, the longing to touch and hold onto something he thought precious wasn't a character flaw. If anything, it made him even more endearing. Marrok had wanted to be the other half of a couple, desired to share his life with a female.

Life under King Brennen was misery incarnate. Any soul worth anything deserved some semblance of happiness in its life.

With this last thought, Evelyn shuffled closer, sliding her arms around his waist. Her forehead rested against his sternum. She loved how his arms automatically came around her in return. In this space, all was right in her world. In this space, they belonged to one another.

So, of course, she had to go and ruin it.

"Who is Melena?" she asked as delicately as she could.

Under her hands, Evelyn felt Marrok go stock-still, his muscles immediately hardening.

"Where did you hear that name?"

"I dreamt of her."

"She was here? Like Jasper had been here?"

"No. I dreamt your memories again. Quite a few of them this time."

Marrok forgot to breath. What trick of Fate would force his mate to witness his past? It couldn't have been pleasant seeing him with someone else.

"What did you see?"

She couldn't voice it, didn't know where to begin. She feared saying aloud she observed him falling for the she-demon would give the past power. Evelyn wanted to live in the present. Unfortunately, she knew to do so, she would have to understand, and get over, Marrok's past.

"Look at me."

179

Evelyn slowly took in a breath, steeling herself to face him. She was met with bright amber, her indication he was experiencing strong emotion.

"What did you see?" he asked again.

"Take it from my mind."

"What?"

"I saw a lot. Much of it seemed personal. I'm not positive I can articulate it all. Can you pull the memories from my mind?"

"If that is your preference."

"It is. Go ahead."

Marrok splayed his hands on both sides of Evelyn's head. Closing his eyes, he sifted through her mind, searching for Melena. He feared what he would see—feared what Evelyn had seen.

A series of moving images played in his mind's eye. The day he met Melena, some of their early days together. Amazingly, the memories weren't as painful as they used to be. In fact, he experienced them as an almost detached observer.

A niggling ate at him when he saw Melena's mouth occasionally move without sound. He had no memories of her doing so. His demon retreated, wanting nothing to do with the show. He was only interested in his saatus.

When the last memory passed, he released Evelyn. Thankfully, she had not been tormented with the reminiscences of him making love to Melena.

"Let us sit," he nodded to the table.

He pulled out a chair and Evelyn sat, dropping her hands into her lap. Marrok took the other chair and drained the rest of his wine. He hoped the dreamworld's alcohol was potent.

He retrieved the necklace from his pocket, where he'd taken to keeping it, and placed it on the table. He'd not been able to bring himself to wear it once again.

"This was Melena's."

Evelyn glanced down at the medallion. He'd told her he'd been wearing it the night he lost it. This night, it had been in his pocket.

"Melena was my wife."

Her throat tightened. "Was?" she managed to ask.

"She died, decades ago."

Evelyn wanted to ask how, being that demons were notoriously hard to kill. Maybe she had perished due to some disease of the heart. Aside from removing the organ, as Marrok had done with Brennen, ailments of the heart were the only thing she'd ever heard could snuff out the life of a Sundari.

Not wanting to be unkind, she didn't press. "I'm sorry. Truly. I could see she meant much to you."

"She did."

"You kept her memory close. This is why you wore her necklace."

"It is."

"But you do not wear it any longer?"

"No. I've not worn it since the night it fell off."

Marrok's jaw worked, clearly uncomfortable. Seeking to soothe his distress, she put her hand atop his.

"I should have told you, Evelyn. I didn't like keeping it secret. To be honest, since I've met you, her memory has only surfaced a handful of times. It never seemed the right moment to bring it up."

"I understand."

A dubious expression appeared on his face. "How could you possibly understand? I married someone who wasn't my saatus. Doesn't that bother you?"

"A little. I understand why you took her as a lover. I could feel how much you resented your feelings of solitude and how you felt a connection to Melena right away. You also felt responsible for her well-being and protected her from Brennen."

Marrok inhaled, relaxing his posture on the exhale and nodding. "I did."

"Why marry if you knew the two of you could never truly bond?"

"I loved her. I'd never loved anyone, not in that way. So I committed myself to loving her, in every way I could."

Evelyn nodded, appreciating his honesty. His admission, while uncomfortable, didn't spark any sort of extreme reaction of jealousy in her. Instead, she was empathetic to his loss.

Melena had brought him some level of happiness. Evelyn couldn't bring herself to begrudge him for it. She cared for him enough to want his life to be fulfilling, even before they met. Someday, she hoped they, too, would find their way to love.

"I'm sorry she was the subject of your dreams. Fate can be a cruel teacher, but She shows us what we need to learn. I assume it was because I should have told you the truth of it."

"I'm not upset, Marrok, not in the way you think."

"You're not?"

"I thought you could determine truth from lie," she teased.

His mouth relaxed, a slow grin replacing the flat line. "You amaze me, *moj draga.*"

"And why is that?" she replied with a grin of her own.

"You're stronger than I. Wiser."

Evelyn sniffed. "Hardly."

He clasped both of her hands in his. "You are. Do you not remember my reaction to the young male during our last visit? He wasn't even your lover and I was sorely tempted to dreamwalk to him so I could tear his limbs off his body."

183

"Really?" Her response came out husky. Something about his visceral reaction turned her on. She should probably be concerned for Jasper's life, though she couldn't remember why while looking into the heated eyes across the table.

"Most definitely. In fact, I—damnit!" he cursed, jerking his hands away.

"What is it?"

She saw the answer before he responded. A long line of blood seeped into the fabric on the sleeve of his white shirt.

"Someone's trying to wake me. I have to go. My men were instructed not to bother me tonight unless it was a matter of life or death."

He stood, hastily returning the necklace to his pocket.

"If you want to wear it, I understand," she insisted.

Marrok's chest tightened. Evelyn really was a wonder to him, far more selfless than he could ever have been if the situation was reversed. He leaned down to plant a firm kiss on his mate's full lips. Reluctantly, he straightened.

"Another month?" she asked.

"Yes. At least. If I am delayed, I'll try to leave word, if I can."

"Here? In the dreamworld?"

"Yes. If you can conjure a table and wine, I'm sure I can manage a pen and paper. I'll contact you as soon as I'm able."

"Be careful."

He was gone before the words left her lips.

* * *

"Stop cutting me. I'm awake," he groused, compelling himself into consciousness.

"Apologies, Sire."

Favin's worried face came into view. Then Danil's.

"Where is Lazlo?" Marrok inquired. He was usually never far, especially now that Petr was dispatched elsewhere.

"He's gathering the guards," Favin responded.

"No, what he's doing is running around like a nutter," Danil quipped.

Marrok sat up, recalling the last time Favin had to cut him to get him to awaken. "What's happened?"

This was their first night in the fortress in a month. No one should have known they'd secretly returned this morning. Rogues weren't likely to attack what they believed to be an empty fortress.

"We've received word the holding stations are under attack," Favin told him.

"Which ones?"

"All of them."

Marrok's fists clenched, angry heat surged from his core through his limbs. He leapt out of bed, gathering his clothing and dressing quickly.

"Even the one here?" he asked his Second.

"Yes, Sire."

Marrok secured his sword, along with a handful of other blades, striding out the door as he sheathed the last of them. Danil and Favin were close on his heals.

"To attack them all at once means it was coordinated. There are too many for it to be mere happenstance," he thought aloud, making his way down the stairs. "All this work, and now we learn they're organized enough to launch a strategic attack."

The longer he thought, the more enraged Marrok became. To be strategic in this manner, someone had to be controlling the rogues, leading them.

Not all rogues were shells. Brennen had enough of his wits to command his army and play mind games with others. Marrok would find the demon responsible and remove his heart.

"Sire, where are you going?" Favin asked.

Marrok didn't reply. He withdrew his sword as he approached the main doors. "Open them," he yelled at the guards.

They swung open and Marrok took off into the night, his two friends drawing their weapons and running to keep up.

Favin shouted orders to the guards behind them. What they were, Marrok didn't know. His singular focus was to contain the intruders.

Killing them would have been easier. He was tired of running in place, tired of taking one step forward, only to be knocked back ten. He dug deep for the will to fight for them, despite their continuous aggressions.

The courtyard was empty and he made his way west, following the exterior wall. The station was just around the corner. He could hear heavy thuds and the splintering of wood.

The torches lining the high security wall, running parallel to the fortress, would make it easy for Marrok to be seen. He made no attempt to hide his approach. He wanted the rogues to know who was coming for them.

His mind knew there was no chance they would surrender. His heart held out hope they would recognize their king and lay down their weapons. It was foolish to hope such things. He also knew he was incapable of giving up on them.

A figure sprinted towards him, crazed and uncoordinated. Marrok side stepped, snapping his arm out straight to close line the demon. The unarmed rogue landed on his back with a loud oomph. Marrok brought the pommel of his sword down hard enough to render the demon unconscious.

C.A. Worley

"Put him in a cell. I'll disable the rest and check if they're salvageable later."

Favin didn't move. "Sire, let us round them up. I'll then check their minds, as you wish."

"No. Any who were corrupt prior to succumbing will be executed. I won't lay that on you. Tonight, this burden is mine alone."

Marrok didn't want to announce he planned to interrogate the captured rogues—or how he intended to get answers from them. He considered himself a fair male, but he would employ drastic measures to cut off the head of the snake. That was a regret he alone would assume.

Favin started to protest but Marrok had already moved on. Snarls and shouts carried through the air. Metal clashed against metal in the near distance. His instinct was to raise his weapon and defend his king.

He stepped towards the sound of chaos when Danil's big hand gripped him hard. "Leave him be, Favin. No rogue is a match for Marrok in hand-to-hand."

"There are at least a dozen of them, Danil."

"Lazlo's already got archers all over the roof. If Marrok needs help, he'll get it. For now, he needs to work some of this out of his system."

Favin lifted his head to the parapets and saw twenty guards with their bows notched and ready to fly. The cries echoing off the stone walls were not those of his liege. His shoulders relaxed and he returned his sword to its sheath. It was going to be a long night.

Chapter 15

Six months later ...

Evelyn sat hunched at the small table, positioned where the walking trail opened to the meadow. The small piece of furniture had remained since she first conjured it, though, the candles were no longer lit. There was no point in lighting them.

There'd been no correspondence from Marrok this month. Or the last. She hadn't heard from him since the last day of fall, hadn't seen him since late summer.

He'd missed their planned meeting half a year ago. True to his word, however, he had managed to leave a short note telling Evelyn to attempt summoning him once each month. If it was safe enough, he would sleep and dreamwalk to her. He didn't tell her what to do if it wasn't safe, not that she could help him.

The month following his first missed meeting, Marrok left another note, apologizing and instructing her to try again after the next lunar cycle. Then another note came. And another. Four months of letters scratched on parchment, but no Marrok. In each instance, he left his letter atop the table weighted down by a solitary rock.

She'd taken to going to bed early to increase her chances of seeing him. Marrok must have been sleeping during the day because she'd never crossed his path. She feared his recent absences meant he wasn't sleeping for long enough stretches to reach her.

Evelyn mourned the time she could have had to get to know Marrok. She worried constantly. His letters had assured her he was alive and well. Four months in a row of messages helped assuage her fears, though she questioned his assertion of being *well*.

When she found nothing last month, she convinced herself it wasn't the end of the world. Evelyn knew he was facing something far more important than scribbling her a line or two.

She'd left him a note of her own. With her heart heavy, she'd left him only a handful of words, unable to come up with anything of more substance.

Evelyn knew he was alive because she could garner his emotions from time to time, as recently as this afternoon. It felt like Marrok was struggling more this week. Thankfully, she sensed no insanity. The bulk of his feelings swung between fury and frustration.

This morning, she could sense profound sadness to the point his melancholy had become her own. So potent was his misery, Evelyn's resolve started to weaken. She believed it had something to do with feeling his emotions because she never thought of herself as one to give up.

Each time she arrived in the clearing, she did the same thing. She checked for evidence Marrok had been here. If he hadn't, she explored what the dreamworld allowed her to explore and occupied her mind with other tasks.

She also tested her powers here. She could make items appear, such as the table. She could manipulate her clothing, something she'd subconsciously been doing her entire life. Only once before had she shown in the clearing wearing what she'd wore to bed.

These were tricks she could perform only in her sleep. Elementals didn't have such magics in the waking world. No one did. That didn't mean her natural talents weren't improved. Far from it.

During training these long months, her father noticed she'd grown stronger, attributing it to her transition into adulthood. Evelyn suspected it had more to do with the fledgling bond she shared with the King of Sundari—a bond her father knew nothing about.

Every waking and sleeping moment, Evelyn faced the arduous task of controlling her emotions. She'd done well remaining positive most of the time. The lack of a note tonight was another punch to the gut.

Emotionally exhausted, questioning if she should take steps to find him in the waking world, she rose from the chair and entered the forest. There was no point sitting there like a lovesick fool.

As she strolled towards her destination, she pictured what Marrok's reaction might be to what she'd created for them. Shortly after he'd been awoken by blade again, Evelyn had done something for Marrok. Or, really, had fulfilled his pseudo request.

Just into the woods, there was an area where the canopy was sparse and the soft purplish-blue moonbeams illuminated the forest floor. It was enclosed by a circle of trees with just enough space between for a large bed.

A bed not designed for sleeping.

The idea had seemed brilliant at the time, as a sort of amorous way to greet him. She'd added the softest of bedding, imagining tumbling onto it, pinned under his weight.

Ruefully, she doubted they'd be able to share it any time soon. Like the table, she left it here, knowing he would eventually come to her. Eventually may as well have been forever.

Standing mere feet away from her creation, she leaned against a large oak and took in the romantic setting. The moonlight shone on the duvet, making the white material appear to have a blueish tint.

It was an oasis in woods. She liked the idea of it, the feel of this place. Here she found some level of peace, thinking of it as theirs.

The back of Evelyn's eyes started to burn. Her lids closed and she pictured Marrok's chiseled physique. She remembered every cut and slope of definition in his upper body, the bright amber shining from his eyes as his hands and mouth brought her to the height of pleasure.

In the dreamworld, Evelyn felt safe and brave enough to explore her sexuality. She was ready to take the next physical step with Marrok, to share something she knew they both desired, to feel the intimacy lovers shared.

More than that, she wanted to hold him and know he was unharmed. She wanted to tell him she would wait an eternity for him—if she could live that long.

The blood exchange created a tenuous connection between them. If Marrok's assertions were correct, the connection was but a fraction of what it would be when they met in the waking world.

A tear slipped free and she clumsily wiped it away. Crying would do her no good. She blinked several times, regaining her composure.

A low rumbling vibrated through the trees, their limbs shaking and rustling the leaves. The soft purple and blue sky turned bright red, reminiscent of the evening he'd come to her not so long ago, livid at having been apart for two years.

An animalist howl broke through the quiet, followed by the sound of something crashing through the forest. She gasped and turned towards the source.

Slowly, Evelyn eased backwards, halting when the bed hit the back of her legs. Lifting her hands, she used her powers to raise a protective barrier, enclosing the ring of trees with her in the center.

Branches and twigs broke with the movement of whatever was coming. She should have been terrified. She wasn't. Just as the figure appeared on the other side of her magics, she sobbed and dropped her shield.

Marrok barreled into Evelyn, knocking her backwards onto the bed. He landed atop her, adjusting his weight to his forearms. Desperate kisses covered her face, her neck, her collarbone.

He buried his head in the crook of her neck, his arms clutching her body to his. He inhaled her delectable scent, drew it deep into his lungs. It took a moment for him to realize they were both shaking, not just him.

Evelyn's tears wet his skin and Marrok squeezed his eyes shut. Though he reviled her reason for weeping, he would bear it and wallow in the shelter of her arms. His mate was his anchor now. The longer they were apart, the more adrift he felt.

He hadn't had a deep sleep for more than an hour here and there in six months. It had taken this long to get some semblance of control and he couldn't be bothered to celebrate because he was so damned miserable.

He was overtly discouraged, unable to find the culprit who organized the attacks in the summer. None of those captured could give him a name. One extremely disturbed bloke had gone on and on about Sephtis Kenelm setting the world right.

The group was long dead and, even if they were active, they didn't create rogue demons to terrorize other demons. Their purpose was balance. A nation filled with rogues was anything but.

This week he'd hit a wall, his demon driving him to the breaking point. Quadrupling his efforts, and relying heavily on his men, Marrok pushed himself to the point of exhaustion.

With what he hoped was the last of the rogues, he'd locked the gates to the Corak Peninsula's colony, tripled the guard, and headed for the fortress. Nothing, short of death, was going to keep him from his mate this night.

He held Evelyn until he felt her tears dry. She relaxed into his embrace and he rolled to the side, meeting her eyes.

"I got your note," he said.

Evelyn's sad laugh had his heart constricting inside his chest. Every letter he'd left had been short and void of emotion. He'd only been able to drop in for minutes at a time.

When he saw her note last month, he knew he had to move mountains to get back to her. He'd finally been able to feel some of her emotions and he knew Evelyn was hurting. Marrok didn't want to hurt his mate. He'd woken before he could reply and hadn't been in a safe place long enough to dreamwalk again.

I miss you. The three words were all she'd written. They were enough.

"I missed you, too, my sweet."

195

Evelyn palmed the side of his face, which had grown thinner. His cheekbones were more pronounced. Dark circles highlighted his lower lids. His blackened hair was longer and unkempt.

Had Marrok not been so large before, the weight loss would have made him look gaunt. Now he simply looked to be of the build of the males of Gwydion, still strong, but lean. Wiry.

A narrow scar was forming from his temple to chin. Someone had cut him deeply. Her magics tingled in her fingertips at the idea someone had dared raised a blade to him.

"Are you alright?" she asked.

"I am now."

A thousand questions entered her mind. The bright, burning, yellowish-brown boring into her, shining onto her skin, dissolved them all. They could talk later. Right now, Evelyn needed to feel.

Images of what she'd been fantasizing teased her, warming her from the inside. Any pretense of shyness died away under the intensity of her demon's stare.

She pressed her front as close to Marrok as she could get. Licking her lips, she hooked a leg over his hip, holding his hardened length to her center.

"Did you not notice the bed?"

"*Evelyn.*"

He'd groaned her name. A warning. A plea. Marrok didn't know which.

Unflinchingly, Evelyn kissed him again, coaxing his lips apart with her tongue. Her left hand pulled at the bottom of his shirt, lifting it so she could place her fingertips upon his skin. Her thumb strummed his nipple and she suddenly found herself on her back.

Marrok rose to his knees, watching Evelyn's chest rise and fall in an increasing pace as he unbuttoned his shirt. She was wearing another flimsy nightgown, her pert nipples pushing out from under the silky material.

He flung his shirt aside, debating where to touch her first. He wanted to see all of her, to roam and taste every square inch of skin. Unbuckling his belt, he forced himself to look upon her face.

"Remove the gown," he commanded.

Heat flicked Evelyn's already too-warm body. His vocals coated her in their magic and she only wished she could have the same effect upon him. She'd imagine his reaction to their combined nakedness a thousand times.

Evelyn wondered what Marrok would think of her lack of underwear. She'd stopped going to bed with them since she'd created their woodland love nest in the hopes her actions could speak if she could not verbalize what she wanted.

Courageously, she sat up enough to lift the gown over her head. His sharp inhale made her feel powerful. Beautiful. He'd seen her breasts before, put his mouth on her most sensitive areas, but she'd never been completely naked with him.

197

Marrok halted his work removing his pants, taking the time to admire his mate. Mismatched eyes watched him intently. One thin brow, a shade darker than her hair, rose in challenge. Had Marrok and his demon not been so desperate for her calming touch, he would have laughed.

Evelyn's dark red hair hung in loose waves, partially covering her chest. He didn't want any part of her hidden from his view. Slowly, he reached for her locks, placing them behind her shoulders.

His knuckles grazed one rigid peak on their journey lower. He felt her abdominal wall tighten under his touch. Lower he went, listening to her breathing alter when he reached his destination. Gently, he rubbed and probed her cleft, growling when he found her already wet.

In the dream's surreal lighting, Evelyn's skin was glowing a tawny gold, reminding him of the treasure she was. Marrok inhaled, her intoxicating arousal was a call he could not resist.

His demon jumped to the surface. Before Evelyn could blink, he had his mouth on her, lapping up her sweet nectar. Her pants and moans had him licking at an increasing speed, demanding her release.

Evelyn whimpered and her temperature soared. Marrok was stoking a fire, driving her mad with need.

"Look at me," his deep voice vibrated against her mound.

His eyes bled black and she knew she was seeing his demon spirit. She watched his sinful tongue lash furiously at the pinnacle of her sensitive folds while one finger gently pushed at her opening.

"Mine," the guttural sound seared its magic against her core, filling her from the inside.

His demon spirit's voice wrenched an immediate climax from Evelyn's quaking body. Ripples of pleasure overtook her ability to move or think. Such was her bliss, she didn't notice the probing of his blunt crown until her orgasm began to ebb away.

Marrok nudged his way between her folds, halting before he fully breached her entry. He waited until he had her full attention, giving her time to understand his intention. His arms shook from the power it took to hold back.

"Are you sure, Evelyn? Is this what you want?"

Take her, his demon demanded, readying to take control once again.

Marrok held back, waiting for his mate to make her choice. They may be in the dreamworld, but it would feel real. Their subdued bond would likely strengthen because he wouldn't be able to halt his demon from fully merging with her soul. He doubted the dreamworld would have any effect on dampening the connection of their spirits.

"Yes."

"The blood bond already connects us. My demon will want more once I'm inside you. He'll want to merge with your soul while we are together in this way."

"I want you, Marrok. Every part of you, and whatever comes with it. For you, I'll accept it all."

His throat felt tight, overcome with something he didn't want to name. His demon hummed merrily, beyond delighted with Evelyn's declaration.

Marrok hadn't been inside a female in three years, not since he'd decided to keep Evelyn when she was eighteen. Worse, he hadn't felt yearning for anyone the way he felt it for Evelyn. Had never felt such blind acceptance, not even when he'd been married.

He lowered his forehead to hers, breathing through the desire to plunge into her tight sheath and take her hard. Evelyn deserved more care than that.

Her small hands glided up his spine and gripped his hair. Lifting herself enough to reach him, she kissed him hungrily, like she was starving for his taste. Marrok lowered his weight, sliding his arms under her body. He rolled his hips forward.

He slid in easily the first few inches. Carefully, he retreated, thrusting forward again, mindful to work his way deeper without hurting her. Evelyn's choked cry halted his movement.

"Are you—"

"Don't stop!" she hissed, digging her fingernails into his back.

Marrok continued his shallow thrusts, working his mate into a frenzy. Evelyn scratched and rocked against him, demanding more. Her eagerness was too much for him to deny and he plunged deeper until he was seated fully inside her constricted channel. She was so tight it was almost painful.

His demon spirit reached for her soul, merging them into one as Evelyn shouted his name. Her muscles clamped him in a vice-like grip. He tried to hold out, but he was no match for his mate's convulsions.

With a roar, Marrok spilled inside her womb, driving into her again and again. His vision blurred as his cock pulsed with his climax. His spirit was so entrenched in her soul he'd surely never get it back.

Their throbbing releases were amplified by the merging of his spirit to hers. A minute passed while his demon coated himself in her essence. All demons could feel ecstasy in such a state. Marrok wondered how it felt to Evelyn.

Her back arched, reeling from the sensory overload. She'd yet to come down from her high. It was almost too much.

"What's happening?" she breathed.

"It's our souls touching."

Evelyn felt like she was on fire, like the slightest movement would push her over again. "Please. Please do something."

Marrok tried to reign in his spirit.

Evelyn's head thrashed. "No! I need more!" she yelled.

When she surged her hips upward, he understood her demand. Letting go of his demon, Marrok used his thumb against her knot of nerves as he continued to stretch her with his still-hardened cock.

With his other hand, he held her face, forbidding her to look away. Delirious, drunk on the experience, he pounded into her unyielding heat. Her nails scored down his ribs, inciting him into a full-blown frenzy.

He watched in amazement as Evelyn's skin reddened, her heart hammering as fast as his. Her lips parted. He was tempted to take her mouth but he didn't want to miss seeing her like this. Mindless in lust. Totally at his mercy. Completely his.

Her sharp intake of air was the only sign she gave before her walls contracted, squeezing him forcefully. The rapture upon her face was the most erotic vision he'd ever beheld. Evelyn's wide eyes and silent scream, coupled with her body's spasms, yanked his own seed from his body, as though it was hers to control, hers to command.

A fissure opened in the hardened shell he'd built around his heart. The pain of it making the moment all the more devastating.

He collapsed on top of her, lying in a stupor. His demon purred so loud she could probably hear it. Finally sated, the spirit retreated fully into its rightful place deep inside Marrok.

He didn't know if he could live without the witch who could so easily touch his soul. Whatever the future held, there was no going back now.

Chapter 16

His vision clearing, Marrok shifted his weight and rolled until his hip hit the bed. Still semi-erect inside his mate, he kept her close, not quite ready to break their union.

He nuzzled Evelyn's cheek, feeling her grin against his skin. Marrok's nose drifted to just below her ear and he inhaled. The air was thick with the smell of sex. Their lovemaking created a unique scent, heady and dizzying.

Like a drug, he wanted more of it. More of her. "How do you feel?" he asked instead of attempting her again.

"I feel wonderful. That was ... more than I could have imagined."

"I'm glad. I wasn't sure, being where we are, if it would be uncomfortable for you. I only ever want to bring you pleasure, *moj draga*."

Evelyn's face flushed, unused to speaking so frankly about anything sexual. Marrok obviously had no such reservations. She found herself liking the fact he spoke this way, as lovers did.

"Maybe a little at first, though I've nothing to compare it to. I suppose I'll have to let you know once we're together. Truly together."

Her fingers traced the thin scar on his face, down the side of his throat. They grazed his collarbone, then stroked the skin between his pectorals. Every inch helped her gather the courage to make her heart's inquiry.

"Any idea of when that may be?" she asked, trying to be nonchalant about it.

"Within the year. Two at most."

Evelyn's face fell and Marrok nudged her chin upward with his hand.

"When I say at most, I mean it. I'll build us a home on sacred ground, if necessary."

"You'll house me away at the Temple of Sanctus Femina?"

"If I must. I also need a plan to approach your father. That will take time, especially if he is resistant. I assume I'll need quite a few months to pursue diplomacy with him."

Sensing her disappointment, he kissed her soundly, then told her, "Though, I'll not be deterred. If necessary, we'll come clean about the dreamwalking."

Evelyn's mouth popped open and he lifted her jaw to close it. "As a last resort. But mark my words, Evelyn, I intend to have you. No one, not even your father, is going to get in the way of that."

Her eyes lit up. Marrok was committing to their future. One or two years was nothing for a being who lived forever. If her life was going to be prolonged by being his mate, she would not make things more difficult by pouting.

The subject of her father was another matter altogether. He'd dealt with demons many times and encouraged trade with Sundari. She didn't think he would take issue with a betrothal to Marrok, but trading with a demon was far different than arranging a marriage to one. Evelyn decided to remain optimistic.

"I'm going to have to test the success of our system's new security measures," Marrok continued. "We have to start over with the introduction stations. A large group of rogues, who have apparently been banding together and hiding out in remote areas, decided to destroy them. They were so far gone, they couldn't understand they could be saved."

"Did you ... what happened to the rogues?"

"Rounded them up and took them to the peninsula. It took this entire time."

"You didn't kill them?"

"I knew you didn't want me to. I also knew if I'd turned, I would want the chance to heal. Or, at the very least, to atone for whatever I'd done without my full knowledge while I was crazed."

Evelyn's heart filled. The more she knew of him, the further she fell. How could she not? His promise to come for her, to build a life with her, had her lips stretching so far across her face she thought she might crack.

"You're happy then?" he questioned.

"Very."

She traced his brow with her finger, then his squared jaw, now covered in a thin beard. Having dreamt of his parents, Evelyn knew he strongly resembled his father, but the shape of his eyes, accented by those thick, dark lashes, came from his mother.

She wondered what their children would look like.

Evelyn froze. Her hand tremored slightly and she quickly balled it into a fist.

"What's wrong?"

"I didn't think. It's so obvious and I didn't think of it," she murmured, her face becoming pained.

"What are you talking about?"

"Is it possible to impregnate me? I know we're in the dreamworld, but I found your medallion and you woke with my panties, so obviously things can be transferred. I can still feel what you *transferred* inside me. It seems like it was a lot. Is that normal? Well, I suppose that's irrelevant. But what about the rest?"

Marrok barked out a laugh, then laughed even harder when her upper lip curled and she slapped his shoulder.

"Do not laugh at me!"

"I'm sorry," he got out in between her smacks against his arm. His entire body was shaking, and it was only getting him more turned on.

"It's not funny, Marrok. What, pray tell, could I possibly tell my father? It's not the sort of thing I could keep secret for two years!"

"Shh, calm yourself," he cajoled, pulling her into an even tighter embrace.

Marrok was still inside Evelyn. Her slick warmth tested his control mercilessly. Fighting his own needs, he merely held her, waiting for his mate's ire to cool.

"I don't know if conception is possible while dreamwalking. From the evidence you so shrewdly presented, it's a distinct possibility."

"Oh, Goddess above," she whispered.

"Evelyn, hush. Now is not a time in your cycle where you are likely to be fertile."

Her entire body stiffened. "Excuse me?"

"There are only certain times when a female can conceive. This holds true for she-demons, vampires, she-wolves, as well as female elementals."

"How do you know I'm not fertile right now?"

"By your scent."

Her stunned expression was adorable. "All beings, of every faction aside from Gwydion, can tell by scent. It's not a secret."

Evelyn remained frozen in place, not so much as blinking.

"Evelyn?"

Her head swiveled slowly, side to side. "I knew others had impeccable senses. I never ... it's just ... so invasive."

The corner of his mouth twitched. "No one calls attention to it. To do so would be beyond rude. It's simply an ability we're born with. So don't look so forlorn. This is a benefit for couples who want to wait for children. Besides, if you ever suspected you were with young before I had a chance to get your father to agree to our marriage, I'd ride to your doorstep with an army to collect you."

"You would?"

"I vow it."

Marrok would never allow her to be alone in such a state, especially not in Gwydion. In his people's eyes, marriage was a formality. The saatus bond was eternally binding. As such, he and Evelyn were already committed. The King of Gwydion, however, would want Marrok and Evelyn to exchange vows.

There was a time where the chance of marrying again would make him physically ill. Now, he could easily picture it with Evelyn. Unable to stop himself, he visualized his saatus heavy with child. Picturing her round belly did something to Marrok.

Melena hadn't wanted young. She'd insisted her visions had shown she would never bear him a child. The future was never set, so he'd assumed she would change her mind after a lengthy period of time.

She'd taken her own life before they'd been able to discuss it further. He'd tried every day since to forgive her for it. Part of him hadn't. He couldn't even bring himself to tell Evelyn how Melena had died.

"Marrok?"

His vision focused on Evelyn's worried eyes. "Yes?"

"Where did your mind wander to just now?"

"Nowhere." He shook his head, upset with himself for allowing Melena into this space, into this intimate moment.

He could tell Evelyn wanted to argue so he kissed her quiet. So easily she softened under his touch.

"Now, tell me all the right things to say to your father before I send him a missive."

Evelyn's lips twisted. "I'd rather not talk about my father while we're still ... joined."

Marrok smirked. "Fair point, *moj draga*."

He flexed his cock and her channel tightened in return. He rolled to his back, pulling her with him. His hands settled firmly on her hips as he thrust upward.

Evelyn inhaled, rocking with him. Her knees tightened against his sides.

"So tell me, shall I continue with this," he thrust again, "or shall we talk?"

She replied by kissing him breathless.

* * *

"Wake up!" Nora panicked, shaking Evelyn by her shoulders.

Her older sister's skin was flushed, covered in a thin sheen of sweat. She should probably go and wake Mara or Eden. Her instincts told her to stay put.

"Stop shaking me," Evelyn griped sleepily.

Nora released Evie's shoulders, waiting for her to fully come to. She scooted a little further down the bed, making sure she wasn't in striking range from one of her sister's slaps.

A series of rapid blinks and Evelyn shed the remnants of slumber. Nora was chewing the inside of her cheek. Her hands fidgeted in her lap.

Evelyn pushed herself upright. "What's happened? Are you unwell?"

"Am I unwell? Really? You're the one moaning and fussing about."

"What?"

"I got up to get a drink from the kitchen. When I passed back by your room you were thrashing around so much I could hear it. Then you cried out so I came in to check on you."

Evelyn covered her face. She could still feel traces of Marrok's powers, like electric currents running up and down her limbs. She knew exactly what Nora had heard. She'd still been in his arms when she'd been pulled away from the dream.

Anxious to return, she told Nora, "Just a weird dream. I'm fine."

"You're sure?"

"Yes. Go back to bed."

Nora didn't move.

"Really, I promise I'm fine."

"Okay. Yell for me if you need me, though, alright?"

Evelyn's embarrassment disappeared, filled with appreciation for her little sister. She heaved Nora into a tight embrace.

"I will," she said into Nora's blonde hair.

"Can I get you anything before I go?" Nora asked, rising and stepping towards the door.

"No. Goodnight."

"Goodnight, Evie."

When the door clicked, Evelyn got out of bed and entered the bathroom. She filled the basin and splashed her face, trying to cool down.

As she dried herself with the hand towel, a cool dampness tickled between her legs. She lifted her gown and gasped.

Small smears of red lined the creases where her inner thighs met her trunk. Despite Marrok being a kingdom away, he had most assuredly taken her virginity while they slept. Dreamworld or not, what they'd done was real.

Evelyn smiled to herself, finished cleaning up, and returned to bed. When next they met, she'd need to tell him how best to approach the King of Gwydion.

Chapter 17

Six Months Later ...

Quietly as she could, Evelyn hovered just outside her father's study. Today, a missive from Marrok had arrived. It was the third one he'd sent, the first of which arrived three months ago.

Father had yet to mention any of them to Evelyn. Nor had he told Eden, the daughter he trusted most with matters of diplomacy. Since Eden's broken engagement, he'd been grooming her to be his successor. Keeping this from Eden wasn't a good sign.

"Will you not even consider it, Edward?" her grandfather, Flynn, asked.

"You think I should?"

Evelyn's stomach tightened. From Marrok, she'd learned her father had delayed his response to the first inquiry of a possible engagement. When he finally replied, it had been a polite declination.

The second message from Marrok was more pragmatic, offering to visit and court Evelyn, to see if they were compatible. Edward wrote back, citing some nonsense he felt his middle daughter was not mature enough to consider marriage at this point in time.

Evelyn had been furious. She was only two short seasons away from turning twenty-two—less than half a year. Soon after Evelyn's coming birthday, her younger sister would turn twenty and be married off to the King of Burghard.

Marrok had talked her down and promised to continue his endeavor to broker the marriage. He also made Evelyn promise not to confront her father.

"I think it's something to think about," Flynn replied, breaking Evelyn out of her memory. "This letter is different. He has no reason to lie about his reasons. He's given you cause to consider his offer. Besides, your argument over her maturity was quite weak, my son."

"It was all I could come up with at the time."

"Why are you so opposed?"

"Have you met Marrok?"

"I have."

"Do you know how he came to be on the throne of Sundari?"

"Brennen passed away and left no heirs. Marrok was the only surviving royal, so he inherited his title by birthright."

"He didn't simply pass away. Demons are immortal and, thus, notoriously difficult to kill. Brennen, who was not someone I looked upon favorably, mind you, did not die of natural causes. Everyone in Imperium knows he lost his heart. What we don't know is how."

"You think Marrok did it."

"Who else would have been strong enough?"

A chair creaked. Evelyn could picture her grandfather shifting in his rickety old seat, the one he refused to get rid of.

"Brennen was a blight on Sundari, Edward. You know it. If Marrok had the courage to eliminate his uncle from further damaging the Southland, I would think that would be a testament to his character. Sometimes we must do things we detest to protect that which we hold dear."

"You mean, greater good and all that?" Edward complained.

"Yes. Don't hold Evelyn back from her future because you are dreading Nora's move to Burghard."

Evelyn's pulse quickened. Finally, someone was being the voice of reason.

"That's not what I'm doing."

"Aren't you?"

Edward sighed. "Not purposefully."

The silence stretched. Evelyn thought she might have heard drawers opening and papers shuffling.

"I will hear him out, but I want to see him face to face. Reply back. Tell him, the first new moon after the summer solstice, I'll expect his arrival. We'll discuss it then, not before. I'm inclined to worry about only one daughter at a time."

"I assume you don't want me to write that last part?" Flynn jibed.

"Just send the damn message."

Flynn laughed again and Evelyn tiptoed away.

* * *

"How many this month?" Marrok asked, pen and paper in hand to add to the tallies.

"Five, Sire."

He set down his pen. "Only five?"

"Yes."

"Any new saatus discoveries?"

"Yes."

Marrok stared at Favin, waiting for him to elaborate. "Well, then? How many?" he prodded, only slightly exasperated.

"Fifty-seven."

"Come again?"

"He said, 'fifty-seven!'" Danil shouted from the corner where he was currently helping himself to Marrok's favorite whiskey. "Surely you're not so old as to already be losing your hearing?"

Favin snorted.

"You," Marrok pointed at his stocky, white-haired friend, mildly annoyed the male was pilfering his best spirits, "knock it off. You know demons don't lose their hearing. Not from age, anyway."

Danil lifted his glass. Favin laughed outright this time. Marrok couldn't help but give in to a smile. Things were going well. Better than well. Great. So great, it was difficult to trust it.

Marrok knew the number of new rogues had been in steady decline these past months, heading to ever smaller sums. He hadn't known there'd been a dramatic increase in newfound mates.

Fifty-seven was more than all the previous months combined. It meant one hundred fourteen demons had been paired with their destined mates. It hardly made a dent in the rogue population, but it was nothing to scoff at.

Marrok quickly entered the new tallies and closed the ledger. "It seems our plan is working, gentlemen."

"Indeed, Sire."

"Favin, it's just us. You can stop with the formalities."

"Sorry. Habit."

"Anything else before I turn in for the night?"

Tonight was his night with Evelyn. He hadn't seen her in a week. Though they could meet more often now, he still refused to dreamwalk every night. He visited a different station each week to check in, and he never risked a deep sleep while on the road. Once a week was manageable.

"This arrived just before your return this evening."

Favin handed Marrok the missive. The dark green wax seal marked it as King Edward's. It took Marrok a second to reach for it.

He'd approached the elemental three times now. The first time, Marrok was very direct, offering an alliance in exchanged for Evelyn's hand. "Regretfully, I am not entertaining any marriage offers at this time for any of my children" was his short reply. Marrok had thrown it in the fireplace.

The second reply was plainly insulting to Evelyn. Marrok suspected Edward's negative view of his daughter's maturity was just a ruse to get Marrok to back off.

With the third letter, the last one he told himself he'd send before riding to Gwydion, he'd been honest—mostly. He'd confessed to Edward that he'd had dreams of Evelyn and suspected she could potentially be his saatus.

It should have been enough for Edward to consider. No beings of Imperium dared to mess with Fate unless absolutely unable to do otherwise. Even Marrok had learned his lesson.

He simply wanted a meeting with both Edward and Evelyn. If he could get that far, Marrok could emphatically confirm for Edward what he already knew, that Evelyn was his destiny.

"Well, are you going to open it or burn holes in it with your eyes?" Danil goaded.

"I don't recall inviting you in here," Marrok responded.

"Standing invitation, Sire. You said it once, some fifty years ago. I didn't forget."

"What a wonderfully long memory you have," Marrok muttered as he snatched the parchment from Favin and broke the seal.

Danil quietly approached, more interested than he would ever admit. He and Favin watched Marrok's eyes scan the lines. Neither had found their own mates, nevertheless, they were happy for their friend.

Unfortunately, if King Edward could not be brought around, diplomacy would get thrown out the window. Things hadn't gotten that far. Yet.

Marrok lowered the letter to the desk. His expressionless face told them nothing.

"Well?" Danil blurted.

"I've been invited to the royal residence."

Favin inclined his head, delighted. "I'll make preparations—"

"No. He'll not see me until the new moon after the summer solstice."

"That's six months away."

"I'm aware, Favin. It's just after his youngest will be married off to the Wolf King of the North. I assume he's not inclined to let go of all his daughters until he has to. Out of respect for their familial bond, you will reply we are agreeable."

"As you wish."

"Thank you. I'll be in my quarters the rest of the night."

Marrok rose and exited his study. He hadn't realized the weight he'd been carrying over Edward's unwillingness to consider him a suitor. It bothered him far more than it should have.

He didn't need to be liked by the male. Rather, he wanted to be deemed worthy of Evelyn. He'd had enough wretchedness in his life. It was time for some degree of happiness.

When he reached the stairs, he was already unbuttoning his shirt, jogging up the incline. He wanted to see Evelyn and give her the good news.

Aside from his issue with Edward, these past few months had been some of the best of his life. Things in Sundari were calmer. His kingdom had willingly jumped on board with his plan for them to find their mates and hopefully save the rogues.

Dreamwalking was now effortless. He only had to think Evelyn's name and he entered her dreamworld as soon as he fell asleep. The nights they spent together were filled with passion and a natural state of togetherness. Being with Evelyn was easy.

Unlike Melena, Evelyn wasn't reserved. She didn't hold herself back where he had to constantly guess what was on her mind. She was an open book, speaking more frankly with him than anyone ever had. They discussed anything and everything.

When they weren't talking, they were in the bed she'd made for them. Her appetite for him was staggering. When he finally retrieved her from Gwydion, he intended to lock them both away for days, reacquainting himself with every facet of her form.

Entering his chamber, he removed his clothing as he walked, tossing each item aside on the way to the bed. A soft clank echoed off the stone floor.

Crouching to lift his trousers, he noticed the chain of Melena's necklace poking out. He'd continued keeping it in his pocket all this time. Neither wanting to wear it nor to put it away.

It had become more habit than need. Marrok picked it up and looked around the room. Finding what he needed, he strode to the desk in the corner and tugged the small handle on the front. He spared one more swipe with his thumb across the cool silver then lowered it into the drawer.

It was time to let go of the past and run straight into his future.

* * *

When Evelyn materialized in the meadow, she didn't see Marrok. She could feel him through their bond so she knew he was near.

Allowing her senses to lead her, she rounded their table and started on the path that led to their little haven. Cylindric lanterns, hanging from branches, were lit all along the trail. Marrok must have added them when he arrived.

Her bare feet grazed across smooth velvet. Frowning, she bent and picked up a pink oval off the ground. Petals. He'd covered the trail in flower petals.

Just ahead, surrounding their oasis, at least a dozen more lanterns swung gently in the night breeze. Evelyn could see Marrok's large outline, backlit by the rays of light breaking through the trees. Tonight, he came to her in nothing but his unbelted pants, which usually meant he was in an eager mood.

She ran into his awaiting arms, as they did each week now. He lifted her easily and her legs wrapped around his waist. The movement caused her nightgown to ride up. Electric currents zapped wherever their skin touched. His fingers dug into her backside where he held her aloft.

Evelyn bent, rubbing the side of her face against his. Marrok had told her this was how demon mates typically greeted one another and showed affection. Then, lovingly, they shared a brief kiss.

He sat with her straddling his legs, lifting her gown over her head. She could feel his erection through the fabric of his trousers and she shifted to center the pressure against her core.

Marrok nipped her lip. "Patience, my mate."

"Says the male who stripped me naked the second I was in his arms."

"Someone is feeling saucy this night."

Evelyn rocked her hips, groaning. "I am."

The amber of his eyes flamed bright, yet his hands stilled her motion. "We'll get to that in a moment. We need to talk first."

"Oh, yes! I have news."

"I do, as well."

Evelyn beamed. "You heard from my father."

"I did. Did he tell you or were you spying on him again?"

"Does it matter?"

"Spying, then."

She playfully slapped his arm. "Fine. I overheard he was inviting you for a visit after Nora's binding ceremony."

"Yes. Wait, binding ceremony? Are they not having a formal wedding?" They were royalty, joining two kingdoms through marriage. It was almost expected to have a large wedding.

"No. They've decided they will ride to Castle Burghard immediately afterwards and neither Nora nor Kellan wanted any fanfare about it."

Marrok hadn't considered anything other than a full-scale royal wedding for he and Evelyn. Though Melena hadn't been of royal blood, Marrok was a prince when they wed and Brennen had forced the entire kingdom to celebrate and acknowledge it.

"And what do you want, sweet Evelyn? For us?"

Her mouth twisted in that adorable way she always did when she was thinking. "I'm not sure. I haven't really thought about it. I only think about a life with you, not about a wedding."

His saatus wasn't like other females he knew, especially those who came from wealth. Evelyn humbled him with her admission. He'd wrongfully assumed she'd been dreaming of some grand ceremony when she'd only been thinking of him.

"Think about it, then. I want you to have whatever you want. I'll be knocking on your door before you know it, and I have no intention of waiting months and months to call you my wife."

"And what Marrok wants, Marrok gets," she teased, feathering her lips across his while reaching down to unbutton his pants.

"So it would seem," his gravelly voice pushed into her skin. He could scent the flood of her arousal, calling to him.

Flipping them over, he tore off his trousers and pushed deep inside his mate. They could discuss trivialities later.

Chapter 18

Two days before the summer solstice ...

For what felt to be the twentieth time, Evelyn rolled to her side and tried to fall asleep. As Nora's wedding drew closer, sleep had become more and more difficult.

She'd believed that once her father had agreed to meet with Marrok, her problems were solved. She found, however, the closer the date came, the more anxious she became. The more anxious she became, the more intruding her dreams became.

She'd been dreaming of Marrok's past off and on for well over a year now. Evelyn had gotten used to it and sometimes looked forward to knowing his life. The opportunity to learn his thinking and emotions reinforced what she already knew—his strength of character was absolute.

Most of the time, the experience was positive, making her feel like she knew him inside and out. A glimpse into his psyche here and there was something she could look forward to seeing. Lately, she'd been pulled into his past more and more often, sometimes several times in a night. Now, she dreaded it.

Over the past month or so, she dreamt almost exclusively of Melena. It was never easy feeling Marrok's love for another. Evelyn did her best to tamp down her jealousy and watch each scene objectively. There had to be a sound reason these particular memories were surfacing.

She always informed Marrok of what she'd seen, allowing him to pull the memories from her. He was very open and it helped when they talked through it.

Neither of them had professed love for the other, but Evelyn knew she loved him. She knew he was capable of feeling the same and she hoped that was the lesson she was to learn.

The only awkwardness between Evelyn and Marrok were the few times the dreams had shown Melena moving her mouth without sound. It bothered Marrok he had no recollection of it and he would retreat inside himself for a short time, processing. Evelyn had a nagging suspicion it was a significant part of his past.

Irritated, she rolled again and focused on her breathing. Eventually, sleep pulled her under its dark veil. When the blackness faded, she found herself in the same hall where Marrok had first been introduced to Melena.

Marrok was standing at the foot of the dais, facing the back of the room. The entire space was packed with demons. Greenery accented with bloodred lilies hung on the walls and along the benches.

A harp played a haunting melody somewhere nearby. It was familiar—an ancient wedding march used in old-fashioned ceremonies. A figure clad in gold was gliding up the aisle. A female.

Evelyn could feel Marrok's tightening throat as if it were her own. His palms were sweating, his heart thumping. *Nothing shall ever compare to this moment. In this moment, I am complete.*

His thoughts were tiny daggers stabbing at Evelyn's heart. She fought against the pain. It was his wedding. He was marrying his love. Marrok was entitled to these feelings, had earned them with his good deeds and unpolluted heart.

It's in the past, she told herself. Evelyn would not allow her jealousy to grow and affect their future. She would be better than that.

Melena approached alone, without a male to give her away. Her face was visible through the sheer fabric covering her head. Her eyes stared straight ahead, towards the throne where Brennen currently sat. Not so much as a glance was awarded to the waiting groom.

Despite Marrok's internal joy, Evelyn felt everything about it was cheerless. Wrong, even. No one smiled. No happy faces or tender gazes endorsed this rite.

The atmosphere was akin to a funeral march. Marrok appeared to be oblivious, his love for his bride outshining the shadows of the day. Before Evelyn could put her finger on why she felt this way, the dream dissolved away and she arrived in a different scene.

Melena's face was close to hers. No, she was staring at a reflection in a full-length mirror. Evelyn's essence was inside Melena, not Marrok. Helplessly, she watched Melena adjust her tight-fitting red dress and smooth down her long black hair.

Evelyn caught sight of a male's face. His narrow nose and arched brow were the same as Melena's.

"You'll not tell him, Melena."

"Really, Cousin. You overstep."

Melena's voice was clear and sharp, but she was having difficulty locking down her fear. Evelyn couldn't decipher enough to understand what was scaring Melena.

Her hand reached for the top of her strapless gown only to have it snatched away into her cousin's painful grip. "Do not test me on this. You'll not like the consequences."

Melena's fear morphed into anger. "Brennen is the king. Not Marrok. Even if Marrok was on the throne, I'm not stupid enough to get either of us killed. Although, I doubt he'd lay a hand to me. You, however, might want to worry about your own neck."

"And what do you think will happen if I die? You're my heir, Melena. Don't ever forget it."

The male let go of her and stormed away. Melena lifted her shaking hand and pressed the palm to the skin over her heart. *Over my dead body*, the she-demon vowed.

Again the scene dissolved and Evelyn was thrust into another. It was dark and she was outside, next to a large stone wall, the kind built to keep invaders out. A nearby torch emitted enough light she could see a cloaked figure standing far closer than was polite.

It handed her a corked vial. The cool glass chilled her fingers. The liquid within hummed with power. Dark power.

"I have your assurance this will work?" Melena's voice whispered.

"It will. You know I want what you are to give me. There's no reason for me to swindle you. Only, be sure to drink it all if you want it to happen quickly."

Evelyn couldn't see the face but the voice was distinctly male. Melena's chest was rising and falling far too fast. Her trembling hands lowered the vial into a small pouch tied to her waist.

When she turned to step away, the male's hand grabbed her wrist. Firmly, but without aggression.

"You are his wife, Melena. His love is obvious. So much so it's nauseating to behold. You don't have to make this choice. If he remains in Sundari, the odds of him finding her are slim to none."

"I don't expect you to understand, Bogdan."

"No, I don't understand. If you go through with this, you know we will be forced to act. It is our duty to Imperium."

"No, you won't. Marrok is *not* the king. There will be no need for anyone to do anything to him as long as Brennen holds the crown."

"Marrok is Brennen's only heir."

"Brennen may yet produce one with his saatus. I've seen snippets of the future, of rogues finding their mates in mass numbers. He could be one of them. It would settle him."

"The future is not set in stone, Melena."

"You're right. My visions alter over time. Only one has never changed. Marrok and I will never produce a child."

A haunting ache rolled through Melena, her hand settling over her abdomen, over the womb which would never carry young.

"When," Melena swallowed, "when I've seen his young, they're not mine. His first has a head of auburn hair, which means his mate is not demon. The vision alters in location, in clothing, in time of year. It *never* alters with the child's odd coloring or with whom he has created life. I'm not ..." she shook her head, eyes glassing over.

She sniffled and took a cleansing breath, getting the upper hand on her emotions. "One way or another, his fate lies elsewhere. Who am I to stand between Marrok and his saatus?"

The male released her wrist. "Would that we all could love as selflessly as you, my lady." A note of respect hinted in his deep voice.

She laughed without humor. "Better my heart explode at my own hand than force my husband to do it for me."

Melena turned and walked into the shadows of the wall. Evelyn's mind was spinning, her heart breaking for both Marrok and Melena. The she-demon had taken her own life. She'd done it to ensure Marrok could be with his mate.

The guilt was a crushing weight. Did Marrok even know? Suddenly, the dream shifted. She was standing in front of a white stone structure. A tomb.

Evelyn was inside Marrok again. One hand resting on the cool marble, his other tracing the inscription with his fingertips. She could easily make out the dark lettering contrasting with the white. The phrase below the deceased's name stood out the most.

SAKANA ZENA, UVEK. Beloved wife, always.

His mood was dark, his grief overwhelming, accented with a heavy undercurrent of rage. His breathing was ragged and his eyes burned, though no tears were shed.

Marrok's despair was Evelyn's. She couldn't escape it. It stole her breath—Marrok's breath. It twisted and pulled his insides, tying them both in knots.

I loved you, he spoke in his head to his wife. Evelyn felt like an intruder, like she shouldn't witness this private moment.

I will never love another. Never. There is nothing left in me for anyone else. I didn't care that your visions never showed us with young. I was content to merely hold you forever. It was all I ever wanted. I may very well find my mate. Goddess help her because all she'll get is the shell you left behind.

"Damn you, Melena," he whispered aloud, bowing his head. "Damn you for condemning me to this hell."

Evelyn awoke, her face covered in tears, her heart torn wide open for the male who mourned his lost love.

Chapter 19

Marrok appeared in the meadow. His upturned lips flattened when he saw the state of his mate.

Evelyn was fully clothed, head to toe. A cloak buttoned high on her neck. Her hair was in a severe braid when she only ever wore it down for him. Though her skin was tan, he could see the distinct feature of dark circles under her eyes.

Striding to the table where she sat, he knelt in front of her. His hands landed on her knees just above her tall black boots. His fingers pressing into the soft fabric of her riding breeches.

Evelyn wore nightgowns when they met. Small, dainty, flimsy coverings he could easily remove. She hadn't worn daytime clothing in so long, he almost forgot what she looked like covered.

She also hadn't ran into his arms the second he appeared, which troubled him more than the outfit she wore. His eyes searched her troubled face.

He hadn't felt any severe distress through their connection. The only sign she might be upset came a few nights ago. The flicker of jealously and sadness he'd experienced in the middle of the night was the same one he always had whenever she dreamt of Melena.

It had rarely affected Evelyn to the point she was standoffish with him. *Damnit*. She must have seen something she hadn't wanted to see. He wanted to curse Fate for inflicting such suffering onto his saatus.

"Tell me what you saw," he urged, without any preamble for what he was asking.

Evelyn drew in a slow, purposeful inhale, gathering the air like it could fuel her courage. "I think it best if you take them from my mind. There were quite a few this week."

Marrok lifted his hands, gently placing them on each side of her face. He could see without touching her, but touch allowed him to feel the emotions she felt in the memories.

Memories, many long forgotten, played out in his mind. Most of them were innocuous. He waited patiently for the ones he knew had hurt his mate.

He flinched when he saw Melena in her wedding gown, marching down the aisle. How had he missed her eyes upon the throne, not upon him? The hit to his psyche came hard.

The memory altered and it took him a second to realize he was seeing from inside Melena. Her cousin, Caleb, was behaving as his usual self. Detestable.

He was threatening Melena, warning her to keep some secret. It raised Marrok's hackles despite the fact both Caleb and Melena were long dead. Caleb had been killed by Kellan for his misdeeds in helping to poison the wolf's father.

His life ended the day before Melena took her own. She wasn't fond of Caleb, so Marrok had never seen the timing as anything other than a sad coincidence.

Marrok had to wonder why Caleb's mention of Melena being his only heir sounded like a threat. He'd left behind no offspring and his assets had been spread among his living family, though the bulk of it was to go to Melena. The entire exchange was baffling.

The image of Caleb's sneer gave him pause. The bastard had been the demon member of Sephtis Kenelm. Few knew of this fact. Only Brennen and a handful of his people, Marrok included, were present when it was revealed.

Kellan had needed permission to hunt Caleb down on Sundari land. With King Edward at his back, Brennen could only grant permission or else risk the wrath of the other kingdoms. Even The Heartless King of Prajna had acquiesced, and he bowed to no one.

Melena must have known Caleb was part of the brotherhood. It was the only logical explanation for their discussion. She took her cousin's secret with her to the grave.

He had no time to think on it before the scene changed once more. He watched Melena put away the vial of poison that would later take her life.

Old wounds reopened listening to Melena tell Bogdan about her visions. By accepting the poison, she was giving Marrok a chance to find his saatus, to have children, something he cared nothing about at the time. Had she really thought he would have ended her life in order to be with another?

Then, the worst of them, for Marrok, at least, was the night he entombed Melena's corpse. The night he vowed to never love another, not even his mate. Evelyn had heard it all.

A warm hand wiped something damp from his cheek. Marrok blinked, Evelyn's face coming back into focus. He pulled out of her reach, unwilling to allow her to clean up the evidence of his sorrow. She'd been subjected to more than her fair share of his heartache.

"Those last few were different. Obviously. They felt ... I don't know. Ominous?" she guessed, unable to come up with a better word.

"You probably have much you need to think on," she continued. "Before I go, I need to ask you something. It's completely selfish of me, but I need to ask it anyway."

"Ask it," he encouraged, sinking his weight onto his heels, still on his knees in front of her.

"If you'd known I was your saatus, and I was here in Gwydion, would you ... would you have ..." she cleared her throat, wracked with guilt for even thinking to put him in this position. It wasn't fair of her. She bit her tongue to stop the rest from tumbling out of her impious mouth.

"Are you asking if I would have come for you?"

"Yes."

"No. Had my wife lived, I would never have come for you."

Evelyn shook her head, hiding the stabbing cold needles perforating her soul. "No, before she was your wife, before you made promises. If you'd known you would meet your saatus in the future?"

"No, Evelyn. I loved Melena. I doubt I could have willingly abandoned her, even knowing my mate would be waiting for me in Gwydion."

She nodded, accepting his reply with her eyes glued to his throat. She understood. She didn't blame him. How could he choose a stranger over his lover? Evelyn felt stupid for even bringing it up. He would have honored his affections for Melena, as he should have.

She closed her eyes, bracing for the answer to her next question. "Could you ever love me the same way you loved her?"

Her breath froze, suspended in her lungs.

Marrok wiped the corners of his mouth, trying to think the best way to answer, to explain to Evelyn without hurting her. How could loving two different women ever be the same?

"I don't know."

Evelyn shot up out of the chair and moved to the other side of the table. Marrok rose, calmly approaching her like he would a wild animal.

239

"Don't," she pleaded.

"Let me finish, then, before you run from me. It's not the same. What you and I have? It cannot be compared to what I had with Melena."

Evelyn lifted her hands to keep him away, her eyes glassy. She didn't want to hear anymore.

"I'm not saying this right. With Melena, I chose to court her. I chose to love her. I'm sorry you had to witness it, but she was a choice I made, one that made me very happy at the time." Then later destroyed him.

"And I was never your choice," she whispered.

"No, a saatus is not a choice. With you it has been far different. It was an instant connection, my soul wanted you immediately. Protecting you was instinct. Bonding to you was instinct. Once I accepted that I could keep you, everything just sort of fell into place. With you, it's been effortless."

"So, you want me because it's easy for you to be with me? Because of the bond?"

Marrok ran his fingers through his hair, shaking his head. "I'm still not explaining myself very well."

"No, you're not."

His lips twitched. Even in her sadness, his mate never lost her edge.

He should tell her what he felt for Melena couldn't come close to what he felt for Evelyn. Yet he couldn't bring himself to do it, not without feeling like he had somehow soiled the love he'd felt for his wife.

240

"I don't know how to articulate this—"

"I love you," she blurted.

Marrok didn't move a muscle. His tongue felt thick and his heart pounded furiously in his chest. His instant erection jerked to full attention, as though it was trying to punch its way out of his pants.

"Can you say the same to me?"

Marrok balked, caught off guard by her courageous proclamation. Though, it shouldn't have been a surprise. He already knew she loved him. He felt it every time they touched, felt it in the way she looked at him when he moved inside her body.

It was a precious, precious gift he did not deserve, not when he wasn't able to easily say it in return. He could feel Evelyn's severe disappointment with his hesitation.

The words were a reminder of what he could lose, what he had once lost. Marrok had told Melena he loved her. He'd handed his heart over on a silver platter and his wife had ripped it to shreds the second she uncorked that vial.

He'd told his parents he loved them and Brennen murdered them. Marrok never wanted to give another being such power over him, almost fearing if he said it aloud something terrible would happen. Loving Evelyn, then losing her, would surely end his existence.

Evelyn cleared her throat. "I'm sorry. I shouldn't have asked."

"It was a fair question."

"Was it?" she snapped, her tone woven with the regret currently burning holes throughout her insides.

"I pounced the second you finished seeing my dreams. I'm ashamed I'm struggling with this, Marrok. I know the saatus bond is the driving force for demons to mate. I just thought—I hoped—eventually, you would feel the same way I do."

"Who says I won't?" Or that he didn't? It shouldn't be so difficult to convey what he felt for her.

Love didn't quite cover the gnawing obsession that never seemed to lesson in the slightest. She was becoming the center of his universe. Why couldn't he voice it?

Evelyn was a part of him in a way no other female ever could be, she lived inside his very soul. He was glad it was her, that she was his saatus. If he could have picked the traits of the female destined for him, she would come out looking and acting just like Evelyn.

Though young, she was clever beyond her years. She was interesting and good-humored. She made him laugh more than he ever had. He craved her body, her touch, her undivided attention to the point he worried it wasn't normal.

Marrok ignored her need for personal space and pulled her into his arms. She allowed it and he hugged her tight.

"Evelyn, what I feel—"

"Please don't. I know you have a lot to sort out with what you saw. Just hold me for a little while, okay?"

He rested his chin upon her head. "Okay."

Marrok swayed gently with Evelyn pressed tightly against him. He didn't want her to wake still feeling as she did now. "Tomorrow is Kellan and Nora's binding ceremony. We only have a little longer before I arrive in Gwydion."

"I know."

"Will you meet me tomorrow night?" he asked hopefully.

Once a week was as often as they ever met now. Evelyn needed to clear her head, which was impossible to do while in Marrok's presence.

"I need a little time, Marrok. We can meet next week, as planned."

"You mean you need some space. From me."

"Yes," she admitted. "Moreover, I think you need to think on this set of memories. Something was going on with Melena. Maybe Fate is trying to tell you to figure it out."

Maybe if he did, he could move beyond his past, and, thus, so would she. Evelyn knew how hard it was to accept that Melena forfeited her life to give Marrok this chance with Evelyn. Evelyn would not throw away such a sacrifice. She would work to kill the guilt eating away at her soul.

She didn't dare bring up the fact Melena had seen him with an auburn-haired child, with Evelyn's child. She batted away the image. It was too much for her heart to handle tonight. She knew he cared for her even if he couldn't say the words she wanted to hear. For now, it would have to be enough. She could worry about the future later.

"As always, you are the wiser of the two of us, *moj draga*."

Evelyn almost smiled. "Can we stay a little longer, like this?"

"Of course. I'll hold you the entire night if it is your wish."

Evelyn squeezed her eyes shut, willing back the tears surfacing with his bittersweet offer.

* * *

"This is it? Everything?"

"Yes, Sire. Melena came to you with very few belongings."

Marrok took stock of the single trunk Favin had pulled out of storage for him. Melena's entire life pared down to nothing more than a few pieces of jewelry, some books, and several paintings she'd done on small canvases.

She'd inherited land from Caleb. Dying within a day of her cousin, she'd never been able to claim it. Marrok told her father to keep it for himself.

"It might help if you tell me what you're looking for, Marrok."

The king rubbed his eyes. "I'm not exactly sure, Favin."

Liar, his inner demon taunted. He was looking for any clue as to why Evelyn had been privy to Melena's life outside of Marrok. The demon went along with it in order to please its mate, not because it had any interest in Marrok's former wife.

"Alright," his Second said, settling into the chair across from Marrok. "Let's start with why you want to dig up ghosts from the past. Is it because you ride to Gwydion soon? Are you seeking closure?"

"No."

Marrok stood and went to the table in the corner. He poured two glasses of whiskey and returned to his desk.

Favin eyed the glass Marrok had all but slammed down onto the dark wood. "Should I be concerned?"

Marrok ignored the question. "I need you to pull a memory from my mind. Evelyn's dreams have altered. She dreamt of Melena last week."

"I thought she'd been dreaming of her for a while."

"This was different. Evelyn dreamt it from Melena's perspective. I wasn't in it."

Favin cocked his head. "I didn't even know that was possible."

"It shouldn't be. Pull the memory."

Marrok shoved the recollection of Melena and Caleb's interaction into the forefront of his mind, then the one of her with Bogdan. He didn't invite Favin to touch him. They didn't need to share emotions for this.

Once the scenes played out, Favin reached for the whiskey and took a drink. "You want to know if she knew about Caleb."

"Yes."

"Does it matter?"

"To me? No. I seek to discover why these are the memories in Evelyn's dreams. Melena's knowledge of her cousin means nothing. Additionally, I already knew of her visions and why she believed she was doing me a favor by ending her life. The question is, why does anyone need to see these two memories? I can guess about Caleb threatening her not to tell anyone he was Sephtis Kenelm. It's irrelevant."

"I think you need to look more closely at the night she was given the poison."

"Why?"

"Because Bogdan said he wanted what she would give him. I don't think he was referring to money."

"What would a stone trader want from Melena?"

Bogdan was renowned in Imperium. His knowledge was vast and he was in high demand. He traded with every faction, especially with the elementals, and worked hard to build his wealth. Coin should have motivated him greatly.

"What, indeed. Of the three in those dreams, he's the only one still alive. Why don't you ask him?"

"Send for him. I want him here by the week's end."

"You'll be on your way to Gwydion by then."

"Then hold him here until I return."

"As you wish," Favin replied, then left the study.

Marrok poured the rest of his friend's whiskey into his own glass. Taking it in sips, he stared at Melena's belongings, replaying Evelyn's dreams.

It had only been one day and he missed his little mate. He scratched at the skin over his heart, downing the rest of the alcohol to numb the ache.

Chapter 20

Four days after the solstice ...

"If you keep dressing like a male, I'm going to start thinking you don't want me to touch you."

Evelyn turned to the reverberating voice behind her. She'd felt Marrok arrive. Sneaking up on her now seemed to be an impossibility.

She walked into his awaiting arms, offering her cheek for him to nuzzle. The sparks of static that had yet to die down tickled her skin where it met his.

"You don't like my riding breeches?"

"I like them fine. If you were going riding. When we're together, I like you in your silky night things. Or out of them."

Her face flushed and her belly tightened with need. Unfortunately, they had things to discuss, and little time to do so.

"I am going riding. I'll be woken any minute."

His smile died. "It's the middle of the night, Evelyn."

"I'm aware. Sit," she stepped back and motioned to the chairs at the table. "This has to be fast. We don't have much time."

Marrok's eyes narrowed. His mate's voice was off, almost hoarse. Her eyes were rimmed red.

"I think I'll stand and you'll tell me immediately what has happened."

"Fine. An attempt was made on Nora's life, during her welcoming banquet at Castle Burghard. She was— she was poisoned," she hiccupped, wrestling with the impulse to breakdown. She'd cried enough earlier in the day.

He reached to comfort her and she stepped to the side, waving him off. His hands clenched, but he gave her the space she seemed to need.

"We received word as soon as Kellan could get it to us. She is alive, though I don't know much more than that. Father says we're leaving tonight, he fears Eden and I aren't safe."

Ideas flew through Marrok, considering any immediate steps he needed to take. Evelyn's mother had been murdered by members of Sephtis Kenelm. They'd poisoned her. News of a similar attempt on Edward's youngest child carried echoes of that past event.

Though the brotherhood had been wiped out, Edward was right to worry. If it were Marrok, he'd hide his children away from everyone. Even from a powerful king who wanted to court one of them.

Marrok couldn't allow her to be taken from him, even temporarily. They'd waited long enough and he'd no longer deny his need to have her close and protect her himself.

"I'll come for you now," Marrok insisted.

"I won't be here by the time you arrive. That's not what's important right now, anyway. I need you to take my dream from last night. I haven't told anyone about it, but I think I'm going to have to say something to Father in light of what's happened to Nora."

She reached for Marrok's hands and lifted them to each side of her face. "Hurry."

The panic in Evelyn's voice spurred Marrok to comply. He concentrated until he had Evelyn's dream in his mind's eye.

Melena was staring at herself in front of a full-length mirror, the one in her quarters. She brushed her hair methodically, counting in her head. One hundred strokes, as she did every night before bed.

Pulling her long mane over her right shoulder, she braided it and tied it off with a white ribbon edged with gold. His stomach rolled. He remembered that ribbon. Covered in red.

Nimble fingers unbuttoned the top of her yellow dress, stopping just below her breasts. She pulled the loose fabric apart, exposing her chest. Ample cleavage heaved with her quickened breath. She unclasped her necklace, the one Marrok had worn after her death, and hung it on the post of the mirror.

He could feel hints of fear overshadowed by her resolve. Trembling fingers reached for a knife on the table to the right. When she stood erect once more, her focus zeroed in on the reflection of dark swirling script written across the skin above her heart.

Marrok inhaled sharply. Melena didn't have any markings on her skin. Anywhere. He knew every inch of her and he'd never seen this tattoo.

He watched in horror as she squared her shoulders and slashed the sharp blade across the offensive letters. Over and over until nothing but ribbons of mutilated flesh, oozing with blood, remained.

She'd gritted her teeth, but made no sound. He felt her perverse satisfaction at defiling the design.

Melena wiped off the knife on the fabric of her dress, cleaning both sides before dropping it back onto the table. She took two irregular breaths, then pulled something from her pocket.

Holding it up, Marrok could see it was the vial she'd taken from Bogdan. Melena uncorked it and held it up to her reflection, as though she was toasting it. "See you in Hell," she whispered.

She emptied the contents into her mouth, holding her lips tight to force the revolting concoction down. She stumbled to the large fireplace and threw the cork and glass into the flames. She sank to her knees, waiting for the dark magic to work.

Marrok's mouth went dry. He felt like the world was dropping out from under him. The vision dissolved and he released Evelyn as though she was made of fire.

"Marrok?"

He held up a hand, recalling the black swirls marring his wife's chest. There was no mistaking the words. Sephtis Kenelm. Of course, Caleb had been a part of its plotting and evil deeds. His membership in the brotherhood made sense. It went hand in hand with his contemptible personality.

Melena would never have offered herself up to such a cause willingly. He would not believe it.

The group came be long ago, possibly a millennium or more, to stop warring factions. To ensure the fair and just rule of each race, to balance the power of Imperium so no one group would rule the other. It's entire purpose was to keep one faction off of the throne of others, caring little for those who suffered for it.

If Marrok was to believe what he just saw, his wife had all but guaranteed he would find his saatus. So long as Melena was alive, he would never have looked for his mate.

His wife knew his saatus was not a she-demon. Melena's death put Evelyn in danger because the brotherhood would never allow an elemental to rule the Sundari demons.

We'll be forced to act, Bogdan had said. Melena insisted they wouldn't need to. She didn't know Marrok was going to kill Brennen and take the throne. He'd never confided in her, choosing to keep her away from the ugliness of his secret plans.

The conversation now made sense, but Melena was not a she-demon who would be part of a group willing to murder for the sake of their own twisted views of fairness. She wasn't like Caleb. She wouldn't have taken his place in the group when he died, earning the mark. It wasn't something she could hide.

It's possible, the demon spirit murmured. *She died the day after Caleb. She wouldn't have had it on her body for long.* No, Marrok's inner voice denied. Melena would never agree to participate in such treachery. He couldn't reconcile it with his knowledge of who she was as a person.

He stared at his mate. "That wasn't real. I do not believe it."

"It's what I dreamt, Marrok. Everything else has been a memory, most of them yours. You've seen them. You know I experience your past."

"Yes, I can validate the parts that involved me. These parts with Melena, where I am not around, I think your imagination has made them up."

Evelyn recoiled as if she'd been slapped. "You think I've made them up? To what purpose?"

"You tell me," he snapped before he could stop himself.

He immediately regretted his tone. What was wrong with him? He knew Evelyn would not act with malice towards him. She gained nothing from planting false dreams in her head for him.

They are not false. Trust our mate, his demon spirit hissed.

Marrok scrubbed his face with his palms, trying to get his bearings. He was feeling dizzy, spinning out of control. His demon was trying to surface, to take over. It took most of his energy to maintain his hold over it.

Nothing made sense. He needed to think straight, just for a moment, then he could sort this out.

"I would never lie to you Marrok. You can hear any falsehood I could come up with. The truth never dies, remember?"

He closed his eyes. He knew she was right.

"When you found her, after she died, was she in a yellow dress? In front of the fire?" Evelyn pressed.

"Yes." It had been saturated with her lifeblood. The poison had flooded her heart with its dark magic to the point the worthless organ had exploded right out of her chest.

"How could I possibly know that?"

"I don't know."

"I'm not trying to hurt you, Marrok. I'm trying to show you everything I have seen. I think they're warnings. There were other dreams this week. I think I finally learned why she was so often moving her lips without sound and why you have no recollection of it. She spelled you somehow."

"Evelyn," he warned.

"I'll be awoken any second. You need to pull the other dreams. She was a Seer. Did you know she could also manipulate minds with her power?"

"All demons can manipulate minds."

"It wasn't the same, at least from what I saw in the dream. She spelled you—or something of the sort. She did it to others, as well. Think about it, Marrok, you have one of the strongest minds of any Sundari, and yet you can't remember a single instance of seeing her do something so odd."

"Evelyn, stop."

"I don't know her motivations," she continued. "I do think she loved you, so whatever her plan was I doubt it was to harm you. She was desperate. Couldn't you feel it? I know you saw what she cut from her skin. You can't tell me it's mere happenstance she bore the mark of the group that poisoned my mother. That infected Kellan's father with sleeping sickness. And now Nora's been poisoned. I'm being given these memories as some sort of message. A warning. Something!" she wailed, her voice escalating higher with each word.

"I said, stop!" he shouted. "Just, give me a moment to think."

Evelyn gripped his hands, imploring. "Pull the memories, Marrok, I think someone's waking me."

"You want me to believe that my *wife* manipulated my mind? No, I don't think I want to pull that from your head."

"Marrok, please—"

She disappeared. Marrok tried to wake himself and couldn't. He paced angrily. An hour ago all was right in his world. Now it was all turning to shite.

He needed to get out of the dreamworld. Evelyn was being pulled from her bed to ride off to Goddess-knew-where. Edward would send them into hiding and Marrok wouldn't know where she was.

He conjured a blade and sliced it down his forearm. He'd cut it deeply in his haste. *It's just as well. I deserve to feel the pain.*

He did it again, breathing through the burn. He could feel himself coming back into his own body. He jumped out of bed, yelling for Lazlo.

The door flung open and Lazlo's hulking figure stood in the doorway. "Sire?"

"Fetch Favin. Ready the horses. We leave for Gwydion immediately."

Laszlo spun, turning into Favin who was running towards the King's chambers. Jumping to the right and avoiding the near collision, Favin moved speedily into the room.

"Sire," he greeted Marrok.

"Favin. It's time to retrieve my mate."

"We have a problem ..." he scowled, seeing that Marrok was wrapping his arm. "Why are you bleeding?"

"It's nothing. What problem?"

"The gate to the colony. Someone's blown it."

"Bloody hell!" he growled in frustration. "They had to do it this night? Of course they did. It's like the damned universe has conspired to make any sort of victory impossible."

He'd just found out his deceased wife might have been part of some immoral brotherhood of assassins, which he'd basically accused his mate of lying about despite the fact he could hear a lie if she spoke one, or, in this case, dreamed one.

An attempt had been made on Nora's life, an elemental currently sitting on the throne of Burghard. Evelyn might also be in danger and was now being moved to an unknown location where he could not protect her.

To top it all off, his mind chose now, in the midst of his fit of rage, to logically sift through Evelyn's dreams. Fate would only show her things of importance. The last few, and the timing of them, were probably the most important.

Melena must have promised Bogdan her place in Sephtis Kenelm, which meant the group did not die out under Kellan's sword. It also meant, if he claimed her, Evelyn would be a target. Fate had sent a warning. Many of them.

Marrok picked up the closest thing to him and threw it against the wall. Then he did it again. This time, it was a vase. It shattered easily, its blue and white pieces clinking against the stone floor.

Melena's vase. One of the few things of hers he'd kept in his room. He grabbed two fistfuls of hair and roared at the ceiling.

"Are you done?" a rumbling brogue called from the doorway.

"Danil, I swear if you come in this room with your usual drivel I'll rip every single one of your white hairs from your giant head," Marrok threatened.

"Ah, I knew you were jealous of it. The hair, that is, not the large skull."

Favin stepped closer to the doorway, worrying he might need to shut Danil's mouth for him. They'd never seen Marrok in such a state, aside from the night he'd found Melena's body. Danil knew better than to poke.

"Sire, are you unwell?" Favin dared.

"Bullocks to this," Danil pushed his way in. "He's fine. He's had a night. He's let it out. It's over."

Marrok's gaze sharpened. "How do you know what sort of night I've had?"

"I pulled your memories while you were carrying on like a she-demon in labor. And before you get your panties too tied up, I did it to make sure you weren't hit with a fit of actual madness. Congratulations, you get to keep your head. You're welcome."

Danil lifted Favin's hands and cuffed his own ears with them. "Take the memory from me and get caught up, already."

Favin looked to Marrok who nodded. A minute later Danil dropped Favin's arms.

"Well," Danil clapped his hands, "now we're in the know, let's get to work. The only question is, are you hunting rogues or are you hunting your mate?"

Marrok's claws flexed, knowing what he should do was not what he wanted to do. "We ride to the peninsula. Edward will get Evelyn to someplace safe. I'll help round up rogues while the gate is repaired. Favin, make sure we have enough men to deal with both."

"Yes, Sire."

"Wait, before you go. Have you found Bogdan?"

"No. Word came he's been away for business."

"Where?"

"Gwydion. Then on to Burghard."

Favin's eyes widened. "Sire—"

"No. Edward is more than capable of protecting his daughters. Go."

Favin bowed and exited. Marrok had spoken with such insistence, he almost believed his King's words.

Chapter 21

Two weeks later ...

"Are you sure you won't come with us?" Eden asked Evelyn, hugging the side of the giant vampire towering over her. Nora and Kellan had already departed and Eden was hesitant to leave.

"I'm sure," Evelyn responded dreamily, having trouble looking away from the pretty male. He really was such a perfect specimen of beauty, like a seven-foot-tall marble statue carved by a master artist.

Eden, just like her sisters, had mismatched eyes. One was the distinct forest green of the elemental people. The other was a beautiful bright emerald, the exact same shade as Viktor's, the King of Prajna. Of course this masterpiece of a male had beautiful irises. Nothing less could adorn a face of art.

She silently sighed. Evelyn wanted to go with them to Prajna, to be close to Eden, but Theron had warned her she needed to stay. Much was happening very quickly and he insisted the temple was the safest place for her.

Oh, how fast things were happening! The Vampire King, Viktor, had come to the temple shortly after they'd arrived. One look at Eden and he knew she was his sieva—his vampire mate.

Watching them together now, Evelyn doubted he'd ever looked away from Eden for a moment since. It was terribly romantic.

"Okay," Eden's motherly voice broke through. "You know how to call for us if you need us."

"Yes, Hale will deliver my messages."

Theron had asked Viktor to station a vampire here. Because they could teleport, they could send word to the Eastland quickly. Viktor agreed and immediately assigned Hale to this post. He was a beefy, silent creature and she'd yet to crack his shield with her antics.

Eden hugged Evelyn and kissed each of her cheeks. "Be safe, Evie."

"You do the same, sister."

Viktor looked down at Evelyn. "Hale can get you out of here in a heartbeat, little one, should you need it. I'll be sending another guard to check in daily, just in case."

"I can't hear you all the way up there."

Eden laughed and one of Viktor's lips lifted. It was more like a grimace but maybe that was how he smiled.

He didn't look like he really knew how to flash a grin, anyway.

"Behave while we're gone," he rumbled and patted her on the head.

"I'm not a puppy."

He chuckled. "No, you're worse. I think you might actually have the teeth to break skin."

"I'd never bite my new brother."

He'd almost tripped over his own two feet when she'd called him *brother* at his arrival today. He was mated to Eden, so of course he was family—he simply didn't seem to realize it until she'd claimed him as such.

Viktor laughed again. "Very well, little ... sister."

The last word came out a little forced, but Evelyn liked it. After the fiasco with Marrok and the happenings since the solstice, it was nice to have something positive come out of the whole mess.

Evelyn waved, watching as they disappeared and ported back to Prajna. The giant and her sister, wrapped tight in each other's arms. Evelyn was thankful her sister had found someone so doting. She was also thankful Eden's male could teleport around in the blink of an eye. It would make visiting so much easier.

Their father had not reacted well to the news Eden was Viktor's mate. When Edward saw both the vampire and Eden bore the matching birthmarks all fated vampires shared, there was nothing he could say. Viktor teleported Eden away that very day.

Evelyn was without a sister nearby for the first time in her life. The day Eden departed, Evelyn was left with a temple full of males: her father, his men, and a few wolves Kellan had sent to help comb through old prophesies for clues of what was to come. Everyone knew each faction was facing hardships and had been for some time. What they didn't know was how to stop them.

This was why Edward had picked the Temple of Sanctus Femina. It was not only believed to be safe, it held information that might prove useful. Her mother, Elora, had a number of prophesies here. Thus far, none had been helpful.

Evelyn wished her father had stayed. Unwisely, he'd set out on horseback last week with some others to get to Castle Burghard. Theron had received a letter from Kellan stating they'd been betrayed by those they'd trusted and King Edward rushed to his aide.

She rubbed her forehead. Thinking of it gave her a headache.

"Evelyn?"

She turned to the elderly male calling from the entry to the temple.

"A word, if you don't mind."

Theron turned and walked into the building, his grey robes billowing into the air. Evelyn followed him into his study, where they'd just had their last meeting with her sisters and their males.

"Please sit," he asked and shut the door. Instead of going to his large chair behind his desk, he sat in the one next to her.

"Marrok responded to my message."

She nodded. Theron had sent a missive two weeks ago, briefly informing the demon of a meeting Theron had held with Edward, Kellan, and Viktor.

"He's on his way here." Theron pulled at his grey beard, staring at her, as though waiting for a reaction.

Adrenaline spiked her blood. Half of her was dying to see him, the other half felt she still needed time. After so long of waiting for them to be together, the timing couldn't have been worse.

Furthermore, Evelyn hadn't seen Marrok since the night she'd shown him the dream of Melena carving up her chest. It had been hard for him to see and he'd lashed out. She could sense his frustration occasionally, but that was all she was picking up.

"Does he know I'm here?"

"No, though I'm sure he could figure it out easily enough. He's riding to Gwydion first."

"Why?"

"Why do you think?"

"For me? He knows I'm not there."

Theron's violet kaleidoscope eyes swirled with magic. He looked at Evelyn, but if felt like he wasn't seeing her, like something else was in his field of vision.

264

She wondered what he wanted to discuss. He already knew everything. As soon as her father left for Burghard, Evelyn told Theron of her dreamworld, starting with the first time Marrok had entered it and ending with their last visit.

The morning they'd arrived, he pulled Evelyn aside and told her it would be best not to mention anything she'd been dreaming. He'd *seen* what would happen if she did and so she'd kept quiet.

Because he already knew about her dreams, she felt comfortable discussing them. She'd hoped he could give her insight on the last ones she'd had of Melena. He'd said he needed to think on it.

"It's the new moon. He is riding to Gwydion to request access to you. He knows Edward has taken you away, but your father and Flynn do not know that you told him as much. Flynn is waiting for him."

"When will he arrive here?"

"Sometime before nightfall."

Evelyn clasped her hands tightly together. She was nervous. Her father and sisters were kingdoms away. Flynn had stayed behind to handle things in Gwydion. There would be no buffer for her when Marrok arrived.

Theron's warm hand settled atop hers. "Do not fret."

"Because it will all work out?" she asked, hoping one of his visions had shown a positive outcome.

"Ah, that I do not know. What I do know is that faith can go a long way. Have some faith in Marrok. It is not

265

so easy for him to have faith in himself. He'll need you to help him with that."

"I can do that."

"I would also advise, when you see him, you do not touch him."

"What?" she chirped, pretending not to know his meaning. There wasn't enough gold on the planet to get her to discuss the concept of a mating frenzy with a male older than dirt.

"Trust me. Please."

"I do."

"Good. Now let us go to our evening meal. All this drama has left my belly empty."

Evelyn laughed. "You're always suggesting food."

"I'm always hungry," he clucked and she laughed again.

* * *

"Shall I stable the horses, Sire?"

Marrok dismounted and shook his head. "Get them watered for now, Favin. We may have to ride out again, sooner than we'd like."

"Very well."

"Shall I accompany you or go with Favin?" Danil grunted hopping off his horse. "Don't figure you need me to hold your hand, but I will."

"Go with Favin."

"Right-i-o, my liege," he sang and sauntered off towards the stables.

Marrok didn't know how Danil could be so chipper after eight hours in the saddle—and that was only from Gwydion to here. It was a two-day ride from the peninsula just to reach Gwydion's border with few stops.

He stretched his back and rolled his head around his neck. He needed to bathe. He needed to eat. And he needed to find his mate. He was hoping she was here, though, he had planned on coming here no matter what. Theron's message had been too alarming to ignore.

"Welcome, King Marrok!" Theron's voice echoed from the top of the stairs.

The older male's bright irises, filled with shades of purple and silver, stood out starkly against his weathered skin. Even from twenty paces away, Marrok could easily see them.

Marrok jogged up the steps and inclined his head to the priest. "Theron. I came as soon as I was able."

"Of course, of course. Come, you've spent too much time on your steed. My stable boys will take care of your companions. We've much to discuss."

"Thank you."

Marrok followed Theron. Instead of heading to his study, he took him into a large sitting room. A table was already set with refreshments and he realized just how parched he was.

"Your timing is perfect, Theron."

Twinkling eyes met his and a hand clapped him on the back. "Of course it is."

The priest took one of the chairs and gestured to the other. Marrok thought the male looked older. His long grey hair was now showing strands of white. Though his face still held mirth, as it always did, it also looked tired.

"Is everything alright?" Marrok asked, sliding into the chair opposite Theron.

"It will be. Goddess willing."

Marrok waited for more, but Theron said nothing. Instead, he filled them both a glass of water and then uncorked a bottle of wine.

"Please," he nodded at the food. "I have already eaten. I can hear your demon stomach eating itself. Refuel while we chat."

Marrok filled his plate and Theron relaxed into his seat, sipping on his wine. He waited for Marrok to start eating before speaking.

"Thank you for coming so quickly. The past couple of weeks have been trying for all of Imperium, though, many are unaware."

"I'm aware, generally speaking, of the issues."

Theron lifted one eyebrow. "Such as?"

"Power drains in Gwydion. I had reports the scents of magics on the elementals had diminished to the point my informant couldn't pick up on them unless he was close."

"This, thank the Goddess, has ceased to be the case. Since Nora left Gwydion, there's been no draining."

Marrok lowered his fork. "Edward's youngest was the cause?"

"So it seems."

"Then what effect is she having in Burghard? Their forests have been slowly dying for years. She could put a strain on it, if she was pulling power from it."

"Quite the opposite, it seems. Kellan reported, since their mating, the forest has started to heal."

Marrok held very still, digesting more than just his meal. "You're saying both Gwydion and Burghard are on the mend."

"Yes."

Marrok wiped his mouth, his attention returning to his plate. "And what of Prajna?"

"Viktor found his sieva."

Marrok's eyes snapped to Theron's. His knee bounced, renewed energies coursing through his limbs. There had been no newly mated pairs in Prajna in a century. This had been the vampire's struggle. No mated pairs and no live births.

The tide had turned for three of the four factions. It all started with Kellan finding Nora, his true mate. Then, for Prajna with Viktor finding his true mate.

Marrok poured himself a glass of wine and took a huge gulp. He, too, had found his true mate. Lately, there had been fewer rogues, as well as a multitude of saatus matches. They still had challenges, but did meeting Evelyn change the fortune of his people?

"Aren't you going to ask me who Viktor's mate is?" Theron smirked.

"Does it matter?"

"I'd say it matters greatly, considering our continent's history."

"Who is it?" Marrok asked, a twinging sensation prickling his neck.

"Eden, Evelyn's sister, is Viktor's sieva."

Marrok sat back, stunned. His dinner suddenly felt like a brick sitting in his gut. He knew what Theron was hinting at, why it mattered greatly.

Nora on the Northland throne, an attempt already made on her life. Eden on the Eastland throne. Evelyn ... his saatus on the Southland throne. An elemental in power in every kingdom.

Assuming Melena really did transfer her mark to Bogdan and Sephtis Kenelm was active, they would be out for all three of Edward's children, possibly Edward himself.

"You know Evelyn is my mate, don't you?"

"I do."

"Is Edward here? I assumed he would come to you, possibly seeking help in protecting his daughters."

"He did come here to search the prophecies for clues. Something important came up and he rode to Burghard last week."

His demon spirit howled. It wanted its saatus. Hell, Marrok wanted her. Burghard was not safe, not with someone poisoning the king's mate. Marrok needed to see Evelyn immediately, see for himself she was unharmed.

"Where is Evelyn?" his voice dropped an octave, proof of his chaotic emotions.

"We'll get to that in a moment."

"Tell me where she is!" his fist pounded on the table, making the dishes jump.

"I'm right here," the sultry voice announced from behind him.

Chapter 22

Marrok had Evelyn off her feet and in his arms before she'd even realized he'd moved from his seat. How he'd gotten from the table to the doorway so quickly she didn't know.

His arms shook as she was compressed up against his front. He pushed his face into the fabric covering her chest as he held her aloft. Marrok hugged her so tightly she had difficulty breathing.

Evelyn did the only thing she could, she held onto him, her feet dangling inches above the floor. Her eyes burned. He was real. He was tangible. There would be no waking up from this.

A throat cleared and Evelyn lifted her watery eyes to Theron.

"Might I suggest, before your skin touches his, you retreat to your rooms for the night? We can meet in the morning. I'll leave you two to ... talk things over while I find Marrok's men a place to sleep."

Marrok snorted, not bothering to turn towards the priest. There'd be no talking tonight. He held his ear to Evelyn's chest, listening to the rapid beat of her heart, waiting until the elderly male vacated the room.

"You can put me down now."

"No, I cannot. Just tell me where your rooms are."

"Marrok—"

"Evelyn. The second I touch your skin, and I most certainly will be touching it, it could start the mating frenzy. It might not be as intense because of our bonding in the dreamworld, but trust me when I say you won't want to be in this room. It's the only reason I haven't kissed you."

"Fine. Exit the room and turn left."

"Wrap your legs around me," he demanded impatiently.

"Anyone could see us."

"I don't care."

"Several of my father's men are here, as are two of Kellan's wolves and one vampire. We are not alone."

Marrok adjusted his grip, his hands holding her aloft by her backside. He lowered Evelyn enough to allow her to feel his erection. She was now at eye level and he could see the flush of her skin, smell the sweetness of her sex.

"Wrap them around me or I'll have my fingers buried in you faster than you can say please."

"Marrok," she breathed, licking her lips, staring into his rich, honey-like gaze. They were close enough to share breath, a whisper away from touching. Her insides clenched and she was tempted to rip away her clothing herself.

Her legs lifted, locking behind his back. A satisfied rattle emitted from his chest and her panties grew damp. His bulge was notched right where she needed it most.

"Please," she whispered, arching her chest.

"Not yet."

Marrok walked out of the room, carrying the center of his universe in his arms. He turned left, entering a long corridor. Halfway down, she told him to turn left again into a darkened hallway leading to a separate wing.

Torches lit the way, but the only light he saw was the golden hue smoldering in his mate's right eye. It marked her as his. He liked seeing her marked, even if it wasn't of his doing. He wanted her branded in every way.

Fevered anticipation to fully complete the bond, to lie with her in the flesh, besieged his body. He was dangerously close to taking her against the nearest wall.

"How far down?" he grumbled, still staring at his saatus, unable to tear away from the trance she held him in.

"Last door on the right."

"Are there others in this wing?"

"No. Why do you ask?"

"Because you're going to scream my name loud enough to shake the heavens."

Marrok opened the door and swept them inside. The heavy wood swung shut on its own weight, closing with a loud click. As he reached for the lock, Evelyn's mouth slammed into his, immersing him in a kiss contrived of pure longing.

Electricity shocked their systems, as it had in the dreamworld. Only, where before it was static charges dancing on their skin, now it was lightning bolts piercing deep, a hundred times more potent.

Evelyn gasped. Compared to the dreamworld, everything was now sharper, more concentrated. The way Marrok tasted. His scent. The heat radiating off his frame. They were an impossibly addictive combination.

She felt off-balanced. Drugged. Heat razed her body, setting her core ablaze and consuming her mind, driving her to a single purpose to have her male inside her.

Marrok pressed Evelyn's back to the door, tearing and ripping her long skirt while she fumbled to undo his belt. An easy tug tore her underwear. Using his body to pin her, he lifted both of Evelyn's arms above her head.

He kept one of his hands on her wrists and used the other to free his cock from the confines of his trousers. His fingertips played with her folds, finding her saturated. She tried to angle her hips enough to take him further into her body, crying out in frustration when he instead removed them.

"Even in reality, you're so wet for me, so eager," he praised, aligning the broad head of his shaft with her opening.

"Always," she panted. Her tongue pushed into the cavity of his mouth, seeking connection to his.

"This will be fast," Marrok warned before he plunged deep inside.

His mate was so tight, so warm. She squeezed him with such delicious pressure he might never retreat from it. Every time they made love in the dreamworld had been perfect, better than anything he'd ever experienced. Marrok had trouble believing anything could have felt better. The reality was far superior.

His demon reached for Evelyn, merging with her soul while Marrok drove inside her body. Her moans grew louder, spurring him to go faster. He sliced her shirt with his claws, exposing her firm breasts.

Pinching and pulling at one of her nipples, he sent her over. Her climax was hard and fast, matching his rhythm. Her wide eyes held his, luscious lips parted in a silent scream.

The sight of his mate's face shrouded with ecstasy from what he was doing prompted a severe tingling at the base of his spine. Instead of fighting it, he pistoned himself in and out at demon-fast speed, craving the release he could only get from his female.

Marrok erupted inside her channel, groaning Evelyn's name. His hips continued working, prolonging both their releases. He let go of her arms and they dropped to his shoulders in a loose embrace.

He spun them towards the bed, carefully lowering Evelyn to her back. Slowly, he withdrew. He removed her boots and stockings, then peeled away the remaining rags of her clothing.

Marrok stroked and kissed her skin as each mouthwatering inch of bronzed flesh was revealed. He wanted to touch as much of her as he could, from the top of her head down to her sexy little toes.

For two years, one of them would disappear shortly after their erotic sessions. This would be the first time he could hang on to her, to sleep beside her. He wanted to be gentle but the urge to take her ruthlessly was rising again.

Once she was completely bare, Marrok stood, taking in his fill of her supine form. Evelyn started to close her legs and he pushed her knees apart.

"No, I want to see you like this. I want to see what's mine."

His bold little mate spread her legs for him. Marrok's fiery eyes held hers, then dropped lower. He stared at her cleft as he removed his own clothing. Their mixed fluids glistened on her mound and he growled in male satisfaction.

Unable to resist, he lowered himself to taste her honied elixir. His tongue stroked her sensitive skin and he hummed his approval.

"Nothing tastes like you, *moj draga*. Nothing. I'll never get my fill."

Evelyn's hands went to his hair, pulling as she ground her hips into his face. His demon chuckled, loving her ardor. He sucked on her swollen pearl and she whimpered.

"Look at me."

Evelyn opened her eyes.

"Say my name when you come," his demon voice demanded, allowing its magic out.

Marrok pulled her hardened nub between his teeth and licked at it with the tip of his tongue. His thumb fondled her entrance, teasing her. He rubbed small circles and massaged her to orgasm.

"M-Marrok!" she shouted as she flew apart, undulating so frantically he had to hold her down by her thighs.

Once Evelyn's spasming slowed, Marrok climbed onto the bed and entered her slowly. The electric feel between them hadn't diminished in the slightest.

Marrok unsheathed a single claw. Drawing it across his lower lip, as he had done two years ago in a dream. The shallow cut's sting only added to his desire to taste her blood again.

Evelyn watched, mesmerized by the drops of Marrok's dark blood beading on his mouth. It smelled like he tasted, like earthen spice. Before he dropped his hand, Evelyn grabbed his finger and used his claw to slice her own lip.

"Careful," he chastised, jerking his hand away.

Evelyn ignored him. She fisted her hands in his inky mane of silk and yanked his face to hers. Their lifeblood blended, their powers fused. Rays of light flooded the room from some unknown source, thickening the air with tension and electric power.

"Ah, Goddess," Marrok gnashed, fighting an overwhelming desire to pierce her flesh with his small fangs. He withdrew and flipped her over to her hands and knees, quickly plunging back inside.

The sound of flesh slapping on flesh echoed in the room. Evelyn mewled and pushed back against him, meeting him thrust for thrust. It was too much. He was going to break her and she was going to love every moment of it.

Instinct took over and Marrok lowered his front to her back. He grabbed a handful of dark red hair and pulled, exposing the curve of his mate's delicate neck, where it met her shoulder. *Now*, his demon susurrated. *Do it now.*

Marrok bit into her flesh and Evelyn's sultry cries turned into high-pitched wails of pleasure. He could feel the pulsating ripples of her climax as she detonated around him.

Evelyn's body accepted everything he gave. In this position, she could take him deeper than ever before. Marrok gave in and allowed himself to take her as his demon demanded. His hips surged with urgency as he found his own release.

On and on it went until they both collapsed. Marrok licked the two wounds he'd left and rolled to the side so he wouldn't crush her. The diminutive healing properties of his saliva should be enough to close the tiny perforations.

A sheen of sweat covered them both. He cupped the side of her face, no longer assaulted by bolts of lightning. The bjesnilo had passed. Not that he didn't still want to take her. Even after all that, he was still aroused. At least now it wasn't a compulsion he couldn't control.

They laid in silence, catching their breaths. Marrok tenderly stroked her face, brushing her auburn hair away.

Evelyn shifted to her side, fully facing him.

"It's very nice to meet you, finally," she quipped.

Marrok's lips stretched, grinning like a fool. He leaned across and kissed her gently. "And you, as well, little mate." He kissed her once more then asked her how she felt.

"Good. A little tired, but I feel good."

"Just good?"

"Amazing. Marvelous. Astounded. Beyond impressed by your sexual prowess. Is that better?"

"Much."

Evelyn smirked. She reached for a pillow to put under her head and winced. Gingerly, she rubbed across the scars already forming on the two small puncture wounds.

"I didn't realize demons bit."

Marrok grimaced. "They don't. Usually. It's an archaic practice male demons used to insist upon so the world would see their female was marked."

"So then, why did you bite me?"

He trailed his fingers over the twin marks. "I couldn't stop myself. My demon wanted it. I wanted it. Archaic or not, I wanted to mark you as mine. Does it bother you?"

She shook her head. "No. I enjoyed it, actually. Is it something we can do again and again?"

His chest shook. "You might be the most perfect female ever created."

Evelyn blushed but didn't respond.

Marrok pulled her close and rolled to his back, tucking her in to his side. Her arm came around his waist and she hooked one leg over his. She fit perfectly alongside him.

"You should try to rest, Evelyn."

"Don't you think we need to talk first? I doubt you had enough time for Theron to tell you everything that has happened." Or to talk through his reaction to their last shared dream.

"I didn't, but we can address it in the morning. Rest for now because I've not had my fill of you yet. I'll be waking you soon."

"Oh."

"Yes. *Oh.*"

He kissed the top of her head and rubbed up and down her spine until her breathing evened out.

Chapter 23

"Did Evelyn share what's occurred these past two weeks?" Theron asked from the other side of the desk.

Both Evelyn and Marrok were seated across from the priest, having finally emerged from the bedroom. It was late morning, yet Evelyn was yawning repetitively. Marrok hadn't allowed her much rest. He'd even taken her in the bath earlier, after having had her multiple times throughout the night.

"We didn't do much talking," the demon responded, watching with amusement as his mate blushed furiously.

Theron snorted. "Yes, well, you may not want to speak so freely in her father's presence."

Of the four factions, elementals were the ones with the strictest views on sex. Pre-marital intercourse wasn't forbidden, it just wasn't encouraged as it was elsewhere.

Wolves, vampires, and demons had very different opinions on casual coupling. Marrok thought it was because their lifespans were much longer and it could take centuries to find one's fated mate. Hundreds of years of celibacy wasn't anything anyone would choose to withstand.

"I promise I'll stay on Edward's good side," Marrok swore and reached for Evelyn's hand, squeezing it.

"I think that wise," Theron agreed.

"Speaking of, why did Edward leave?"

"To get to Nora and deal with ..." Theron looked at Evelyn who was twisting her mouth nervously. "Kellan figured out who was responsible for the poisoning. I didn't add specifics to the message I sent to you on the off chance it was intercepted."

"Who would bother to intercept correspondence between us?"

"I'm sure you already know the answer to that. It seems the brotherhood is still active."

"Sephtis Kenelm," Marrok said aloud, feeling the weight of the declaration sit heavy upon his shoulders. Talking of it in the dreamworld was one thing. Having Theron confirm it was another.

Marrok's thumb brushed across Evelyn's knuckles. He debated pulling her into his lap, then thought better of it after how red her face had been a minute ago.

"Who poisoned Nora?" Marrok finally asked.

"A she-wolf. One under compulsion."

"Only demons can put others under compulsion."

"Technically, vampires can hypnotize others, but it's usually short-lived. You're correct, however. She was under a demon's compulsion."

Marrok inhaled. Evelyn's dreams implied Bogdan was the one who would have inherited the marking. Favin's intelligence had informed them Bogdan had travelled to Burghard.

"Was it a demon named Bogdan?"

"Yes. I'll not ask how you know. Rather, I would ask if you have any other information coming through your network, you share it."

Marrok glanced at Evelyn then nodded. "Of course. In turn, I would ask to handle Bogdan personally."

"I'm sorry to say you'll not be getting access to that male."

"Why not?"

"He's already dead. As is the elemental involved. Kellan took care of one and Nora the other. The she-wolf, a healer named Agatha, got away. We've not identified the vampire involved."

Evelyn let out a shuddering breath, caught somewhere between sorrow and fury. Her fear of what her dreams had been showing her was realized. It was Sephtis Kenelm.

Almost worse was the news Kellan's missive contained, the one prompting her father to ride to Burghard last week. The identification of the elemental member of the brotherhood was something King Edward could not ignore.

"Evelyn?" Marrok's questioning eyes bore into hers when she lifted her face.

"You knew him, didn't you? The elemental Nora *took care of*?" he guessed, both scenting and feeling her wave of emotions.

"Her. I knew *her* very well. She was our governess, Mara. Father sent her with Nora so Nora wouldn't feel alone. We treated her like family and she deceived us all. She raised Nora from birth," her voice cracked. "I'd kill the traitor myself if she was in front of me."

"Come here, little mate," he coaxed, pulling Evelyn onto his lap so he could wrap his arms around her.

She settled easily against him, allowing him to soothe some of the rage threatening to rise. He tucked her head under his chin and gave what little comfort he could before turning his attention back to the priest.

"Bogdan and this Mara are dead. Unless they had plans in place for their replacements, that would mean there is still a wolf and a vampire at large."

"Yes. Kellan and Viktor have made plans to track them. The wolves caught their scents already near the border to Prajna."

"When will Edward return?"

"He won't," Evelyn squeaked, her emotions getting the best of her. "Not for a while, at least."

"Why ever not?"

"The scent they found? Of the vampire? It came from the forest ... from where my Father and those traveling with him were attacked. He was almost killed."

Marrok tried to keep his muscles from tensing under her. His mate needed a soft place to land right now, not a hardened warrior out for vengeance.

"I'm sorry, *moj draga.*"

"Don't be. It's not like there was anything you could do. Luckily, we were assured he was on the mend when Nora and Kellan visited."

"Good. I'm glad."

He kissed the top of her head, thinking. Stroking her back, they sat in silence for long minutes. Marrok felt her relax and her breathing even out. He wasn't surprised, not after their night-long exertions.

"What's coming, Theron?" he asked quietly. "What should we do?"

The old man's kaleidoscope eyes spun. "That I cannot tell you."

Marrok exhaled. "Can't or won't?"

"Both. I cannot steer the ship. It is forbidden. I can give you information on the wind, on the swells, but I cannot steer you through the storm, nor can I see if you make it through to the other side. There are rules to the universe, Marrok, and the full revelation of a vision comes with a price."

"Tell me what you can, then."

"Evelyn needs to return with you to the Southland."

"It's not safe."

"Do not forget what I told you of Gwydion, Burghard, and Prajna. Choices were made for those kingdoms. Nothing about them came easy, but in the end, the *choices* made all the difference."

Theron's gaze lingered on the beloved female in Marrok's arms. "It's time for you to choose, Marrok."

"Choose what?"

"Your saatus."

"A saatus isn't a choice. You know that," Marrok bit out, aggravated with the priest's riddles.

"Isn't she?"

Marrok started to argue and stopped himself when Theron went rigid, the purple and silver of his eyes spinning oddly.

"You need to return to Sundari," Theron insisted, coming out of his stupor.

"I will."

"No, you need to go now. I'll have Viktor's man port you to the palace. Favin and Danil will bring the horses and her things."

Marrok didn't like the idea of travelling without his guards. He also didn't like the idea of taking Evelyn to the home Brennen once occupied.

"The fortress—"

"No, I think you need to be closer to the border for now. Trust me on this. Please."

His insistence gave Marrok pause. He inhaled Evelyn's essence, knowing it would calm him. He needed to be logical right now. If the Seer was insisting Marrok take his mate to the palace, it wasn't without a valid reason.

"If you insist."

"Thank you," Theron replied, visibly relaxing. "Also, when you're in a secured location, you need to let Evelyn show you her most recent dreams."

Marrok's lips pressed tight. "Alright," he grated.

"Wonderful. I'll go fetch your transportation."

* * *

Evelyn rolled and stretched under the heavy comforter, coming out of a dreamless sleep. After weeks of dreaming others' memories, it was a welcome way to wake.

She reached for Marrok, her hand hitting cool sheets. Not only was he not beside her, he hadn't been for some time. She forced her eyes open, not recognizing the large canopy above. Evelyn's bed in the temple's living quarters didn't have a canopy.

She bolted upright, searching the dim room—a room she'd never seen before. The space surrounding her was large and felt empty. The bed was the obvious focal point of the chamber. A couple of chairs and a small settee, covered in a sheet, were the only other items of furniture.

"I'm here," Marrok assured, rising from one of the chairs next to the bed. He sat beside Evelyn and nuzzled her cheek with his.

"How do you feel?" he asked, reluctantly putting a little space between them so they could talk.

"Refreshed. I was exhausted. I've not been sleeping well."

"I'm sure."

Her head swiveled around the room once more, this time taking in the rich earthen colors, accented with deep browns and golds. The walls appeared to be covered in a muted rainbow of painted clay.

One contained a mural of a desert at sunset. She'd never been to Sundari, but knew it was the only kingdom with any sort of arid land, mainly in the far South.

"Where are we?"

"Piatra."

"We're at your palace?" she asked skeptically.

Marrok nodded, unsure how he felt having her here. He'd always thought of this as Brennen's home, despite it having been the residence of each of the royals before. Even Marrok had lived in this wing as a lad, with his parents.

"How did we get here?"

"Viktor's guard ported us here."

"And I didn't wake?"

He tucked a strand of auburn behind her ear. "You were out of it and I hadn't the heart to wake you."

Evelyn's eyes narrowed. "You woke me continuously last night."

His sensual smile had her coiling with need. Marrok inhaled and his smile stretched further. She slapped him playfully on the arm and he laughed.

"Why?" she asked.

"Because I couldn't resist you, little mate."

"No, why am I here?"

"You belong with me."

"Suddenly it's that simple?" she replied dubiously.

"Theron also saw something he couldn't share, but he basically pushed us out the door. For now, this is where we need to be. Favin and Danil will be here soon."

"They weren't allowed to hitch a ride with Hale?"

She didn't know the two males, but she knew how much they meant to Marrok. He'd spoken of them fondly during their many nights together in the dreamworld.

"No. They have the horses and are bringing your things."

291

"My things? Wait ... how long am I to stay? My father has no idea where I am."

"Indefinitely." His tone brokered no argument.

Admittedly, Evelyn liked his answer. She felt like they were on the precipice of something of great magnitude, of starting their life together. They had a few things to clear up between them, and a malicious brotherhood to contend with, but she was finally with him. Evelyn would fight with everything in her to keep him.

"This isn't your room," she assessed, shifting the conversation.

"What makes you think that?"

"There's nothing in here."

"I don't stay here very often. I prefer the fortress in Terenuskit. It's closer to the peninsula and I can better keep an eye on things from there. For now, though, we will stay here as Theron requested. There are a number of rooms to choose from. You can have whatever you want to decorate them."

Evelyn twisted her mouth side to side. "I'm happy to sleep wherever you sleep. I don't need much, so as long as there is space to put some clothing away, I'll be content."

Marrok felt the same. He had no ties to this place. His only desire was to be with Evelyn in whatever home they made together.

So unlike Melena, his demon taunted. Though the spirit had never been fond of his wife, Marrok couldn't argue there were significant differences between the females.

Melena had wanted two chambers, one for him and one for her. He'd believed it was because she came from wealth and needed the space for her belongings. She was fond of the finer things in life and he was only happy to fulfill her requests.

Truth be told, he was acknowledging more and more the things about his late wife he'd chosen to forget. It was difficult to accept she had characteristics he would never seek out in a life partner.

Marrok needed to stop comparing the two females. There was no comparison, not anymore.

"Theron is going to write to your father," he informed Evelyn. "I know it's not how we planned it, but it's how he'll find out you've been confirmed as my mate."

"He'll be upset he wasn't there, that we've not had a ceremony."

Marrok shrugged. "We're bonded. Fully. It's far more binding than *any* wedding could ever be." He gave her a second to let his words sink in before continuing.

"However, if you want a wedding, and to have your father watch you take your vows, you shall have it."

Evelyn shook her head stubbornly. "I've decided I do *not* want a royal wedding."

She didn't say why. She didn't have to. Marrok knew she'd suffered having to live through the memory of his emotions as Melena walked down the aisle to him.

He would have done anything to spare Evelyn from it. He questioned Fate's decisions where those dreams were concerned, though he knew he should have told Evelyn about Melena from the start. The fault was his for those particular memories.

"Then we'll do a binding ceremony, if you want. We don't have to decide today. We have time."

"Alright," Evelyn agreed, fidgeting her hands on the blanket. Her focus remained on her lap.

"Evelyn?"

"Yes?" she whispered. She felt like she was about to burst into tears for no apparent reason.

"Look at me."

When she didn't lift her face, Marrok tilted her chin with his fingertips. She hated the sting she felt as her eyes filled.

"I'm sorry," he told her earnestly. "The way I reacted during our last dream together ... I shouldn't have treated you like that."

"It's okay."

"No. It's not. I wasn't prepared for it and I reacted poorly."

Marrok embraced his saatus and rocked her slowly, trying to take away a little of the hurt he'd caused.

When her small hands slid around him, the knot in his chest loosened.

"What do we do now?" she asked.

"I think it's time you show me the things I didn't want to see."

Chapter 24

Marrok slid under the covers next to Evelyn, lying so they were facing one another. He pulled her hands up to rest on his chest then wrapped one of his arms around her waist.

He was completely nude, as was she. His erection, thick and heavy, rested against her hip. Evelyn battled the urge to reach for it.

"I thought you wanted to pull on my *memories*," she tried to joke.

"I do. Skin-to-skin allows me the clearest picture."

"Can demons lie?"

Marrok chuckled. "Yes, but other demons always know."

"I'm not a demon."

"I know," he said with a glint in his eye. "I like it, makes things more interesting. Now, as much as I'd rather roll you over and have my way with you, I need you to concentrate on the dreams."

Feeling suddenly very serious, Evelyn swallowed. "These memories were different, Marrok. I think—I think they might hurt you."

His face softened and he kissed the corner of her mouth. "The past is the past, Evelyn. I promise not to react as I did. Once I can glean anything important from the memories, I'll bury them, leaving them where they belong."

Trusting him, she closed her eyes and concentrated. She tried to remember things in the order they'd come to her. If they occurred chronologically, she didn't know. Marrok would have to be the one to figure out if the order mattered.

Marrok rested his forehead against his mate's, giving her a few seconds to push the memories into the forefront of her mind. The first few came fast, snippets of Melena moving her mouth without sound. With him. With Favin. Even with her father.

Finally, the vision settled, just outside of the small chamber adjacent to the throne room. He was looking down, smoothing out the silken fabric of a bright blue dress. He could tell from the bracelet adorning his wrist he was seeing from Melena's viewpoint.

Voices carried from inside the chamber. Brennen often met here with small groups of demons, so it wasn't surprising. Melena waiting to meet him, however, was.

As far as Marrok knew, she'd never worked directly for the king. She'd told him her family had offered up her services and Brennen swiftly gifted her to Marrok.

The door opened and she looked up into the face of her cousin, Caleb. "Come," the male commanded.

Melena entered and the heavy wood slammed shut behind her. Her head jerked and Caleb stepped in front of the door, as if he meant to block her exit.

What have you gotten us into, Cousin? she silently wondered.

Two other males were seated at the worn table. One had black hair and beady dark eyes with black covering the places where she should have seen amber. Something about him was not quite right.

He was dressed in fine silk as opposed to the leathers most of the Sundari wore. His fingers were covered in jeweled rings, the sizes of the gems were ridiculous. He was soft, like a female.

The King, her mind sneered a second before her eyes swung to the other male. Messy tufts of sable stood out in all directions from his scalp. His clothing was old and tatty, the brown leather faded to light tan in places.

The juxtaposition of the pauper next to the sovereign was stark. Melena's expression blanked as the Prajna's bemused emerald green irises looked her up and down obscenely. She was used to being ogled by demon males. She was not used to the probing attention of a vampire.

"My liege, may I introduce my cousin, Melena. The Seer I was telling you about."

Almost forgetting herself, Melena swiftly bent into a low curtsy. Brennen stood and she tracked the movement of his feet. They stopped in front of her and she waited for him to allow her to rise.

"By the Goddess, Caleb. Your description wasn't hyperbole. She's exquisite."

"Yes, she is, Sire. Still, I believe it is her visions you will be most attracted to. Knowledge is power, after all. You know our purpose. You know we seek to—"

"I wouldn't finish that sentence if I were you," the vampire harshly reprimanded. "We don't speak of such things where others may overhear, demon."

"Of course, D—"

"You fool!," the vampire interrupted again. "I told you not to use my name! Learn to hold your tongue or I'll be promoting this beauty to your position immediately," he seethed.

"M-my apologies!" Caleb stammered. "Melena will be discreet. She is my heir. I'm sure Brennen knows we serve his interest, and his interest only."

The air in Marrok's lungs halted. Melena did know she was next in line after Caleb. She'd been in league with them from the start, or at least complicit with the group.

She'd been complicit with Brennen, as well. This meeting had to have occurred before the day Marrok met Melena, if she was being introduced to Brennen.

Marrok's uncle had used his words carefully that day in the throne room when he'd announced she was a gift.

299

He'd implied it was the first time he'd met the female he'd heard much of from her father.

"Gentlemen. Let's move on from such topics. Rise, Melena, and join us at my table."

Melena straightened and moved to the chair Brennen had pulled out for her. The others took their seats, as well, and Caleb gave her a meaningful glower.

"So, Melena. Caleb tells me you've seen something I won't like. I'd like to hear it straight from the source."

"I'm not sure what Caleb told you, my lord. He neglected to inform me he'd spoken to you."

Brennen planted both hands on the table and licked his teeth. "Don't play coy with me, female," his low voice groused. "You saw Marrok would take the throne. I want to know when."

"My visions don't reveal time. I only know they are future events."

He continued licking his teeth in that disgusting way he did. "Very well. Tell me what you can."

Melena folded her hands atop the table. "I saw him with his saatus. He called her his *wife* and his ... *Queen*."

"It could have been a term of endearment," Brennen guessed.

"Not when she was sitting on the throne next to his. I've had many random pieces thrown at me. From what I could gather, once he meets her, he will take the throne."

Brennen growled and Melena held very still. He was known to be impulsive and he didn't like the answer she gave.

"Are you able to see at will?"

"Most of the time."

"Caleb told me he's run through different scenarios with you already? Of decisions I may or may not make?"

"Yes, my liege."

"Then tell me, love, if I give you to Marrok, without conditions, what will happen?"

Her swift intake of breath was unmistakable. Marrok supposed she hadn't expected the question. Her eyes darted to Caleb and Marrok could pick up on the heavy dose of betrayal she felt towards her cousin.

Demons couldn't lie without detection. Melena would have to tell Brennen the truth. Resigned, her eyes closed.

Marrok felt power as it built from inside Melena, clicking and whirring like the insides of a clock. Her spine straightened, held stiff by the magic. If she could call forth visions at will, she was far more powerful than she had led him to believe.

She'd never shared this part of herself with Marrok and he'd never pried. The only time she'd spoken of her visions were when she'd been adamant they would never produce offspring together.

When Melena slumped, she was breathless.

"Well?" Brennen prompted.

She head shook in disbelief. "We," she gulped, "will marry."

Brennen clapped his hands with delight, laughing wickedly. Both Caleb and the vampire relaxed their posture.

"Oh, my dear. This is far better than what I had originally planned. What a surprise you are. Marriage?! Who would have ever thought it could have been so easy to keep my nephew from his saatus? You are going to be perfect for this. Absolutely perfect!"

His snigger reminded Marrok of a depraved madman who just discovered he'd gotten away with murder and planned on doing so again.

Melena waited for Brennen's laugh to die down before speaking. "If I may be so bold as to request, Sire, what exactly are you asking me to do?"

"You'll marry him, of course."

"This is a ... command?" she dared.

Brennen grabbed her arms and jerked her out of her seat so fast she got lightheaded. "If you want to keep your pretty little head attached to your shoulders, you'll do as I say. Understood?"

"Of course, Sire," she exhaled.

"Good. Then we have an understanding. Caleb, pour the wine. I'm in the mood to celebrate."

He shoved Melena back into her chair and she bit her tongue to keep from crying out. Her eyes tracked Caleb as he carried out his master's command.

"You'll need to be on guard, Melena," her cousin warned, sliding a glass in front of her. Melena stared at it, saying nothing.

"Did you hear me?" he snapped.

"Yes."

"You'll use your magic to shield or to erase memories. Perhaps try planting some, if necessary. Do whatever you have to in order to remain undetected. I know how persuasive your powers can be with unsuspecting dolts."

"Ah, yes, I almost forgot," Brennen mused. "Caleb tells me you can prevent others from reading your thoughts and even plant suggestions in their minds. Quite easily. That must be quite handy."

"It can be."

His hand came down on top of hers, none to gently, crushing it between the table and his palm. "You'll not shield from me or attempt to manipulate me. Ever. If I discover you have, I'll find creative ways to punish you, maybe even imprison your father. I'll let you watch as I tear him apart one piece at tim."

Brennen slid his hand away and returned it to the arm of his chair. "The choice is yours, of course," he grinned wickedly.

Still staring at the glass of wine, Melena whispered, "I understand."

Brennen crowed at his own dark humor and the memory dissolved into another. It took Marrok a second to recognize they were now in the palace garden. Brennen was pacing anxiously in front of Melena.

"You're sure?" he spat.

"Yes. The vision was of his child. One with dark red hair, like its mother. Marrok will still be king."

"I don't understand. You are his *wife*! I've done everything short of finding this female and cutting her into pieces."

Marrok's demon bellowed with rage—they were speaking of Evelyn.

Brennen stopped pacing, his face lighting up as though he'd had a life-changing epiphany. "That's it. I'll find her and then I won't have to worry about Marrok if she'd dead."

Melena flinched, a storm of panic brewing in her belly. "There's still time, my lord. I'm not even sure she's been born yet."

"Hmm. Yes, I suppose I can't kill something that's not alive. You'll tell me when you're certain you know who she is."

Nausea moved through her abdomen and up her throat. "As you wish, Sire," she forced out, swallowing back the bile threatening to come up.

Brennen watched her doubtfully. "You don't like the idea of me killing the child, do you?"

"I—I'm not fond of harming children, no."

"Then change the outcome, Melena. Wrap him so far up in your cunny he can't see his way out or I'll be forced to take action. One of them will die if you can't change it. The girl will be easier for me to dispose of. I'd prefer not to take the life of my sister's child, as well, but I will."

Melena nodded, still waiting for her stomach to settle. The vision faded and Marrok was once again looking into the eyes of his mate.

"Are you okay?" Evelyn murmured.

Marrok vaulted out of bed and ran into the adjoining chamber, emptying the contents of his stomach into the privy. A cool, damp cloth pressed to the back of his neck.

He hadn't even noticed Evelyn when she entered. He turned, sinking down to the cool floor. The stone felt good on his heated skin. "I'm sorry. I promised I wouldn't react the same."

Wrapped in a sheet, she knelt beside him. "You didn't. This reaction is … different."

He huffed. "I'm not sure if it's from Melena's nausea or if it's my own."

Melena's duplicity was a slap in the face. Marrok could concede she'd been coerced and didn't have much of a choice—it didn't make her deceit any easier to swallow. He would never betray someone he loved in such a manner.

Marrok was starting to accept his wife might not have ever returned his feelings. If she could have manipulated his mind, he'd never know if she lied when she told him she loved him or even if his feelings were his own.

It should have been a crippling blow. He should have been raging over having loved someone who was only playing a game.

The reality was, his reaction to the memory, the panicked revulsion, had little to do with Melena and everything to do with how lucky he was Brennen had never gotten his hands on Evelyn.

"Do you want to talk about it?"

Marrok shook his head. "We can get into the details later. I need to mull some of it over. When Favin and Danil arrive, we'll sit down with them. Then I'll need to talk to Hale so he can carry a message back to Theron."

"He won't be back today."

"I know."

"Okay. What shall we do until then?"

"I think I'd like to bathe."

Marrok got up and added heating stones to the bath, thankful he'd had the foresight to warm them while his mate slept. He opened the spigot and the water whooshed down the chute and into the bathing pool.

Evelyn moved to exit and he tugged on the sheet.

"I think I'd like you to bathe with me."

When he'd said the same words this morning, they were playful and full of naughty promises. This came out more like a boy who didn't want to be alone.

Dropping the sheet, Evelyn enfolded him in her welcoming arms. She could feel his emotions more clearly through their bond. She wasn't surprised he was swinging between sadness and rage.

"For what it's worth, I do think she cared for you. She went to great lengths to remove herself from it all. In a way, she tried to protect me."

"Don't."

Marrok wasn't ready to discuss it. He wasn't even sure he could figure out what he was feeling aside from his fury over Melena putting Evelyn's life in danger.

Any attempt on Melena's part to protect Evelyn was weak at best. The fact remained Brennen had invaded Evelyn's dreams. There was only one way he could have known who she was.

Evelyn nodded. Instead of speaking, she held him until the bath was ready. Marrok led her into the water and they washed in silence.

Chapter 25

"You're staring," Marrok accused his friend, whose eyes scarcely left Evelyn's head of hair. They were seated at the oval table in his study, finishing dinner.

"So I am," Danil replied snippily. "You'll forgive me, but it's not everyday I get to see a being with hair that's not black as night."

Evelyn cocked her head at the white-haired male. "Do you not ever look in the mirror, then?"

Danil howled in delight. "Not if I can help it, my lady. I'm the only one in the King's guard with this coloring. Everyone around is covered in the color of midnight, including the King. Biased he is towards particular colorings."

Marrok smirked, tugging on the tail of Evelyn's braid. "Guilty. Though, I must confess my preference is for red."

Evelyn pressed her lips over her teeth, trying not to blush.

"Very smooth, Sire," Favin chimed in and Evelyn snickered.

"I thought so, too," Marrok shot back, causing the men to laugh, as well.

She was enjoying watching how Marrok interacted with Favin and Danil. She'd never expected them to rib one another so. They acted more like brothers than king and guard. She was glad Marrok had them.

He'd lost so much in his life he deserved to feel like he still had family. Everyone needed connections like these.

Marrok had told her there were two other males in their close group, Petr and Lazlo. Petr had found his saatus and was stationed in her town, a boon Marrok granted to ensure his friend had time with his female.

He'd left Lazlo at the fortress in his stead. He'd sent a messenger and hoped to hear back that all was well. He worried about the security of the peninsula and if Lazlo could handle it on his own.

A knock on the door turned her head.

"Enter," Marrok called.

The door to the study opened and a kitchen maid with short dark hair came inside, pushing a trolley. She made quick work of clearing away the plates. The men grew somber and no one spoke.

Evelyn thanked her but the girl didn't reply. She started to ask the girl her name and Marrok's warm hand touched hers, patting it firmly. She looked up and he gave a subtle shake of his head.

When the girl left with her load, Evelyn turned to Marrok. "Did I do something wrong?"

"No, *moj draga*. That wasn't about you. That was Yana," he said, as if it explained everything.

Evelyn waited, looking to each male for further information. It was Danil who clarified.

"We found her two years ago. Rogues had taken her and her sister from their village."

Her eyes flitted to the closed door, picturing the girl. She couldn't have been more than thirteen or fourteen years old.

"Her sister?" She didn't clarify. They all knew exactly what she was asking.

Danil shook his head. "We were too late. There was no saving her. Yana was close to death herself. We were able to kill her captors, to remove her from the cave where they'd held them for over a week. She hasn't spoken of it. She hasn't uttered a single word since we removed her from that hell, as far as we know."

"Why didn't you return her to her village? To her parents?"

"Because, little mate, there wasn't a village to return to. It was a small farming community, no more than forty demons living there. The rogues slaughtered them all. Yana and her sister were the only younglings. We assume that's why they took them, to feed off their terror."

Evelyn's fingers itched. Her magics wanted out, to protect those around her from the enemy. The bottles of liquor in the corner clanked together.

"Easy," Marrok soothed, lifting her hand and kissing her palm. "Two years have passed. The ones responsible were unsalvageable and have paid for it with their lives. There's nothing to be done to them now."

"We have to stop it. All of it. The rogues. The brotherhood."

"Brotherhood? So it's confirmed, then?" Danil asked.

Marrok hadn't caught them up on his meeting with Theron or on what Evelyn's most recent dreams had revealed.

"It has."

Danil got up from the table.

"Where are you going?" Favin asked.

"I have a feeling this is going to require whiskey."

He grabbed the bottle and four tumblers before returning to his seat. He poured each of them a glass and settled back into his chair.

Evelyn, whose fingers were still itching to take action, downed the spirits and slammed the glass back on the table.

"That tastes terrible!" she exclaimed in between coughs.

"It's supposed to be sipped, poppet."

Evelyn eyed Danil as though he'd just called her a trollop right to her face. Making a decision, she nodded and shoved the glass towards him. "Fine. This time I'll sip it."

Danil grinned, pouring a smaller amount this time. "You know, Marrok, I think I'm going to enjoy having a Queen."

"I couldn't agree more," the King replied, warmth spreading through his chest that had nothing to do with the whiskey he'd swallowed.

* * *

Marrok watched his friends as they sifted through the memories he was sharing. He focused on his discussion with Theron, as well as Evelyn's dreams.

A minute ticked by. Then another. Their faces didn't show much. It was their body language that gave them away, especially Danil's.

While Favin's knuckles went white as he gripped the table, Danil's fingers flexed and closed and flexed again. His head swiveled back and forth and a low rumble emanated from the back of his throat.

Once it ended, Danil's face had gone ruddy. "That bitch sold you out, Evelyn. Pardon my language," he quickly added, peeking at Marrok for any reaction to his assessment of the King's late wife.

"I don't see how she had any other choice," Evelyn defended Melena, ignoring his profanity. "She was under duress. Brennen was holding those she cared about over her head. I don't know what I would have done if in the same position and someone was threatening Nora or Eden."

Danil scoffed. "You wouldn't sic a murderer on a child."

"Enough," Marrok intervened. "Melena's motivations are immaterial at this juncture. What does matter is that we know Sephtis Kenelm had access to some of her visions. They knew about Evelyn, at least in the abstract. They knew if I met her I would take the throne. They were trying to intervene. It's how Brennen found her when she was six."

"I think that, too, is beside the point, Sire."

"What do you mean, Favin?"

"The dreams are past memories. Decades ago. No one even knew the brotherhood was still functioning. Now we have confirmation and two of the four members are confirmed deceased. The wolves have identified the she-wolf."

"They also know of the vampire," Evelyn interjected.

"The wolves know his *scent*, not who he is. We know what the vampire looks like. Between him and the she-wolf, he's the greater threat because he can teleport. The wolf you might see coming. The vampire? Doubtful.

313

I think this is why you had this particular dream. It gives you an advantage to recognize a previously unseen foe."

"I wish I also knew the face of the she-wolf."

"Don't need to. No she-wolves reside in the Southland. You see one, you kill her or run away."

"Thank you, Danil. Very insightful," Evelyn deadpanned.

"I live to serve."

"What about the other dreams, Favin?" Marrok questioned. It still didn't sit right with him, his mate having to experience his wedding to another.

"The same. Warnings. Clues. Explanations, perhaps. They seem to be more important for you than for Evelyn."

"A blessing is what they are, Marrok," Danil decreed firmly. "You deserve the truth about your wife. Fate delivered."

Marrok wouldn't concede the revelations were helping him get over the loss of Melena. It was Evelyn who was doing that. Yet Evelyn had been the one Fate had chosen to reveal the harsh truths of his past, and she'd suffered right along with him.

While he appreciated facts coming to light, he would rather it not be at his mate's expense.

Evelyn took another sip of whiskey, thinking more would calm her nerves. It didn't. "I feel like I keep asking this, but what do we do now?"

The guards and Evelyn looked to Marrok. It was up to the King what happened next.

"Theron insisted we come here. He didn't say anything more on it. For now, we shore up the palace's defenses. I've already made plans to send home any unnecessary staff and called for extra guards. There's more than enough supplies and food here to last half a year. I assume this will be resolved much sooner than that. Hale will teleport back and forth daily with updates. Kellan and Viktor are searching their shared border tomorrow. Hopefully they'll find the traitors and that will be the end of it."

"Cheers to that! Hunting and capturing our criminal brethren is old hat for us. Let someone else take it on for a change," Danil crooned and saluted the table with his drink in hand.

Marrok forced a smile at Danil's toast. He didn't share his friend's sentiments. Marrok wanted to go hunting with the other kings, as was his right and duty. He wanted to lay waste to anyone involved in the plan to take Evelyn away from him.

He stared at her profile, at her pert little nose and plump pink lips. She threw her head back at something Danil said and Marrok stiffened. He didn't want Evelyn to give Danil her attention. He wanted it for himself.

Marrok stood and held his hand out. "Come."

"Where are we going?"

He pulled her up and led her out of the room without answering, half dragging her in his haste.

"Seems you're off to bed, my lady!" Danil's shout echoed into the hall just as the door closed behind them.

Evelyn stopped and pulled her hand from Marrok's. "Is that true? You yanked me away from the table to take me to bed?"

"Yes. Is that a problem?"

Evelyn jumped up, wrapping her arms and legs around his large frame. "No. I was just double checking."

"Cheeky female," he purred, nipping her lip as she giggled. "You resisted me in the halls of the temple, but will allow me to carry you around in the halls of the palace?"

"You've shown me the error of my ways, demon. Maybe I'll demand you carry me around everywhere we go from now on."

She tightened her legs and pressed closer, meriting a low rumble from his chest. The predatory sound heated her core.

"Now," she said saucily, "show me what else I have to learn."

Marrok turned and jogged the rest of the way to their chambers, anxious to teach her what happened to sassy little mates who teased.

Chapter 26

"Is all this really necessary, Marrok?"

His grip tightened on her hand, the one he held everywhere they went. "Yes. You wanted to see the palace grounds. This is what you must endure to do so."

Evelyn swung her head around, seeing nothing but broad shoulders and heads of hair under helmets, all dressed in the silver and black colors of the King's guard. Four in front, four to the rear, and four on each side of them as they strolled through the garden.

"What palace grounds? I can't see anything," she complained.

They had been here for four days now. She'd merely wanted to see something beyond their quarters and Marrok's study, which were only a few doors apart.

Marrok had made some effort to keep her busy with choosing new furnishings for their bedchamber. He'd told her it had been the room he'd stayed in as a boy and he refused to take the King's suite. Evelyn didn't blame him for not wanting to lie in Brennen's old room.

The study, however, had been Marrok's father's. Marrok spent much time in it as a child and had the space duplicated, almost exactly, in the fortress.

She wondered if she'd ever see Terenuskit. She couldn't even see five feet in front of her.

"Did you hear me?" she goaded. "Or have you aged so much you've lost your hearing?"

The male to the right of Evelyn choked, playing it off with a fake cough.

"I heard you, little mate. I won't change my mind, so I decided not to argue."

The same male snickered and Marrok shot him a look that had the guard straightening his posture. "Apologies, my liege. I've not had this much fun protecting you since the time you fell in the—"

"Stuff it, Danil."

"As you wish, Sire."

Evelyn snorted loudly and several of the guards tried to hide their amusement. Marrok's disgruntled face made her laugh harder, which only made the guards transition to full-blown belly laughs.

She was having such a fit, she stopped walking, bending at the waist and holding her abdomen. Evelyn laughed until her side hurt. She drew in air, wiping away the gleeful tears which had surfaced in her merriment. Something about the stolid King getting razzed by his royal guard was hysterical.

Finally, her vision cleared and she chanced a once-over of Marrok. He was standing stoically with his arms crossed. It reminded Evelyn of how her father looked when she and her sisters got into trouble when they were younger.

"Are you done? Now that you've reduced my elite guard to nothing more than playful children?"

Evelyn bit her lip. "That depends."

"On?"

"Are you going to spank them for bad behavior?"

Danil's horselaugh was so loud several birds flew out of the bushes ahead. Shoulders all around her shook. Evelyn knew the guards might be in trouble for their gaiety. It wasn't something warriors were supposed to fall prey to while on duty.

Sheepishly, she peered up at her demon lover. His eyes were bright gold and she could tell he was fighting a grin. Whenever he looked at her like this, like she was something dear to him, her world felt right and everything else fell away.

Marrok stepped into Evelyn's personal space, yanking her hard to his front. Lowering his mouth to her ear, he whispered, "There's only one person who needs a spanking. I look forward to delivering it."

"You wouldn't," her breathless voice managed.

"I would."

"We can hear you, you know."

319

"I swear to the Goddess, Danil." Marrok bent his head back, looking to the sky and praying for patience. "You're fired."

"So you've told me. Many times."

Evelyn grabbed Marrok's shirt, pulling him down to eye level. "I think you should keep him."

"You do?"

"Yes."

"You're in luck, Danil. My mate says you're rehired."

"And what your mate wants, your mate gets?" Danil teased.

"Something like that," Marrok replied, winking at Evelyn.

Rapid footfalls came down the stone steps behind them. The jovial atmosphere died immediately. The guards shifted, closing in tight around the royal couple. Turning, Marrok tucked Evelyn behind his body.

"It's only Favin," Marrok announced, knowing Evelyn couldn't see past the protective circle.

The guards relaxed and spread apart so their King could speak to his Second.

"Hale is here, Sire. There's news you'll want to hear immediately."

Marrok and Evelyn shared a look. She felt a pressing weight expand from within her ribs. Her entire family was caught up in this, having done nothing other than be marked by Fate.

"I'm sure your family is fine, *moj draga*. Come on," Marrok assured, sensing his mate's anxiety.

He grabbed Evelyn's hand and escorted her up the stairs. They entered the palace through the large doors they'd exited out of only minutes before.

Hale was waiting for them just inside the back entrance. He bowed and Marrok went on alert at the grim look on the vampire's face. Whatever news he carried, it wasn't good.

"In my study, Hale."

"Of course," he replied, falling in step behind the royal couple and their guards.

When they reached the study, Marrok asked his men to remain in the hall, then quickly ushered Evelyn, Favin, and Hale inside.

Before closing the door, he turned to Danil. "No one gets inside this room."

"Nothing will get past me, Sire," Danil promised, the seriousness in his tone sounding lethal.

Marrok nodded and shut the door. Turning, he saw the others standing behind seats at the table.

"Please," he gestured for them to sit. "Evelyn, I want you beside me."

Swiftly, she moved to the chair he held out for her. He pushed it in then took his own, preparing himself for

321

the worst. He wanted Evelyn close in case she was about to hear something had happened to her family.

"Hale, Favin says you have news?" Marrok held out his hand, expecting a scroll.

Hale tapped his temple, "It's all up here, Sire. There wasn't time to write. I was told to come immediately."

"Very well. Tell us the message."

"The she-wolf, Agatha, has been found."

"Where?" Marrok asked, knowing she was likely dead. Kellan's wolf would have demanded retribution for his mate's poisoning. If the Wolf King got to her first, she'd have been torn to shreds.

"At the bottom of a shallow pond in Western Prajna."

Marrok's knuckles knocked on the table. "Shallow pond?"

"Yes."

"That's odd. Wolves are strong and can swim. Was she dead before she went into the water?"

"No. It is believed Dmitri killed her, possibly hypnotized her to take her own life."

"I'm sorry, who?" Evelyn interrupted.

"My apologies, I've gotten ahead of myself. Agatha is dead. Drowned in shallow water. No markings were on her body so there was no evidence of a struggle. The scent of the vampire the wolves found in Burghard, when King Edward was attacked? They found the same scent in the dwelling the she-wolf was inhabiting, deep in the woods of Prajna. Viktor confirmed it was Dmitri, an advisor he believed had died a century ago. Both Agatha and Dmitri's scents were all over the shelter. It was obvious they were there together."

"Dmitri," Marrok sounded out slowly, as if the name made him ill.

"It makes sense, my lord," Favin said. "In the memory, Caleb had started to say the vampire's name. It sounded like it started with a D, and he didn't appear keen to have his name said aloud. If he needed Viktor to think him dead, Dmitri would have to be cautious about such things."

"Memory? What memory?" Hale asked quizzically.

"I'll write a message for you with the information Theron may need. The short of it is Evelyn has dreamt of members of Sephtis Kenelm. One was a vampire we did not recognize. It might be this Dmitri."

Marrok rested his hand on Evelyn's knee, squeezing it in reassurance. "Unless there are heirs to the others in the group, Dmitri is the last one alive."

"Which brings me to the second part of my message," Hale told them. "Dmitri might be dead, as well."

"*Might* be?" Marrok pressed.

"Viktor's brother, Luka, managed to get an iron manacle on Dmitri's wrist, which would prevent him from teleporting."

Marrok leaned forward. "And just how did he manage that?"

"I don't know. I was told Dmitri showed up at Castra Nocte, took Viktor's mate—"

Evelyn gasped, covering her mouth.

"Your sister is fine, my lady. I should have led with that. I apologize. Again. I'm usually carrying written word, not memorizing a thousand words to regurgitate."

"Continue with the message, Hale," Favin instructed, noticing Marrok was distracted by Evelyn's reaction.

"Yes, well I was told only that Dmitri had taken Eden, Luka slapped on the iron manacle, and Dmitri couldn't port away. It's not clear how, but he fell from Diavol Crest. It's the highest cliff in Prajna, overlooking a dangerous whirlpool that all vampires are warned away from. If Dmitri couldn't port and he got caught in the whirlpool, it would eventually kill him."

"Without his body, no one can be sure, right?" Evelyn asked.

"Right. Viktor has men scouring the beaches. If the ocean killed him, it will likely spit him back out on shore."

"And if it didn't?" she whispered.

Marrok clasped her hand. "Then we will be ready. We'll continue on as we have. I'll not leave anything to chance when it comes to your safety, little mate.

Hopefully, if the traitor lived, the vampires will still find him first since he'll have to swim to shore."

"Only if he still has on the iron cuff. Otherwise, he could teleport to anyplace he's ever visited in Imperium," Favin interpolated.

"Then it's a good thing he's never been inside the palace," Hale declared, visibly relieved.

"Unfortunately, it seems he has," Favin corrected the vampire. "The meeting in the vision took place in a room next to the throne room. We don't know what other spaces here he was able to visit, if any. At the very least, he could get into that wing, quite easily."

Evelyn turned to Marrok. "The male is likely Dmitri, I want to assume he did not survive the fall, but …"

"We'll assume nothing," Marrok spoke adamantly. "I'll not risk it. We'll block off that section of the palace. It's on the opposite side of the building and there's no need for us to be there. We'll remain diligent. Nothing changes until we have confirmation he is dead."

Marrok almost hoped Dmitri wasn't, only so he could kill the vampire himself. If Evelyn could be safe in the palace on her own, he'd already be out there searching.

Chapter 27

"Do you think my sisters and I should return to Sanctus Femina?" Evelyn pondered out loud, resting comfortably on her lover's bare chest.

As soon as Hale departed, Marrok quarantined them both to their bedchamber. He'd yet to make good on his promise of a spanking. In fact, he'd been uncharacteristically gentle in their lovemaking this evening.

"No. Some of the rogues wouldn't care if it was sacred ground. They cannot think rationally and would risk the wrath of the Goddess, likely not even able to consider it. Plus, Theron said you needed to be here. Maybe he saw Dmitri attacking the temple or intercepting you from there. Whatever it was, he was insistent you remain here."

"Dmitri might never be found, Marrok. Is this how we will live if his body is never recovered?"

"It's not how I want to live, either, my sweet. It's only been a matter of days. Let's let it play out a little

326

longer before we worry about the rest of our lives, alright?"

"Alright," she agreed, her warm breath blowing across his skin.

"What's bothering you, Evelyn, aside from the obvious?"

"Nothing."

"Damnit, Evelyn," he cursed, sitting up and pulling her with him. "No lies, remember?"

"It's a truly inconvenient skill you demons have," she huffed. "For future reference, when a female responds to your inquiry with the word *nothing*, it means she doesn't want to talk about it. How did you know, anyway?"

"I pay attention and I could feel it through the bond. Furthermore, if you don't want to talk about it, use those words. Exactly."

"And you'll drop it?"

"Not a chance."

"You're impossible!"

"As are you."

Evelyn covered her face, close to laughing at their absurdity. He could feel her concern, but he had no way of knowing what had her in turmoil. She wouldn't want him to conceal anything from her, leaving her to worry and draw false conclusions.

"No hiding, Evelyn," Marrok commanded, pulling her hands down.

Evelyn rolled her eyes. "Alright, Demon King, you win. You want to know what's bothering me?"

"I wouldn't have asked if I didn't."

"You haven't talked about it."

"About what?"

"Don't be obtuse. Melena. The memories? Aside from analyzing facts about the brotherhood, you've said nothing about how you feel. I know this has shaken you to the core, Marrok. You must feel something about your wife's actions."

"*Late* wife," he staunchly corrected.

"Yes, your late wife, the one who took her own life. The one who was manipulated by your uncle and by her cousin. The one you loved dearly."

"Did I? Or did she manipulate my mind into forming an attachment?"

His eyes had grown hard, his jaw set. He'd been holding in whatever he was feeling. Evelyn could sense his tumult through their bond and she thought talking it out might help him navigate his emotions. He obviously had a lot of resentment towards Melena right now.

"Marrok, she was in a difficult spot. You know this. You know what Brennen would have done if she'd refused to play his game. I think you need to forgive her. I don't think you'll get past this if you can't."

He stood from the bed, pacing. "You want me to forgive the person who helped Brennen find you? Who knew you were only a child, yet promised him information he demanded to obtain your identity and did nothing to stop him from reaching you?"

She grimaced. "I know it sounds terrible, but there was more to it. You're just too angry to see it."

"What is it you think I need to see?" he seethed, turning his back and staring out the darkened window.

Evelyn pulled the sheet higher. He was irate. Not with Evelyn, but with his past.

"You want me to see her betrayal? I see it. Her inability to handle being Caleb's heir? I see it. Her visions which always pointed in one direction when it came to my future? I see it. Her promising to tell Brennen who my mate was if her visions revealed your identity? Trust me, I see it, and I refuse to see anymore. If I do, I might find a necromancer for the sole purpose of bringing her back so I can kill her again myself!"

Evelyn stood, slowly approaching his shadowy figure outlined in the moonlight. Her palm fell upon his muscular back and he stiffened.

"You've every right to feel deceived, Marrok."

"Well, thank you for your blessing that I'm entitled to my own feelings," his sarcastic tongue lashed out, moving away from her touch.

It hurt, but Evelyn wouldn't back down. Like a festering wound, it needed to be flayed open and debrided so the healing could begin.

"I see some things, too, Marrok. I see that she ensured you *would* find me. If she hadn't done what she'd done, I would not be here with you now. I'm not convinced if you were still happily married, you'd have been able to come to my aide that night. Fate wouldn't let you fall in love, let you remain married to that person, and then find your saatus."

"Then you have more faith than I," he ridiculed. "Fate's been nothing but cruel these past years. Even you've suffered at Her hands, Evelyn."

Evelyn blinked away the tears forming, despising the pain in his voice.

"I disagree," she countered. "I think Fate has been very generous with me."

"How can you say that? I've seen what you had to endure, night after night, reliving my memories, my thoughts. You felt me fall in love with someone else. You were forced to watch it happen. It was callous at best. If I was to see the truth of my past, it shouldn't have come at a cost to you. How can you possibly think Fate gave you a godsdamned thing?"

Her eyes filled to the brim, spilling over in rivulets streaking down her face. "Because I have you, Marrok. Whatever the price for that, I would gladly pay it. I know it's not the same for you, that you don't feel the same, but that's how I feel about it."

The air left his lungs in such a rush he was sure he'd taken a blow to his gut. His little mate took no issue with suffering whatever pitiless twist Fate threw at her.

Because they were together, Evelyn accepted all the moments of heartache.

He'd been so wrapped up in the brutality of things hidden from him years ago, he'd failed to acknowledge the one beautiful truth in his sad existence. Evelyn was his. Melena's death, as difficult as it was for him, set in motion the path to his mate.

"Evelyn—"

Someone hammered a fist against the door, startling them both.

"We've got problems, Marrok!" Danil's muffled voice called through the wood.

"Get dressed. Hurry," he marshalled, collecting his own clothing with demon speed.

She quickly threw on a dress, not bothering with her underthings. Once Evelyn was lacing her boots, she heard Marrok open the door.

Favin and Danil stood in front of a dozen others whose faces she couldn't see. The two entered and Danil barked out orders to the others to be alert.

"What's happened?" Evelyn asked, coming up beside Marrok.

"Lazlo sent a rider. The peninsula's wall has been compromised. The barrier ..." Favin took a breath.

"Which part is down?" Marrok asked impatiently.

"It's gone. The entire colony rushed it at once."

Marrok went still. The wall was gone. There was nothing holding the rogues on the peninsula. "It was coordinated. There's no other way that would have happened. Someone has rallied them."

Evelyn's nervous gaze fell on Marrok. "Do you think it was Dmitri?"

"Maybe. They might be easily influenced by a vampire's power of hypnosis. Those who are really far gone would have followed the crowd, feeding off the frenzy. Or Bogdan could have had an heir in place, planting ideas. Or both."

Danil ran a hand through his white hair. "Bloody hell, this is bad. There are thousands of them."

Marrok looked at Favin. "Is Lazlo alright?"

"Nevin, the rider, said the rogues were about a mile out from the fortress, on foot, when he departed. They would have reached it in minutes, and that was almost eleven hours ago."

Demons could move incredibly fast. Slower than the rider would have been on horseback, but not by much. The fortress would have been inundated by the sheer numbers shortly after Nevin exited the outer gates.

He prayed Lazlo had either escaped or had secured himself and the men in the secret rooms under the tombs. Marrok and a handful of trusted males had built the hiding space themselves shortly after he took up residence in Terenuskit. Few would think to look for the living underneath the dead.

Marrok's head was already running through defense plans he and Favin had hammered out days ago. They'd started preparations for a worst-case scenario.

Evelyn worried her bottom lip with her teeth. "Marrok, how long until they can reach Patria?"

"A few hours at most."

"At best?"

"Within the hour."

Evelyn's stomach rolled. They were about to be swarmed by rogues.

"I need to change."

"What?" all three males look at her as though she'd lost her mind.

"If we're to stand our ground, I'll not be doing it in this flimsy dress. Get out so I can change."

Favin blinked. Danil smirked. Marrok frowned.

"You will not be fighting against rogues, little mate."

Her eyes flashed, her hands pulling at the air inside the room. She created strong enough currents to push them back towards the door.

"I will not be a sitting target, either. If one of them gets past our defenses, I'll need every advantage to protect myself. As the only female currently on the property, I would prefer to not be caught by a madman while wearing a dress with easy access to things he has no right to. My leathers will make it easier for me to move and better protect my skin from weapons, should they have any. If nothing else, I'll feel covered and less vulnerable. Now, if you don't want me to knock all three of you on your arses, get out."

"Favin, Danil. Leave us."

"I think I'm in love with your saatus, my liege."

"Danil!" Marrok's demon spirit thundered from deep within.

"Right. Apologies, Sire," he bowed, backing out of the room.

The door clicked and Marrok turned to meet Evelyn's heated glare.

"Go ahead, my little warrior. Change."

"Why are you suddenly so accommodating?"

"Because you just gave me a reminder of how strong you are. You almost knocked three formidable demons to the floor, and you weren't even exerting yourself. You've not used magic around me outside of the dreamworld, so it's easy for me to forget you're powerful in your own right."

Evelyn beamed at his compliment.

"Now take off your dress."

Her eyes widened and her smile disappeared with his change in demeanor. Now was not the time to be thinking of rolling around on the bed, as much as she would enjoy it.

"Are you just going to stand there and watch?" she mocked.

"Absolutely."

Evelyn rolled her eyes, opening the armoire and pulling out what she needed. She made quick work of removing the dress, feeling her demon's impassioned stare sliding over her curves.

"The world is ending and you want to watch me get naked," she muttered, jerking up her pants.

"I have no intention of allowing our world to end. That said, if we were about to die, this wouldn't be a bad way to go out. Buried inside you would be preferable, but I'll take what I can get."

Evelyn disregarded his claim. She needed to focus on her tasks or else she might remove her clothing again and jump into his arms. She finish strapping her shoulder harness and reached for her sword. Marrok's large hand landed on it first.

"Allow me."

He picked it up and she gave him her back. "Why do you not carry it at your hip?" he asked as he secured it to her back.

"Because I'm too short. If I bend enough, the tip of the scabbard drags the ground. Carrying it on my back, I have more freedom for movement."

She added a short blade to her leg harness and turned to face him.

"You look ..."

"Comfortable?" she offered. Unlike her sisters, Evelyn would choose to dress this way everyday if her father would have allowed it.

"Sexy. I was going to say sexy."

Evelyn laughed. "I thought you didn't like me—how did you say it? Dressed like a male?"

"I didn't say I didn't like it. I said I was going to start thinking you didn't want me."

Marrok cupped her cheek and lowered his lips to hers. One gentle brush and he nuzzled her cheek with his own. "I preferred your nightwear in the dreamworld because it was so easily removed, *moj draga.*"

Reluctantly, he took a step backwards. "We'll explore what we can do with your leathers once this is over."

"Seriously, how can you think about that when we're about to be overrun?"

"Easy. It gives me something to look forward to and I have no intention of losing."

Chapter 28

"Promise me you'll remain out of sight, Evelyn," Marrok requested, sounding far calmer than he felt. The scouts had reported a large mass of rogues were about to exit the woods south of the palace.

"I will," she swore, looking between the arrow slits from her spot on the roof. Though the palace wasn't a fortress like the one in Terenuskit, it wasn't without some structural advantages in case of attack.

"Hale won't be here for hours yet."

After he and Evelyn finished dressing, Marrok had sent for the vampire, asking Thereon for reinforcements. His men to the south were cut off from him and he had already called for those available in the northern parts of Sundari. Still, they would be outnumbered if the majority of the rogues were headed this way, and it would take hours for his missive to reach Sanctus Femina.

He should have asked for one of the vampires to remain with Evelyn at all times, but he'd never thought the entire colony could have escaped at once.

Marrok had also been reassured by the priest this was where they needed to be. He wasn't one for blind faith, but he trusted Theron.

"I want you to leave with Hale if we haven't gotten things under control by the time he arrives. He can teleport you around the entire continent, if need be."

As Viktor's primary messenger, Hale had to be familiar with the geography of each kingdom. He'd visited as many locations as he could in his many years. He would be the best person to keep Evelyn on the move and away from Dmitri.

"I can only keep up the barrier if I'm here, Marrok."

"It doesn't matter." Reluctantly, he'd agreed to allow Evelyn to use her magics to create a barricade, as she had done for years in her dreams.

"I don't want to leave you."

"I know. But Hale will take you away if I tell him to take you away. Understood?"

Evelyn didn't reply, unwilling to lie to him. She slapped her hands on the side of his head and yanked him down for a kiss. She poured all her feelings into it, all her passion, her love, and her worry.

Marrok groaned, his heart constricting. His mate's sugary lips unraveled him. Panting, he rested his forehead on hers.

"You'll do whatever you have to do to stay alive, *moj draga*. I don't care who you have to maim or kill, you'll do it."

"The same goes for you, my love."

His eyes closed, basking in the sweetness of his mate's affections. He wanted to return the sentiments. He would, after this was over and she was safe. For now, Marrok needed to harden his heart. He would not enjoy killing his own people.

He turned to his men. The archers were in place, one for every other arrow slit. A dozen more were near with the sole purpose of protecting Evelyn. Hundreds more were below, spread along the outer walls, waiting for orders.

Marrok squeezed Danil's shoulder affectionately. He knew his friend wasn't happy to be on the roof instead of in the trenches with him, but he needed someone he trusted to stay with Evelyn.

"Guard her with your life."

"I will, my liege."

Marrok planted one more kiss on his mate and took off towards the stairs. He would be on the ground for this fight, needing to lead his men from the front. Unlike Brennen, Marrok would never hide behind others.

Evelyn watched Marrok's retreating back until it disappeared through the door to the stairs. Four armed men quickly chained it shut, locking out anyone coming from inside.

339

The message on its way to Hale would instruct him to come directly to the roof. Before he departed, Marrok had him enter every wing and any other possible locations where Evelyn might be found, including the roof. The vampire might be the only way off the top of the palace for a while.

The brontide of rolling thunder carried over the large space from the woods to the outer wall. Evelyn could feel the vibrations under her feet and she placed her hands on the stone in front of her.

Danil's shoulder brushed hers as he moved close to peer through the slit. "Here they come," his low voice announced to those on the rooftop. "Hold steady."

They'd rigged the ground with explosives, about fifty yards from the palace's outer wall. Favin had instructed Evelyn to place her partition between the minefield and the wall.

Evelyn lifted her hands, gathering her powers to erect a barrier of air currents. The Southland was far more arid than the rest of Imperium so there wasn't much water to pull from. She hoped she could move the wind fast enough to slow the rogues' progression.

"Not yet, poppet," Danil cautioned. "Let as many as possible set off the explosives first."

"What if some of them make it through before I can get enough wind speed?"

The corner of his mouth lifted. "Let them. A handful is nothing for your royal guard. Your mate alone could take on twenty if he doesn't have to be careful about keeping them alive."

"Danil, I don't want them to die. They cannot help themselves."

"It is always the innocent who suffer in times of war, Evelyn. Sometimes it cannot be avoided. You've nothing to feel guilty about. This whole mess is a symptom of a plague hitting the entire continent. Blame whatever or whomever brought it about. Word is, the other kingdoms are mending."

"So why isn't this one?"

Danil shrugged. "Who says it isn't?"

"But—"

"Move!" he hissed, pushing her from the slit. "The first ones are out of the forest. Do not let them see you."

The rumbling deepened and she could hear shouts and cries of the approaching herd. The noises came out as unintelligible nonsense, reminding Evelyn of wounded animals instead of grown males.

A series of explosions rocked the night. Evelyn's hands flexed, gathering more power from the elements around her.

"Tell me when, Danil."

The seconds ticked by. More and more mines detonated, the sickening screams echoing off the stone palace.

"Now!" Danil whisper-yelled over the noises from below.

Evelyn released her magic. A thick current of air picked up speed, circling the entirety of the palace, just beyond the external security wall.

"Holy Goddess above!" Danil exclaimed when the first few rogues hit Evelyn's magic. They were picked up immediately and thrown by the sheer force of the currents.

"You've created a tornado out there. I think I might be a little afraid of you now."

Evelyn tried not to appear too smug, taking Danil's words as a compliment.

"How long can you hold this?" he asked, watching her hands pulse and stretch.

"Hours, maybe? It hasn't been tested, really. Not in my waking hours."

"No battling thousands while living the good life in Gwydion, eh?"

"No. Though it did keep Brennen away from me in my dreams when I was six."

"You could hold off Brennen at age six? Are you sure you're fully committed to Marrok?"

"Yes, Danil. Utterly and totally."

"My loss."

Evelyn shook her head, blushing. A loud thud landed on the other side of the stone from where she was resting the back of her head. Then two more, causing her to flinch with each one.

"What was that?" She wanted to turn and look out through the narrow space, but she'd promised to stay out of sight.

Danil leaned forward, looking over the edge. "Ah, that was the body of a rogue demon and two of his friends. It appears they are throwing one another over your vortex."

"They can do that?!"

"Our race is a strong one, my lady."

"Apparently."

The explosions had tapered off, presumably because they'd already set off most of the mines. Evelyn concentrated on giving her barrier more height. She was the only thing between the rogues and the perimeter wall.

The clink of metal hitting metal started, which meant some of the rogues were over the wall.

"How many have gotten in?" she asked.

"Nearly forty. The guards below are easily handling them. Hundreds were taken out or maimed by the landmines. Your magics are holding off the bulk of the bastards. You come in quite handy, little witch."

"Can you see Marrok?" she inquired, paying no heed to the witch comment.

"No. He's fine, though. If he wasn't, you'd feel it through the bond."

"I'll feel his pain?"

"No. If he was in trouble, you'd feel his panic."

"Marrok doesn't seem like the sort of male to panic."

"He's not, not unless he thought they were going to get past him and get to you. The alarm would be out of concern for you, not for himself."

Evelyn's hairline dampened, a bead of sweat rolled down her temple. She wiped it on her arm.

"Problem, my lady?"

"No, not yet."

"You said you could hold it for hours."

"I can. If a thousand demons weren't bashing their powers against it simultaneously."

Danil looked again and cursed a litany of creative words. "They got smart. Or someone told them to attack collectively."

He scanned the grounds, looking for anyone not in royal guard attire who might be giving out orders. He could see no one leading or directing the militia.

That's when he saw ten demons appear out of nowhere, right in the middle of the walking path behind Marrok's soldiers. Each had a hand on a male in the center of the group. Releasing their hold, they charged towards the door and the male who'd been in the center disappeared.

"Bloody hell. Archers! Fire! Fire! Ten count at the main entrance. He's teleporting them inside!"

Evelyn whirled away from the stone, pulling her sword. "Dmitri's here," she breathed.

"I don't know if it's him, but it's definitely a vampire. Stick close to me, Evelyn."

Danil circled the roof, looking through the slits after each archer fired and reached for another arrow. Ten more rogues were teleported near another entrance. This time, Danil got a better a look.

"It's him! He's in all black. Dark brown hair. Glowing green eyes. Aim for the green!" he ordered, hoping one of them could catch the bugger in the head.

"Green eyes, you say?" a voice lilted next to Evelyn's ear.

Evelyn launched her head to the side, aiming for his nose. A sickening crunch came from the contact and something warm splattered her face.

She swung her blade at the same time Dmitri and Danil both made a grab for her arms. Suddenly, she felt compressed the point her lungs could no longer expand.

Dmitri had gotten to her first.

* * *

Hundreds of rogues clambered over the wall and jumped down into the palace grounds. The soldiers were holding their own, but they wouldn't be for long if the rest of the rogues made it over.

"Evelyn's shield is down!" Favin called from nearby.

Marrok's stomach dropped. There was no way Hale had arrived yet. Something had happened.

He looked to the roof and could make out royal guards engaged with rogues. They'd made it to the roof. Terror ripped through the bond he shared with his mate.

He tore through the crowd, dodging and carving his way inside the palace. Marrok sprinted up the stone stairwell to the top level. Bursting out through the door on the rooftop, he searched for Evelyn's dark red mane.

He easily caught site of Danil as his friend's blade sliced through the rogue attacking him from the side. The rest had already been put down by the time Marrok had reached the roof.

"Danil," he snapped.

The male turned, meeting Marrok's eyes, his mouth tight.

He shook his head. "Dmitri. Less than a minute ago."

Marrok's roar was so loud, so heart-wrenchingly full of despair, the rogues below paused, feeling the pain of their King. Some fed off of it, some dropped to their knees covering their ears. The soldiers took advantage, slaying only the ones still fighting.

Favin looked around, perplexed at the rogues who were submitting. It reminded him of how wolves yielded to their alpha.

"Secure the ones kneeling, kill the rest!" he ordered the guards in the courtyard. Then he turned and headed for the roof, running like his King's life depended on it.

Chapter 29

Evelyn landed hard on her hands and knees, her stomach threatening to empty onto the dirt floor. As she started to push herself to her feet, a large booted foot connected with her ribs and she collapsed, the wind knocked from her lungs.

Gasping, she moved to her back just in time to see the black boot coming for her face. She rolled swiftly, her ribs screaming in protest. Air breezed past, lifting stray strands of hair with the missed strike.

Raising her hands, she called to the elements only to have her arms slammed down to the ground before she could siphon power. Straddling her chest, the vampire held her wrists down by one hand.

With his other, he gripped the fingers on her right hand, her sword hand, squeezing mercilessly. Sounds popped loud enough to echo off rock as he easily broke the small bones.

Evelyn screamed.

"That was for breaking my nose, *witch*. I was just going to kill you and be done with it, but now I think you need a lesson before dying."

Evelyn glared at him through her watering eyes. His nose was swollen from where she'd head-butted him, the blood already drying on his face.

He let go and pulled back his fist. A severe blow landed square on her face and stars burst inside her skull. Her ears rang and her nose bled.

Stay awake, stay awake, stay awake, she chanted inside her mind. If she lost consciousnesses, he would kill her easily.

Evelyn refused to die like this. With her one good hand, she reached down and grabbed his testicles, squeezing as hard as she could. Dmitri howled in pain, and teleported away.

He reappeared to her left, breathing heavily and doubling over. Keeping her eyes on him, she scooted backwards until she felt the cool rock on her shoulder blades.

It was then she noticed they were in a cave. A fire was going a little further inside. Next to it was a thin pallet. This is where he'd been hiding.

The air was tinged with salt and the tranquil sound of ocean waves systematically hitting the shore. They could be on any coast, but she suspected they were on or near the Corak Peninsula. Dmitri was the most likely candidate to be manipulating the rogues.

"You're going to pay for that, witch."

"My name is Evelyn, you horse's arse."

"Doesn't matter. You'll be joining your mother soon, then so will your sisters once I get to them. The threat from the West will be no more."

"What threat? My sisters and I are no threat," she said as her eyes darted around the small space, looking for her sword.

The misshapen reflection of firelight shone just behind the male. He glanced where she was looking.

Dmitri bent and picked up her blade. "Looking for this?" he mocked, pointing it towards her. "You are the threat. Your own mother predicted it. *Northland, Eastland, and Southland quest. Heed the threat from the West.* The king from each of those kingdoms has found a fated mate in Elora's children. It cannot be allowed. Your family will not be allowed to control all of Imperium."

Evelyn kept her hands behind her back, trying to draw on the elements closest. Her right hand was growing numb from the swelling. *Good. It will make this easier.*

"We've no desire to take over the continent. Did you miss the part about fated mates? You're toiling with the will of the Goddess above. You can't possibly win. She'll have her revenge on you, no matter what happens to me and my sisters."

"Enough talking."

His manic green eyes flared, his lips peeling back in a snarl. He pulled a knife from his side holster, waving it around joyfully.

"Maybe I'll cut out your tongue first."

Dmitri threw her sword away, too far for Evelyn to attempt at the moment, not when he could teleport and get there first. She focused her magics, the elements only too happy to answer her call.

The second he advanced, she set him on fire. His screams echoed off the cave walls as the flames ate away his flesh. Evelyn crawled as quickly as she could to the sword, her head still swimming from the vampire's assault.

Dizzy, she rose to her feet slowly, never looking away from the spectacle before her. The stench of burning flesh filled the air and she gagged.

The vampire managed to take two steps closer. She lifted her steel, channeling what was left of her energy into staying upright. With all her might, she swung.

In slow motion, she watched a dagger fly out of the flames as her blade reached Dmitri's neck. His head flopped, then bounced off his shoulder. White hot pain exploded in her chest. She dropped to her knees and her world went black.

* * *

"The palace is secured," Favin told Marrok, who was wearing a hole in the floor of his study with his pacing.

"Those who refused to cease attacking were killed," he continued. "The others we've had to corral into the throne room. There are too many to jail. They've shown no signs of aggression since, well, since you brought them to their knees, Sire."

Marrok glanced at Favin. He had no idea how his cry of anguish brought them to a crashing halt. Nor did he care. He only cared about finding his mate.

"I can feel her pain, Favin. It's coming through the bond hard enough I can feel where he's hurting her." His voice broke, forcing him to swallow past the lump in his throat.

His demon was simmering, just below the surface, wanting to harm. To disfigure. To exact revenge. He could do nothing until he found Evelyn.

"Question them. Start pulling memories," he told his Second. "One by one. I want to know where he is, anyplace he might be."

"Hale and reinforcements will be coming before too long. Not that we need reinforcements now," Danil said. "He can teleport you around if they can give you a starting point."

"I—"

A searing pain stabbed through Marrok's chest, his hand slapping over top of it. The saatus bond pulled at him, his mate's agony blaring loud and clear. He fell to his knees, both Danil and Favin rushing to him.

Quickly, it went numb and he could take in air again. "Evelyn," he exhaled.

Danil held Marrok's shoulders. "Is the bond still in place?"

"Yes."

The white-haired demon relaxed. "Good, then she's alive."

"Good?" Marrok gritted. "I'm not getting anything from her now. I was able to feel her fear and her pain. Now, it's like her mind's shut down. Like ..."

"Like she's asleep?" Favin suggested.

"More likely knocked unconscious," Danil corrected. "Which *is* good, Marrok. If she was in tremendous pain, now she's not feeling it."

"It is not good! She cannot defend herself if she's not awake!"

Favin cleared his throat. "I think Danil has a point, Marrok. If she's not awake, you need to gandeste. Immediately."

Marrok straightened, then hopped to his feet. "Favin, get the valerian powder and bring it to my chambers. I'm not going to fall asleep easily."

"Right away," he said and swiftly exited.

"Danil," Marrok looked at his friend, "stay with me, just in case."

"Just in case what?"

"Just in case those docile rogues decide they're no longer content to sit and stare at the floor."

"I'll gather some of the guards and meet you in a under a minute."

Danil ran off in one direction and Marrok hurried to the chamber he shared with Evelyn. He used the pitcher on their breakfast table to fill a glass with water. Favin entered and handed him a small packet.

Marrok poured only a fourth of the contents into the glass. He needed to be able to wake and feared too much of the sleep aid would hinder the process. He drained the glass, downing it in a single gulp.

Setting it down, he turned to Favin. "Have a blade ready. If I cannot wake myself, you'll have to do it."

"How long should I wait?"

"Five minutes after you're sure I'm asleep. No more."

"Okay. You know I hate doing this."

"And we believe you, Favin," Danil pronounced, full of his usual sarcasm as he breezed into the room.

"Twelve guards are in the hall. Forty at each entrance to the throne room, everyone else is on high alert," he added, closing the door.

"Thank you, Danil."

The male nodded at his king in return.

Marrok moved to the bed, not bothering to remove any clothing or his weapons. He needed to be at the ready in case Dmitri or the rogues decided to attack again.

Danil and Favin moved two chairs to either side of the bed, sitting closely so they could watch over their liege.

Marrok closed his eyes, concentrating on Evelyn. On her dark red hair and mismatched eyes. Her pert little nose and pretty pink lips.

In his mind's eye, he could see her smile and hear her laugh. No one, not even his friends, had brought him such amusement. The little witch had woven a spell around his heart.

Once he found her, Marrok might lock her in their rooms and never let her out. He'd never felt so protective of anything. He needed her to be safe. He needed her to remain as she was. Perfect. Whole. His.

Marrok had fallen into a pit of despair when Melena took her own life. Slowly, he'd crawled out of it and continued on. If something ever happened to Evelyn, if Death rose from the underworld to pull her into its bottomless depths, he'd dive in and follow her down.

It should have scared him how much he needed her. It would have if he didn't know he had her love. Gwydions did not have mates, and still she chose to love him.

He was her choice. Sweet, spritely Evelyn *chose* him. His demon pranced proudly and Marrok felt his chest puff out at the reality that Evelyn didn't have to love him. She didn't even have to accept him.

She'd stood there, after he'd been unable to return those three little words, and chose to love him anyway.

She'd brought him to his knees, and he hadn't been male enough to give her the same assurance.

Marrok had once imprudently believed he could use the bond as a sole means to keep his demon sane. He hadn't counted on the force of nature Evelyn was. Fate or not, she, too was his choice.

As he felt the dark tendrils of sleep wrap around him, he finally let go. He let go of the past. Let go of the treachery. Of the lies. Of the hell Brennen put him through. If, in the end, Evelyn was his, it was all worth it. He'd choose to suffer it again if she was the outcome.

Loving Evelyn was the only thing worth living for. With that final thought, he opened his eyes.

Chapter 30

Marrok stood on a narrow ledge, overlooking the ocean. The salted wind whipped his hair and cooled his skin. He spun to take in his surroundings.

He was standing on the small lip of a cave carved into the face of a cliff. It was over two-hundred feet above the water and at least fifty feet below the overhang leading to flat land. Shades of red clued him in to his location.

Prajna's coastline was full of shiny, black stone. Gwydion's was made up of sandy beaches. The Northland shores of Burghard were heavy with thick vegetation and the climate was cold, much colder than this place's warm temperature.

The red volcanic rock was a trademark of Sundari's southern coast. He was somewhere in the Southland. It couldn't be the Corak Peninsula, whose coast was protected by ancient magics to prevent invasion from the sea. The magics of that place wouldn't allow Dmitri to dwell within the cliffs.

Was this a normal dream? Disappointment landed on his shoulders right before his demon came to full attention. *She is here. Look at the sky.*

The sky was full of purples and blues, shades not made by the natural atmosphere. It looked just like Evelyn's dream sky. It was the first time he'd dreamwalked to his mate in a setting outside of Gwydion.

She was alive so she wouldn't be at the bottom of the cliff. With nowhere else to search, Marrok unsheathed his weapon and entered the narrow mouth of the cave. He moved cautiously, unsure what dark magics Dmitri might have at his disposal, like another demon who could break into Evelyn's dream as Brennen had.

Orange and yellow light flickered ahead, where the passage made a sharp turn to the left. He could hear the mute crackling of a fire. His nose picked up the scent of burning wood combined with something putrid.

He moved faster. When Marrok got to the bend, he lifted his sword, preparing to fight. Silently, he rounded the corner.

The small circular space was well-lit by twin fires. One campfire at the back of the cave, and one blazing lump to his right. It looked like a pile of rags set afire.

The fetid stench of something that had been alive when it burned singed his nose hairs. *Dmitri*, his demon spirit rumbled.

Evelyn was on her side, her back to him. Marrok did a onceover, checking for danger. Nobody else was here.

He sheathed the blade and knelt behind his mate. Dampness soaked into the fabric where his knees touched the ground. Marrok's eyes dropped to the dark shadow under Evelyn's form.

No, not a shadow. Blood.

Carefully, he rolled her to her back and his heart stopped. The jeweled handle of the dagger protruding from her chest shimmered brightly, reflecting the nearby flames.

Marrok debated removing the knife, but he didn't know what would happen if he did. He checked her pulse. It was slow, but it was there. She'd lost a lot of blood and needed a healer.

He needed to wake and get help. Conjuring a short blade, he shifted to lie down beside his mate. As gently as he could, he slid one arm under Evelyn. He hooked one leg over both of hers, trying his best to hold on to her body in any way he could.

Marrok brought the hand holding the short blade across Evelyn's torso, cognizant of not jostling the jeweled dagger. He cut the palm of his hand and quickly gripped the strap of her leather harness, praying to the Goddess he could pull her with him.

If he couldn't, he'd have to search for this location. Even with Hale's assistance, the chances of finding her before she bled out were slim to none.

He waited. Nothing happened.

Marrok sliced his hand again. Still nothing. Frustration and fear had him digging it deep into the underside of his forearm.

Finally, he felt the welcome dissolution of the dreamworld. He clutched Evelyn to him, begging the Goddess to save her, to let him hang on long enough to break her out of this nightmare.

* * *

Marrok's eyes fluttered, the remaining fragments of sleep slowly falling away.

"What the—call for the healer, Favin. Now!" Danil's low tenor barked and hurried footsteps scuttled off towards the door.

The bedding was wet under Marrok's side, as was skin of the body he held. Hair caught on the scruff covering his jaw. Long, red hair.

He'd done it.

A moment of elation ran through him, cut off by the horrified look on Danil's face. He was leaning over the opposite side of the bed, inspecting both Evelyn's torso and his king's arm.

"Slide your arm out from under her, Marrok. One of your cuts is deep and won't stop bleeding without pressure."

Marrok gingerly disentangled himself from Evelyn, sitting up beside her. His right hand stroked her forehead. She felt clammy. He forced himself to remain calm. Help would be here any second.

Danil tore a strip of fabric off from the sheets. "Here," he said, tossing it to Marrok. "Wrap that up until someone can look at it."

Marrok rolled the rag around his arm, watching Danil study Evelyn's wounds. Her face was bruised and bloodied, already swollen. The fingers on her right hand, misshapen.

Danil's eyes lingered on the knife. "Tell me that bastard is dead."

"If the dreamworld was her real memory, then he's dead. My little mate removed his head and set him on fire."

"Let's hope that wasn't just wishful thinking manifesting in her dreams."

Favin bolted into the room, Salix, the healer, close behind. Marrok moved off the bed so the male could tend to his mate.

Salix reached for Marrok's arm and he jerked it away. "See to my saatus."

"Of course, Sire." The healer pressed his fingers to Evelyn's wrist.

"Her pulse is weak. She's lost a lot of blood. With your permission, I'm going to cut away her top."

Marrok nodded.

"Here," Danil offered, holding out his small pocketknife towards Salix. "Cut away the leather and lift the sheet."

Salix took the item and quickly sliced the front of Evelyn's leathers. Gently, he pulled the top apart and lifted the sheet to cover her nakedness.

The healer's hands skimmed the place where the steel entered her flesh.

"I was afraid to remove it," Marrok stated.

Salix's brows slanted downward. "It's embedded deep. She should have lost more blood than she has. Honestly, I'm not sure how she's still alive."

Marrok took a shuddering breath. "Can you save her?"

"I don't know, Sire. I think she may be beyond my help."

"Marrok?"

The King swiveled his head to his Second.

"Hale is here, sooner than planned. He and his entourage arrived right before you awoke. Maybe you should have him take her to Theron. The priest has healed severely wounded beings in the past."

"Bring him to me. Ask if any of the others have been to Terenuskit. If they have, take Danil and check on Lazlo. If not, I'll send Hale back to teleport you."

Favin bowed and opened the door. "Hale? We need you."

Hale came into the room, blanching when he saw Evelyn on the bed. "What do you need?" he asked.

Marrok carefully lifted his mate. "Take us to Theron."

Hale planted a hand on Marrok's shoulder and ported them to the entrance to the temple. Theron was there, waiting with the door propped open.

"You knew this would happen," Marrok accused walking up to the old man.

Swirling violet and silver looked right past him, right down into the Demon King's very soul. "It was one of the possibilities, yes. Of them all, this was the only one where she lived."

Theron looked over to Hale. "Go back to the palace. Favin needs you. Marrok, let's get Evelyn to the infirmary and see about removing the vampire's weapon."

The priest patted the King's shoulder as he marched past. "I knew you would do it. I couldn't see it, but I had faith you would."

"I would do what?"

"Choose her. It was the only way you'd be allowed to keep her."

Marrok's step faltered. He shook it off, refusing to consider the possibility of ever living without Evelyn.

Chapter 31

Evelyn awoke to sunlight coming in through the large window next to the bed. Birds chirped with the sweet song of morning.

She reached over for Marrok and winced, a deep ache radiating out from her sternum. Warm hands pushed her shoulders down to lie flat. Confused, she opened her eyes.

She was in a small, white room. Shelving along the wall held dozens and dozens of flasks and corked decanters. The smell reminded her of the medicines that had been forced down her throat when she was a child.

Marrok was sitting at her hip, his worried eyes roaming her face as his hand smoothed back her hair. *Why did he appear so upset?*

"Theron told me not to take away all of your pain, that you'd need it so you wouldn't move around too much while you finished healing."

The memories came flooding back. Dmitri. The cave. Her hands called to the elements, her defenses rising right along with her heartrate.

"Easy," he soothed, lifting her left hand to kiss each of her fingertips. "You're safe now."

"Where are we?" she rasped, her mouth feeling like she'd eaten a bowl of cotton.

"Sanctus Femina. Hale ported us. Five days ago," he answered, reaching to the side table to pour water from the pitcher into a small glass. "Thirsty?"

"Very."

Marrok cupped the back of her head and helped her raise enough to take a drink. She reached for the glass, finally noticing the splint wrapped in thick bandages around her hand. She wouldn't be able to hold anything in it for a long time.

"Let me take care of you, *moj draga.*"

Something in his voice told her not to argue. She allowed him to hold the drink to her lips while she sipped. When she was done, Marrok lowered her back to the pillow.

He set the glass down, then gave her his full attention. His hands rubbed up and down her arms, massaging tenderly.

"How—how did you find me?"

"I dreamwalked to you. I managed to pull you out with me."

"Like the night with my, ah, underwear?"

His face sobered. "I'd say this was far different a night."

Marrok inhaled a shaky breath. "He took you, Evelyn. He took you right from under my nose and there wasn't a damned thing I could do about it. I thought I'd lost you."

His golden eyes brightened, glassing over, causing her own to do the same. Her demon warrior had been afraid for her.

She reached for his face and he leaned down for her touch. "You saved me, Marrok."

"You saved yourself."

"Not really. I killed him, but I couldn't do anything about the dagger in my ribs. You came for me. Saved me."

"Theron saved you."

Evelyn rolled her eyes. "So stubborn."

"Says the female arguing."

She laughed and winced again.

"Damnit. Don't laugh if it hurts."

"Don't argue with me and I won't," she shot back.

Marrok's mouth twitched. He bent down to nuzzle her cheek, inhaling deeply. He relaxed into the aroma of midnight dew on a desert rose. His mate's scent was as unique as she was.

"You scared the hell out of me, Evelyn."

"I'm sorry."

"Don't be," he whispered, planting a kiss under her earlobe. "It wasn't your fault."

"I know. I just don't like seeing you like this."

"Like what?" he asked, pulling back to see her face.

"Upset. Vulnerable."

Marrok sighed. "You'll have to get used it, I suppose."

"Why?"

"Because I love you more than I've ever loved anything in my entire life. I love you more with each passing day. The more I love you, the more upset I'll be if you are ever harmed. You are my one and only vulnerability, Evelyn. Nothing else in this world matters."

Tears streaked down her face and Marrok wiped them with his thumbs.

"Shh, don't cry or I'm going to think you hate hearing me profess my undying devotion."

Evelyn snorted through her tears, slapping lightly at his arm with her one functioning hand. "Don't be ridiculous. I like it very much and you know it."

Marrok's mouth brushed across hers, featherlight. His tongue glided across the rim of her lips, tasting her tears. Her breathing grew ragged and he caught a trace of her arousal.

"Even injured from a nearly-fatal wound, you desire me."

He pressed his forehead to hers, his heart filled with wonder. She was such a mixture of attractive ingredients. Intelligent. Beautiful. Strong. Fearless. His saatus hadn't needed him, she'd taken care of Dmitri herself.

"I'm so proud of you, Evelyn."

Evelyn laughed, trying to hide the pain from doing so. "You're proud I'm so attracted to you?"

"Smart-aleck. I'm proud of you for fighting him off. You took his head and set him on fire. That was a nice touch, by the way, ensuring he was dead."

"Actually, I set him on fire first. I needed to distract him so I could get to my sword."

"I'll be sure to thank your father for teaching you to fight. He and your sisters will be here tomorrow."

Evelyn swallowed. She'd mated before her father even knew about Marrok. It wasn't going to be an easy conversation.

She yawned, feeling drained.

"Sleep, little mate. I'll be here when you wake."

"I need to tell you what Dmitri said."

"We can discuss it later. Close your eyes and let me watch over you."

"Okay," she replied sleepily, drifting off to Marrok's melodious words whispered in the old language.

* * *

"I think the room's a little crowded," Evelyn whispered to Marrok.

"I think we can all hear you," Kellan whispered back from his spot on the bed closest to the door. The entire group laughed.

"Stupid wolf hearing," she grumbled and they laughed again.

Not allowed to leave the infirmary yet, her sisters, Theron, and all four kings came to her. Everyone had been updated on what happened to Evelyn this past week. To her dismay, her sisters fussed and coddled and she tried to bat them away each time they approached.

To Evelyn's surprise, her father hadn't reacted the way she thought he would. He seemed to take it all in stride and had even congratulated both she and Marrok. Granted, he'd had a week to think on it, so maybe he just needed the time.

None of the others, aside from Theron, had known how bad things had gotten over the years. Each kingdom knew the other faced some sort of plight. Or, at least, they had been. Now, things seemed to be turning around.

"Marrok," Theron spoke, "please continue with the news Hale brought this morning."

"As I mentioned earlier, the majority of the rogues ceased their attacks, simultaneously, when, well, when I reacted to the knowledge Evelyn had been taken. At first, they seemed to be in a sort of a daze. We don't know why or how."

"And now?" Viktor asked, tracing his fingers across Eden's back lazily.

"They seem normal. It's like they woke up from a coma, with no memory of what happened."

Edward leaned forward in his chair, dropping his elbows to his knees. "Power drains in Gwydion. An unknown sickness killing off the forests of Burghard. No mated pairs or live births in Prajna. Growing madness and limited matings in Sundari. Each epidemic ending shortly after my daughters married."

Evelyn coughed into her hand. "Um, technically Marrok and I—"

"Will be married immediately. Maybe today while you are all here," Marrok interrupted.

"I can barely walk, demon. At least let me heal enough to stand on my own two feet."

"Anything you want, my love."

Nora shook her head with humor. "Careful what you promise to Evie. She'll take advantage."

He looked down at his mate, with total adoration. "I don't mind."

"You should," Nora deadpanned, prompting Kellan to pull her against him and nip at her neck.

"Yes, a wedding will be most welcome when Evelyn is up to it. In the meantime, I'd like to return to Edward's point." Theron looked to Edward.

"My point is only that none of it was a coincidence. We knew something was happening across Imperium. Oddly, the king's finding their mates seems to have ended whatever has been going on."

"I think you are correct," the priest agreed. "Which brings me back to Evelyn. Please tell them what Dmitri said to you before he died."

Evelyn licked her lips. "He told me we were the threat, Nora, Eden, and I. He quoted Mother's words."

"Which ones?" Eden questioned.

"*Northland, Eastland, and Southland quest. Heed the threat from the West*," she recited the portent Elora had given when she was a child.

"He said the kings from each of the kingdoms mentioned in that prophecy had found a fated mate, all in the same family, and that it couldn't be allowed. He thought we were the threat because we would be able to control all of Imperium, a Gwydion on each of the four thrones."

"Upsetting the balance of power," Kellan thought aloud. "Too bad they didn't take into consideration your family wasn't out for power and that Fate had chosen each of our mates."

"Messing with Fate and her plans is never a good idea," Viktor supplied.

Eden stood. "Sephtis Kenelm wasn't wrong. There is a threat from the West."

Nora frowned. "Who?"

"Us. Don't you see? We *are* the threat. They were right about that and wrong about who or what we threatened, right Theron?"

The ancient's eyes twinkled. "I would have to agree, yes."

"Explain," Viktor ordered the priest.

"I don't believe Elora's warning was for a broad audience. It was for a very specific group. It warned the brotherhood to watch their steps, to heed the threat that would end them."

"And they misinterpreted what it meant," Marrok mused.

"Wait, so why all the problems? Everyone has suffered in some way," Evelyn's eyes lifted to Theron.

"Fate had to get your attention. Kellan, why did you seek out a bride of Gwydion?"

"For help with the forest."

"Yes, and that one decision led him to his mate, then put Nora's life in danger, which is why Edward brought Eden and Evelyn here. Viktor, why did you come here to the temple that day?"

"For help with the lack of matings and nonexistent birth rate. Instead, I found Eden."

Theron gestured to Marrok. "You may have met Evelyn in the dreamworld, but no matter what you decided about your saatus, you would have come to the temple. Why?"

"I needed help with the rogues," he ran a hand through his hair. "It seems so obvious now."

Theron shrugged. "None of it was certain. Each of you still had to make choices. Fate just set the stage."

"Yes, and you conveniently pushed us out onto it," Evelyn griped.

"My help only got you so far. All of you had to *choose* your path, to open your hearts. Matehood doesn't guarantee love on both sides."

Marrok squeezed Evelyn's hand. Yawning, she squeezed back.

"I think we need to let Evelyn rest," Marrok spoke to the others, but his attention was on her.

When Nora and Eden stepped in Evelyn's direction, their father stopped them, glancing over his shoulder back at his middle child. "You can visit with her later. Let's give them some time alone."

Kellan and Viktor escorted their mates away and Theron followed close behind. Edward limped to the foot of Evelyn's bed, not quite healed from his attack.

"I'm sorry, Evie. If I'd been able to prevent this," he motioned to the bed she was in, "I would have. Of you three girls, however, I will say you'd be the one I knew would not only survive it, but would eliminate whomever dared to cause you harm."

"Really?"

"Really. You're the most blood-thirsty of the lot and that's saying something. I've seen what you girls have done to the training equipment. I've also seen Jasper after you've kicked his arse. Bully for you, young lady."

Evelyn beamed, thankful Marrok had taken the pain from her face so she didn't cringe.

"I'll leave you two to rest," Edward inclined his head and exited the infirmary.

"Scoot over, little mate and I'll hold you while you sleep."

Evelyn shifted and allowed Marrok to pull her into the curve of his body. She easily slipped into a healing sleep, thinking of all the things she wanted to do to him when she was up to it.

Chapter 32

Evelyn snuggled closer to the heat behind her. A band tightened around her midsection and she sighed contentedly.

"Open your eyes, *moj draga*."

She lifted her lids and her world was filled with soft purples and blues. Lanterns swung in the breeze, hanging from the trees above. They'd landed on their love nest instead of in the meadow.

"Well, this is new," she remarked.

Marrok kissed her neck. "Were you thinking about lying with me in bed, little mate? When you fell asleep?"

"Maybe."

His hot breath puffed across the skin where he'd kissed her. Goosebumps broke out on her flesh. Her naked flesh.

"Were you?" she asked.

"Without a doubt."

She started to turn and he held her in place.

"How do you feel? Does your chest hurt?"

Evelyn didn't answer.

"Evelyn?"

"I don't want to lie to you."

"Good. Don't"

She rolled her eyes, even though he couldn't see it. "Yes, it's still painful. My hand is still weak. Though I don't feel the pain in my fingers or from the damage to my face. I can feel the swelling in both. My sternum is sore. I'm a mess, but I don't want to tell you because then you won't touch me.

"You want me to touch you?" he nipped her earlobe.

"Yes."

"Where?"

"Everywhere."

Marrok laughed. His fingertips drifted to just under her left breast. "Tell me if I aggravate the wound."

Evelyn held her breath, shocked he was actually going to give in. She'd tried last night in the infirmary and he'd steadfastly refused. He'd even had Theron give her a concoction to put her in a dreamless sleep so she could rest.

His palm coasted upwards until he palmed her breast. Soothingly, he flexed his fingers and relaxed them, repetitively.

"Tease," she jested.

"Careful, mate. I'm keeping track of your infractions, which we'll address when you're better. I, for one, am looking forward to the spankings you've earned."

"Tease," she repeated and he laughed.

Evelyn needed more than a gentle massage. She wiggled her rear against the erection she felt behind her.

"Don't. This is about you and if you push me too far, I'll stop."

Evelyn froze, not wanting him to stop.

"That's my good little mate," he purred, sliding his hand down her abdomen. "Lift your leg over mine."

She hooked her right leg over his, spreading herself for his exploration. Marrok's fingers traced the swell of her mound, pressing and teasing all around the edges of her sex.

"Please, Marrok."

"I like it when you beg. Do it again."

"*Please*. Please touch me."

His middle finger dipped into her tight heat. "Here?"

"Yes," she panted.

Marrok withdrew the digit and rubbed the sensitive nub at the top of her cleft. "What about here?"

"Oh, yes!"

"You're so responsive. I like that, sweet Evelyn. I like that a lot."

He continued his sensual offensive, finding a rhythm that had her strung tight as a bow. Her hips rolled as Marrok dipped and rubbed, then repeated. He never lingered in one spot for long, building her desire until she dug her nails into his forearm.

"Say my name when you come."

Marrok thrust his finger in and out, using his palm to continue pressure on her knot of pleasure. He felt her muscles contract and she gasped.

"Say it," he gritted between his teeth.

"Marrok!" she shouted as her climax hit and she rode the waves of pleasure.

Marrok watched his mate come apart in his arms. Each time was spectacular, more beautiful than the last. Once she relaxed, he rolled her to her back to check her unbandaged wound.

An angry, serrated scar was forming, marking the spot where the dagger had entered her chest. A few inches to the right and she wouldn't have survived. Marrok bent and kissed the reddened skin, so thankful she made it back to him.

It had been six days since the incident. With Theron's help, the wound had progressed enough to close completely, though the ribs underneath were still repairing themselves. Movement wouldn't harm her, but it would be painful and prolong her recovery.

"What about you?" she bit her lip, invitingly. "You won't hurt me."

"You're right, I won't. So we'll wait. I'm thinking until our wedding night."

Evelyn gave him a withering look. "Are you joking?"

"No. I need an incentive to get you down the aisle."

Evelyn dropped her eyes.

"Hey, look at me."

She lifted her eyes again.

"What's wrong?"

"I don't want a big wedding."

"I know. I wasn't suggesting one. I just want to see you walk towards me."

Her lips flattened and his heart clenched. "I'm not saying this right. I think I never say it right."

Marrok sat up, scrubbing his face with his palms, thinking on his wording. "She didn't walk down the aisle towards *me*."

"What are you talking about?"

"Melena. I know that memory bothers you. Big royal wedding. Bride coming down the aisle to her smitten groom? I've replayed it over and over and the more I do, the more I see how blind I was. She didn't look at me.

379

Not once. Her eyes were on the throne. She walked down the aisle to Brennen, under his command. I hadn't been her choice."

Evelyn opened her mouth and he clamped his hand over it. "Let me finish."

"Okay," her muffled voice tickled his palm and he pulled it away.

"I want to be someone's choice. I want to be your choice, Evelyn. I know you think she cared for me, and maybe she did. You're right about how bleak her options were. Nevertheless, she didn't choose me for me, and I have to live with that."

It didn't hurt as much to admit aloud as he'd anticipated.

"The more I think about it, the more I don't really care what her reasons or motivations were. It happened and, while the truth of it did hurt me, it wasn't as painful as it should have been, not if what we had was real."

"I'm sorry, Marrok."

"Hold that thought," he said. "I have to tell you I think you were right. I have to forgive her. Not because I can't move on if I don't. I have to forgive her because her actions led me to you. Hell, I should probably be kneeling at her tomb and thanking her for the gift she's given me."

Evelyn grinned shyly. He thought she was a gift.

"I understand your aversion to the idea of an actual wedding, but I would like one. Walk to me down an aisle. Choose me. It can be small, just us and your family. I only want to have this one thing from you. To make our own memory."

"You're really quite romantic, you know that?"

"Don't tell Danil or I'll never hear the end of it."

Evelyn shook her head, chuckling, as Marrok slid back down beside her. "Please?"

"Did you just ask nicely?"

"I did."

"Then how can I possibly say no?"

Marrok took her mouth hungrily, his tongue demanding entrance. He stole her breath as she stole his. He broke the kiss and nuzzled her cheek.

"Could you repeat all of that because I wasn't really paying attention?" she asked innocently.

Evelyn watched Marrok. It took him a second to catch on to her devious jest. A roguish grin slowly broke across his face.

"Oh, little mate. You just keep adding to the infractions, don't you?"

"I think I recall you saying you were looking forward to spanking me?"

"I did say that, yes."

"Then it's a good thing I love you enough to give you want you want."

His nose skimmed her temple and down to her jawline. "Say it again," he whispered.

"I love you."

"And I love you, *moj draga*. For all time."

Epilogue

Theron watched Evelyn dance with her new husband. She was glowing with happiness and something else she hadn't yet shared. Perhaps she didn't know.

Nora's small bump could no longer be hidden, though she wasn't much further along than Evelyn. Wolves gestated rather quickly.

Eden's belly was obviously round with child, the first of her sisters to become pregnant. He wondered how Viktor would react when he found out his mate was carrying twins.

Three sisters would be birthing four babes in the coming year. Four tiny, but powerful younglings to lead Imperium into its golden age. It was imperative there were four to herald the new era.

"You've been meddling, Theron," the musically accented voice accused him from behind.

And you haven't? he wanted to reply. Wisely, he held his tongue.

383

Lowering his head, he turned towards the Goddess and bowed. He'd never been physically able to look at her directly. No being had ever described her face because they couldn't.

He'd only ever seen the flowing silver material of her dress and the cream color of the skin on her hands. When he pictured her, he imaged a female with the combined attributes of Edward's daughters.

"Nothing to say to that?" she asked.

"What can I say? There's no denying it."

The Goddess kept her attention on the smiling couple as they twirled around the garden at their small wedding feast.

"You'll have to die for the marks to be transferred," she warned.

"I know."

"Do you intend to?"

"Die?"

"Mark their young as heirs."

"We'll see how things progress, the choices they make as they grow."

They stood shoulder to shoulder, watching the wedding party. It was all that was good in this life.

"You could always give them the choice," she suggested.

"Yes, and that turned out so well these last thousand years."

"Careful, priest. The Sephtis Kenelm were meant to be the custodians of Imperium, to reign in those who would topple the others, to ensure peace and balance. It is a heavy burden to choose who lives and who dies for the sake of all. I refused to force it upon them so I gave them a choice."

"You do so love your free will. Tell me, what happened to the first worthy souls you offered to mark?"

"They refused."

"Interesting." *As well as unsurprising.* Such beings would never hunger for power or assume they should control Imperium's future. Only the easily corrupted would crave the position.

She shrugged. "I still think you should give them the choice."

Theron scratched at the skin over his heart where four lines of black swirling script now existed.

"I'm curious, priest, how did you get them—all of them—to make you their heir?"

Theron was one of her few blind spots. He had to be if he was to control the power of Sanctus Femina and wield it freely. Even she had rules she had to follow.

"I didn't. Not directly. I found their heirs and *requested* these heirs take a blood oath to make me second in line. Then I ensured I was first in line immediately after the pledge was sealed with our powers. As soon as Mara, Bogdan, Agatha, and Dmitri each took their last breaths, the marks appeared, one by one."

The Goddess laughed. He just confessed to killing four beings and she laughed.

"So you skirted direct influence. You cunning fox. I knew you could do it. I couldn't see how, only that you would fix my little problem. Well done."

Theron frowned and she laughed again.

"I'll anxiously wait to see what happens next, Theron," she told him and started down the stairs towards the feast.

"Where are you going?"

"I think it's time to see about the King of Gwydion. Don't you?"

Theron took off after her and she disappeared in a wisp of smoke, her tinkling laugh carried on the breeze. Standing there, stroking his beard, he debated interfering with Edward. He was the only king in the land without a mate.

He sighed and walked back up the steps, returning to his spot to watch the revelry below. He would leave it alone.

After all, the Goddess of Fate could be fought, but She would always win.

The End

Note From the Author

Thank you so much for reading <u>The Demon King's Destiny</u>! It's the final book in my Fate of Imperium Series, though I am tempted to write a few of the side characters' stories. We'll see ...

This series is my first attempt at writing something where humor is not the star of the show. There are snippets, of course, but it's not my usual in-your-face nonsense. This is one of the reasons I released it under a different name.

If you're new to my work, my original publications were penned under the **Cass Alexander** moniker. It's the name I use when I'm feeling the funny—which has been every moment of my life until this series.

Right now I'm working on another novel titled, <u>Shadow's Lyric</u>. It's more modernized than what you've just read, complete with a kickass heroine and lots of bad words. Evelyn inspired this new character, for sure.

If you're interested in receiving notifications for new releases, or joining my team of ARC readers, or just seeing what sort of nonsense I put out into the universe, you can follow my blog (see below). It also has all my social media links.

caworleyauthor.wordpress.com

Lastly, if you enjoyed the book, please, please, please leave a review. Reviews are an author's lifeblood. Much obliged!

Made in the USA
Middletown, DE
26 June 2023